WAR
VALLEY

WAR VALLEY

A HANK GANNON WESTERN

LANCASTER HILL

PINNACLE BOOKS
Kensington Publishing Corp.

www.kensingtonbooks.com

PINNACLE BOOKS are published by

Kensington Publishing Corp.
119 West 40th Street
New York, NY 10018

All Kensington titles, imprints, and distributed lines are available at special quantity discounts for bulk purchases for sales promotions, premiums, fund-raising, educational, or institutional use. Special book excerpts or customized printings can also be created to fit specific needs. For details, write or phone the office of the Kensington sales manager: Kensington Publishing Corp., 119 West 40th Street, New York, NY 10018, attn: Sales Department; phone 1-800-221-2647.

PINNACLE BOOKS and the Pinnacle logo are Reg. U.S. Pat. & TM Off.

ISBN-13: 978-0-7860-4475-7
ISBN-10: 0-7860-4475-6

First printing: March 2019

10 9 8 7 6 5 4 3 2 1

Printed in the United States of America

Electronic edition: March 2019

ISBN-13: 978-0-7860-4477-1
ISBN-10: 0-7860-4477-2

PART ONE
Blood and Vengeance

Prologue

September 17, 1871

"But the *governor*! The *law*!"

The bony black man who had invoked His Excellency Edward J. Davis—who was a Southern-born Union officer, a Reconstructionist, and a traitor without honor as far as the officer on horseback was concerned—the bony man, in a crawling position on the ground, was sweating hard and hot into the dry dirt. Each panted breath shook his thin, filmy cheeks and heaved more perspiration to the ground. Unimpressed with the man's discomfort, the noon sun sizzled it away as fast as it fell.

The long-fingered, almost delicate black hands pushed from the dirt. The bony man was now on his thirty-five-year-old knees facing the ground, one of those knees bloody and still resting on the stone that had ripped the flesh. The sting was bad, but not as bad as the throbbing in his left temple where it had struck the ground, hard, when the black mustang ran him down. His lengthy, cracked fingernails were caked with dirt, having been dug into the earth like a buzzard on a mule rib. His oversized ears listened for the restless clop of a hoof or an impatient whinny—or, more important, the hammer of the .44 Remington being lowered. His brown eyes dashed left and right in search of a shadow, a man, some part of the Texas Special Police officer he could personally turn toward and implore to let him go. He didn't even know which lawman it was, though it was certainly not a black man. Even a black man in a uniform would not have the iron in his voice that this man had.

"Get up, dammit."

"But the governor!" the bony man said again, desperately, his voice a little softer now. There was only so much speech he could force across his dry, limp tongue.

"The governor," said the flat voice from somewhere behind him. It was a voice that fell hard from a granite jaw covered with overnight stubble. It was the voice of a man who had suffered loss, lacked both the spunk and compassion of a greenhorn, did not impress easily. "Mr. Davis says that you freed slaves got the same rights as a white man. I no longer got a quarrel with that. But those rights do not include murder."

"Wasn't *murder*!" the man screamed, though it was more of a rasp. He had not had any water since the day before, and the autumn sun was still baking-hot. "The man . . . he . . . I *asked* him. I gave him a chance to surrender!"

"To *you*," the other said. "Not to the police."

"There was no police there," the black man

replied. "Alls I wanted was him to admit that he was Jack Summerlee."

"To *you*," the rider repeated. "Surrender to you like he was some slob in a barroom dispute because he had a limp like the man who sold your wife and baby son before the war—which I remind you was legal, then, in Louisiana. And when he didn't do that, you stabbed him."

"He was leavin' and he *was* that man," the other replied, sobbing now. "He *was*. I was makin' a citizen's arrest."

"Where'd you hear o' that?"

"We was told by agents of the United States government that such is our right," the man replied. "We got schooled on our new rights."

"I'd say you carried them too far," the rider said. "I'd also say you got mighty amazin' eyes. It was dusk. Dark enough so you'd already put away your chalk, didn't you?"

"Yes."

"All right. Now let's—"

"I seen him well enough," the black man continued to protest without moving. "I felt his evil."

The black man flinched as the horse stomped the ground impatiently. It hadn't had any water either.

"Widow says you were wrong," the voice replied calmly. He would give reason a little more time. Just a little.

"She wasn't there back then," the black man said. "She was inside with the house slaves. She don't know."

The rider said, "Fact is, no one knows anything except that you killed an unarmed man. Now I been plenty patient with you, but that's at an end. Get up."

The man on the ground was Sketch Lively, a name he was given because he had an art for caricature with chalk or charcoal. The voice of the rider belonged to Henry Wilson "Hank" Gannon, and he had no patience for debate, political or otherwise. He was one of the few white men paid to track alongside the Tonkawa and Tejanos who were also members of the Texas Special Police. He was not paid to trade street-corner law with a street-corner artist. This had already taken longer than he had expected and he was not especially sympathetic. During the War, where he had refined his natural skill for tracking, Gannon's Confederate unit, the Pensacola Guards of the 1st Infantry Unit, had encountered many runaway blacks. They were arrested and sent back with Collection men whose job it was to fill their wagons with escaped slaves. During that time, Gannon had heard every story and every variation of every story, including this one. "I'm looking for my family."—"I want to join the Union army." Even, "I'm lookin' for my missin' master." He was willing to bet that Sketch Lively, having heard about Mr. Lincoln's proclamation, simply decided to take off. Perhaps Sketch had gotten close to the Summerlee children, drawing pictures for them, which enabled him to gain the master's trust and flee. Or maybe he was mad with grief, losing his family. That was common, too.

Regardless, at some point, for some reason, he had escaped from Jack Summerlee. Sketch knew how to stay upwind, how to run on his toes to reduce his footprint, how to leave shreds of clothing stuck to tumbleweeds that would blow here, there, and every which way but right. Gannon had seen it all during this pursuit. Gannon was also willing to bet that Sketch had even risked planting his foot near a coiled rattler just so his pursuer would come and investigate the footprint and possibly get bit. Gannon didn't blame him. He actually admired the man's fevered thinking. But the flight was over now and he was going back.

The black man had remained on his knees, as if in prayer. "Legal, sir," he said, thinking back to the rider's earlier comment. "Legal don't make somethin' right."

"You can say that at your trial," Gannon pointed out with a kind of monotone finality, like a dropped rock. "Get up."

The black man seemed to be wrestling with too many things at once. His seemingly hopeless situation, his fate, his anger,

Since Gannon had joined the new Texas Special Police ten months before, he had seen the man work, drawing for pennies on an Austin street corner, for stagecoach passengers. He drew on scavenged planks of wood, of which there were many as old shacks were torn down to make way for a new Austin, and railroad construction got underway in earnest. Gannon had also seen Sketch earn money for races with other freed blacks. He usually won. At night, he helped drunks home from the saloon— for a fee. There was no end to the man's inventiveness when it came to separating visitors from their money. He slept, with other blacks, at the hotel Governor Davis had established for them with state funds. It rankled some that poor whites, mostly veterans, did not have such a place, nor could they stay at the Negro facility. Reconstruction was angering to many that way.

Gannon had not been there the night before when the man from Louisiana and his wife, coming from supper, paused on their way back to the hotel and asked Sketch to create a portrait of the missus. What the gentleman got was a dispute that ended with a knife in his throat, his blood pouring onto unvarnished wood, painting a portrait of death. At the time, Gannon had finished with a late-afternoon poker game at the saloon and was walking with his fiancée, Constance Breen. Constance was the nineteen-year-old schoolteacher who had just gotten home from tutoring a young pupil about the geology of his home state. The boy seemed to be reading his words backward. She and Gannon were puzzling over that, discussing it as a way of awkwardly avoiding their future plans as husband and wife, on which Gannon lacked clarity—though not conviction. They had talked more about where they wanted to be, San Francisco, than about the nuptials that must necessarily come before then. They had seen pictures in one of the school's new books, and it excited the imaginations of them both.

That was when Sgt. Richard Calvin found them. The big man was on foot, having known just where the officer would be. A Union marksman during the Civil War, Calvin got directly to the point in everything he did. There was a cursory "Pardon, miss" and a tip of the hat to Constance, and then the sergeant addressed Gannon. He briefed him on what had happened and what needed to be done. Because Gannon had been a nighttime tracker during that conflagration, Captain Keel wanted him to go find Sketch Lively.

"Why not Whitestraw?" Gannon had asked, referring to the unit's Tonkawa scout. "He likes an adventure, especially if he can use his gun. Or Hernando Garcia? He'll do anything to be on horseback—"

"The dead man had status, Reb," Calvin had said, needling him about his wartime status. The sergeant would not have done that if he hadn't respected the man.

"Dead man?" Constance had said, Calvin having been talking to Gannon privately, quietly, until then.

"No one local, miss," Calvin had assured her. "Old slave feud."

Gannon immediately understood the politics of it. One did not send an Indian in a matter that had political or economic weight. A great many influential whites already felt disenfranchised by Reconstruction. The police had to give the appearance of sending an advocate for the race.

Gannon had turned to Constance, but she hushed him.

"You will call on me after church tomorrow?" she asked.

"Before your mother's first apple pie is cold," Gannon had vowed over his shoulder as he fell in beside Calvin.

Gannon was already going to be late. The pies that she sold from a table outside the Breen home, after church, would already be coming from the oven. He shouldn't have wasted time arguing with Sketch; he should've just roped him and rode him back. If he refused to go, there was a rigid canvas sled, modified from the two-horse litter used during the War, that would be angled down from a harness and dragged behind. It was modeled after the native travois, which was typically pulled by horses or dogs.

"Y'know, Sketch, I am not a heartless soul," the rider said, trying a different tack, the way Captain Keel had taught in one of his manhunting talks. "But answer me—how many months did I watch you out there, playin' around when you could've been searchin' for this family? You hurt so much, why weren't you lookin'?"

"I was savin' money," the exasperated man replied. "Checkin' slave registries—that *costs*. Bein' free don't mean anythin' else is free."

"I'm sorry," Gannon said sincerely.

The black man's shoulders heaved up and down. "I didn't get free to hang! I had a *right* to do what I did! Law says all 'bout res'tution. I heard others say it."

"You heard wrong, or it was said wrong," the man told him. "Restitution does not mean an eye for an eye. It means things get fixed over time, without stabbing, shooting, burning, *or* lynching."

"This wouldn'ta been 'fixed.' He was still wealthy and white."

"I was, too, once. Wealthy. Lost it in Lincoln's war," the voice said. "Guilt is not for an assassin to say. It's for a jury."

"A jury." The black man exhaled a bitter laugh. "A white jury. White men to avenge a white Southern gentleman. In Texas. Justice ain't never fixed. You can't understand. I'm just wastin' breath."

"And wastin' time," the rider pointed out, having

exhausted his talent for conversation. "Look, if you get up now you can come back with dignity. No ropes. If I have to come down, you'll be comin' back in a sled, either unconscious and hogtied or dead."

The black man stayed very still, despite the sun burning on his bare neck and arms, which is from where the torn fabric had come.

"Don't let's make this grow ugly," Gannon said. "Get up, come back with me, and tell your story in a court of law."

The man shook his head vigorously, perspiration flying. "I am free, ya hear?"

"Best get on your feet," Gannon said sternly. "That's about all you're free to do right now. That and sweat."

Without lowering his gun, Gannon turned to his left and reached for his coiled lariat. He hadn't wanted this to get ugly but Sketch was not keen to cooperate.

"Last time I'm askin'," the police officer warned him. "Don't make me treat you like a runaway. That profanes us both, and on God's holy day."

The man on the ground had continued to shake his head. He did that defiantly right up until the moment he pulled his fingernails from the dirt, pushed off from that dirt with his palms, and bolted. He ran with his arms pumping so hard, harder than Gannon had ever seen, that he nearly stumbled forward on the level ground, saving himself with long-legged strides as the ragged sleeves of his once-white shirt fluttered like wings providing lift.

Gannon swore and spurred the mustang forward

at a slow gallop. He quickly came alongside Sketch Lively, who suddenly screamed a sound that rose from somewhere down around his knees. The black man simultaneously stopped hard and turned on the horse, still crying to the heavens. Grabbing the reins, he tried to clamber up the side of the animal. The mustang reared and Gannon held his seat but Sketch jerked up and down, shook and pulled at the leather as though he were trying to drag horse and rider to the ground.

It was right after Gannon holstered the Remington, freeing both hands to try and steady the horse, that Sketch lost his footing. The bony black man dropped on his back with an audible blast of breath, and the horse came down on his chest with both forelegs. The pop of his sternum and ribs was like a thunder crack. The black man seemed to fold in half above the waist, and his dying breath fanned blood a foot in the air. The spray caused the horse to whirl, Gannon working hard to steady him so he could dismount. It took the better part of a half-minute for the officer to regain control.

His lips pressed tightly together, the broad-shouldered six-footer managed to get his polished boots on the ground. Holding the reins in his strong right hand, he coaxed the horse forward just enough so that he could drop to a knee beside Sketch Lively.

The black man's chest was caved in and he had drowned in his own blood; a professional gambler wouldn't bet on which killed him. Sketch lay staring, unblinking, into the overhead sun. Gannon searched for the knife but did not find it. The fingertips of the man's right hand were an incongruous, layered mix of chalk, dried blood from his victim, and dusty earth. The reflected light from Gannon's badge played across the dead man's chest. The white shirt briefly bore the marks of the horse's hoofs, but a growing bloodstain swiftly covered them.

Flies wasted no time gathering. Gannon, removing his white hat and positioning himself so the skittish horse couldn't see the sudden movement, shooed them away.

"*Dammit*, you!" he said to the corpse. His voice was still flat, emotionless, but the tension in his mouth was anger. Sketch Lively was going to die, a jury would have seen to that. The trial would have been used to bring out past injustices and free up money to reunite families. But he had killed in cold blood, and he would have died. Nonetheless, this accident was going to take some explaining. And the two active participants, the corpse and the mustang, couldn't talk. Gannon could not begin to consider how Captain Keel would react. It was not entirely possible to be a good leader, a fair man, and a political adept—but there were times the officer managed all three.

Gannon didn't have a blanket or anything else to wrap the body in. He didn't think the horse would be too happy having the bony man slapped on his back, still dripping blood and smelling like carrion. The officer looked around. He was on a scrubby plain, but there were a few struggling ash trees here and there. Nothing out here grew like it did in his native Florida, the land that had given him his perpetual ruddy complexion and light, sun-bleached brown hair. There were times, like now, when he missed the land of his birth. He used to ride for days in the lush hills between the Apalachicola and Suwannee Rivers. He would stop, for fun and relaxation, in the capital city of Tallahassee within this farming belt. He would also talk to the planters, who spoke with one voice for the Deep South— farmers who were unified by common trade and also by marriage, plantation to plantation, trade to related trade such as farmers to merchants, merchants to seamen or railroaders. He would see the slaves at work as he rode, most of them in either the cotton or tobacco fields of Middle Florida. It was a state where Mr. Lincoln wasn't even on the ballot in 1860. Southern Democrat John C. Breckinridge of Kentucky carried the state by a significant margin.

Gannon was not a political man then, and he was not a political man now. He cared little for those who governed; no land in which he had ever lived or worked or fought bore more than just temporary scars from its leaders. His grandfather Peter used to say that when it is time for institutions to fall, they fall on their own. Gannon was not convinced that the end of slavery required the ghastly spilling of blood he had seen. It would have been replaced soon enough by the age of machines that was coming. He had already seen pictures of horse-drawn reaping devices in magazines. Unlike slaves, they did not require food, clothing, shelter, or doctoring.

And how can one spot on a map, on the border between North and South, know what is best for the growing nation? he thought. *Tallahassee and Austin know better than Washington what is right for Florida and Texas.*

But Gannon was not the President or a member of Congress, nor did he want to be. And Texas was not Florida. Not worse, not better, but with very different needs and benefits. Defoliating any of these trees would set the state back in terms of soil erosion, wildlife, and just looking like something other than future desert. There were even rules about that in the Texas Special Police handbook. But he had no choice.

Walking the horse to a twelve-footer and tying him to the trunk, Gannon used strong fingers to wrench off three low limbs that he used to fashion a hurdle. With rope for a towline, he attached it to the saddle, placed Sketch Lively on top of it, and rode the eleven or so miles back to town.

Austin was preparing for church on this bright and serene Sunday morning. The citizenry had not been happy about the murder in their streets the night before. Austin was civilized, now. Threats from Mexico, from Comanche, and even from the venerated Sam Houston—the capital being his namesake city—were largely in the past. Not just cowboys and ranchers were out at night but, increasingly, families. They mingled with an increasing population of freed blacks and workers from Mexico. The growing city had gone from its pre-war adolescence of wooden wagon sheds, saloons, and makeshift everything else to a city of masonry and brick. The capital was solid and manicured and pointing the way not just for the state but for the restored Union.

But Austin was even more unhappy, on the Sabbath, to see the makeshift cortege come darkly into town, a somber horse and rider with a litter

pulled behind. To the few Irish residents, who crossed
themselves at the sight, it was like the arrival of the
Cóiste Bower, the death coach, of the home land. If
it had been the local undertaker approaching, that
might have had an appropriately funereal, religious feel. This was just the dead.

There were others who were unhappier still to
see a dead black man being dragged behind a
horse. Only the young, eastern-educated editor of
the *Daily State Journal* did not seem disturbed. It was
not the kind of newspaper front page coveted by
either Governor Davis or his agents, which was just
the kind Vance Vale liked to run. It guaranteed him
access to men in power, and that assured a report
that would be sold throughout the nation.

But most unhappy of all was the commander of
the Texas Special Police, whose function was to
augment local law enforcement throughout the
state. The police served at the pleasure of Governor
Davis, who mandated that they pay particular and
very careful attention to racially based crime. There
were pamphlets in the commander's office that the
men were compelled to read, and seminars he personally conducted, instructing the men how to deal
with violent or indigent former slaves, desperate
and bitter orphans, and those who were slow of
speech or unable to read. Many blacks were phys-
ically disabled by their years in bondage: backs
crooked, leg muscles damaged or cut to prevent
escape, broken limbs improperly healed.

Captain Amos Keel was a one-eyed Civil War
legend who had shifted from fighting the North to
fighting Comanche. He was the one and only
choice of Governor Davis to head this outpost, one

of the few who had the temperament to run an outfit consisting of men like Sgt. Calvin who were former enemies. He was wise enough to have a suggestion box for anonymous ideas pertaining to the smoother running of his operation. His men liked and respected him. Citizens admired him. Children cried when he showed them his glaring glass eye. They cried harder when he took it out. He had his own pew at church, which he visited most Sundays when duty did not take precedence. His spinster sister Carol, with whom he lived, was very close with the wife of the governor. Keel was widely read, especially in the area of geology—which, he said, being in a vast state like Texas was useful knowledge to possess. Only a handful of Texas Special Police were stationed in the capital; when men were moved between outposts, or summoned to this one, it was good to know just what crossing a plain, desert, or foothills actually required in terms of supplies and time.

Keel was a big round man, a head taller than most, with a woolly moustache and a hand-rolled cigarette usually poking beneath it. He did not walk so much as orbit, like the moon, moving slowly and with stoic purpose, shedding light and guidance on dark circumstances. That was how he appeared now, when word came that Hank Gannon had returned—not with a prisoner but with a cadaver. Wearing a black vest, white shirt, and tent-wide black trousers, he flung his cigarette aside as he walked up the center of the dirt street that ran through the orderly quadrants of Austin. His usually affable expression was instantly disapproving when he saw the man that was supposed to be a "prisoner" lashed to a sled with the same rope that was looped around the saddle horn tugging the construct with fits and starts. Whatever the explanation—and it could be as reasonable as "Sketch fell from a ledge"—it would run counter to the policy of the governor. The captain's lips moved a little, bobbing the moustache up and down, as he softly prayed that the increasingly large crowd did not raise the governor from his residence. Mrs. Anne Davis was a devout woman for whom Sunday was not a day for socializing—or news-making.

Keel motioned with a thick arm as Gannon approached, but the lawman was already ahead of him. The officer turned off the main street toward the small stone stable where the police kept their workhorses and personal mounts. Gary Bosley, the teenage stableboy, shut the big wobbly doors behind the men as they entered. The only light came from a hayloft with open service doors in the back. A side door, behind the stalls, was latched shut.

The captain's good eye went from Sketch to Gannon, rising like mercury in a thermometer and with the same indication of fever.

"Gary, get the doctor," Keel said, the eye fixed on the tracker.

"Yes, sir."

The thickset man cracked one door to exit, closing it quickly behind him. It rattled in the darkness. When that stopped, Keel could hear muffled talk on the other side; editor Vale questioning Bosley.

Keel turned his head to the closed door. "Vance, let my man be about his business!" he shouted.

"I want an interview with the officer who just arrived!" Vale yelled back. "Gannon, isn't it?"

"You'll get a statement from me!" Keel told him, pulling a box of matches from his vest pocket.

"That's not enough to support a headline!"

"I know that!" Keel replied. "Now leave us be!"

The captain struck a match on his shoe and walked over to the corpse. His expression did not change a whisker. Keel was accustomed to seeing grotesquely dead men. Men who had been too close to cannonballs or too long in a desert, brought down by starving animals or flayed by hostile Comanche. What he was not accustomed to was laying his good eye on fatal incompetence. He shook out the flame, ground it under his toe, and went back to the front of the horse. He did not have to ask to be told what happened. Sliding from the mustang, Gannon faced his superior and briefed him concisely and truthfully. Keel listened without comment until the report was finished.

"How did he take you by surprise like that?" the commander asked.

"Same as a rattlesnake you don't shoot when you first see him," Gannon replied. "Sketch was on his feet and he sprang. I could have shot him point-blank but didn't. Like I said, he grabbed the throat-latch, cheek piece, and my horse panicked."

"What about the busted knee?" Keel asked disapprovingly. "And the lump on the side of his head?"

"That happened first," Gannon said. "He was runnin' and took it hard when I bumped him down."

"You ran him over?"

"No, sir. I wouldn't do that to any man."

Keel said gravely, "So he fell down and then he got up. He ran, *wounded*."

"He didn't seem to know he was hurt, sir. You know how that is. I saw men in the War run with their arms blown away. Sketch—he was down, got up, ran again, I pursued, and then he turned and attacked."

"Why were you still mounted?"

"'Cause Sketch was fast, we all know that," Gannon said. "I knew if he ran I might not've been able to stop him. I was tired an' he was rested. He'd been sleeping other side of the Colorado. He heard me come across and got away. He wasn't too winded when I first caught his scent. But then he'd hide, rest, shoot off in another direction. Smart, an' I was thinkin' that was how he first came to be a runaway."

Keel shook his head. "If I tell that theory to the governor, he won't buy it."

"I can't answer for him, only for me," Gannon said. "I fought for the South, sir, like you, but I have no hatred for the black man, Captain,"

"I know that, but Vale is tool of the governor," Keel said. "By the time he's finished the crime will be what you did, not what this man did. Everything you just said—that'll get buried in courtroom reporting."

"Courtroom?" Gannon's stubble emphasized the sudden darkness in his features. "A trial, Captain Keel? I'm entitled to a police investigation—"

"You'll get that first, and then there will be a trial," Keel said, his voice rising the first time. "Man, the facts are all on this stretcher. There will be a trial, and it will be followed by a conviction. Rebel soldier? Dead freed slave? The governor will have you tried and found guilty of murder."

Gannon's square jaw was set. "That, Captain, is just all balled up. I didn't *want* to kill the man!"

"I believe you. Yet here he lies, dead."

"You're forgettin', Captain—a killer lies here, dead. People saw what he did."

"*You're* forgetting that even a killer deserves a hearing."

The doctor arrived then. Anton Zachary was one of three physicians in Austin. One worked exclusively for the railroad, where a looming deadline made for haste, which made for injuries; the other had a general practice and worked for the general citizenry; and Zachary worked for both the public and the police. When Captain Keel needed his services, a stipend ensured that Keel's project took precedent. The medic was in his early sixties, short and slightly hunched from bending over bedsides, stretchers, and patients passed out on the ground. He was humorless, charmless, but sober. The medic was followed by the stableboy. Bosley grabbed a lantern from the hook by the door, lit it. As they made their way to the body, Keel walked Gannon toward the stables.

The dozen horses were side by side by side like the members of a jury, arranged from the smallest to the largest. Gannon's brain echoed the words he had lately uttered to Sketch Lively: *"That's for a jury to say."*

Keel was thoughtful, silent for a long moment. Gannon dug at the edge of a hay pile with his boot. The officer had already replayed the events in his mind as he rode to town; there was nothing to think about, other than how this was unfortunate but also unintended. Not like what Sketch had done. Surely, Keel had to see that, had to be considering a way to make that point to the governor.

The silence wore quickly on Gannon. He had expected the support of his superior. His successful record of tracking should have earned him at least the man's neutrality. Gannon did not sense he had even that.

"Listen, Captain, I did everything by regulations," Gannon finally broke and said in his own defense. "Takin' him down—hell, you know I done that dozens of times. Never happened like this."

"Officer Gannon—"

"It's 'Officer Gannon' now?" he interrupted. "What, we're no longer friends?"

Keel resumed as if nothing had been said. "Officer Gannon, none of what you just told me is going to impress the governor. Or, more importantly, a jury, which his own attorney general will interview and help empanel." He shook his great, round head. "None of it."

"I did not realize, sir, that pleasin' Mr. Davis was on my list of duties."

Keel fired him an uncharacteristically harsh look. Gannon knew why. There was a narrow, often winding line between the extremes of duty and policy, between vainglory and political gaming. For better or worse, that was the path Keel had chosen.

"*I* am displeased," Keel said. "You did not do what I sent you to do, and I suspect that is because you were in a hurry to get back to your girl."

"I was that, sir, but not enough to *trample* a man to death—"

"Enough to be distracted," the captain continued. "And why in the name of dear, sweet God did you have to bring him in that way?"

"On the sled that you taught us to make?"

"For the injured," Keel pointed out.

"I did that because I didn't want to leave the man under a pile of rocks for varmints to pick at," Gannon told him. "Would that have been better?"

"What would have been better is if you had left the horse and the dead man just the other side of the river, come and got assistance," Keel said, his voice rising for the first time. "Instead you made an entrance like Edwin Booth on opening night. You should have known better—Sunday morning, Officer Gannon? What did you expect?"

"The support of my superior, Captain." Gannon moved closer to the big man. "I'll accept whatever blame is due me, but the real problem wasn't entirely me. What would have been better is if you'd sent one of the black officers to fetch Sketch Lively. Or one of the Tejanos."

"You're the best tracker."

"Well, he wasn't havin' any part of me, personally. Or what I had to say." Gannon shook his head. "Maybe I should've let Sketch Lively get away. I'd be in church, now, and so would you. There'd be only a dead white Louisianan to deal with, and Governor Davis—he'd've been happy."

"That's enough," Keel warned.

Gannon was growing exasperated. No one had ever questioned his judgment before. Not in war, not in peace. In his thirty-seven years he had been a bold but careful man. If nothing else, short of cowardice, that was the only way to survive a war.

The doctor walked over, staying a respectful distance until Keel turned to him.

"Go ahead," the captain said.

"Sketch's chest was crushed by the horse," the bearded physician said. "Hooves have traces of blood. Sternum and at least four ribs shattered, bone tore up the heart and lungs. You can see them in the wound."

"I see. All right—you can take him," Keel said. "Is there family?"

The question was out before Keel realized what he had asked. The doctor did not know what had triggered the attack in the first place and said he would find out. The captain did not say anything else until he turned back to Gannon.

"I want you to resign," Keel said. "This morning."

Gannon stopped kicking at the hay. The rustle and thud of the body being removed from the hurdle sounded very far away. The thud of his own heart sounded very loud. The lawman couldn't even respond, the idea was so unpalatable.

"If there is a trial, and there will be," Keel went on, "this becomes a Reconstructionist nightmare. Every abolitionist with nothing to do will make this a national issue. Politicians will turn over peace-keeping entirely to the occupying Union army. Freed slaves? They will come here and demand government land and they *will* get it. From where? From who? The Comanche. And that war we've been fighting with them for half a bloody century will have to be fought all over again."

He jerked a thumb over his shoulder. "All because a horse got spooked."

"I don't believe any of that," Gannon said. "People are smarter."

"I'm sixty-two, got a score of life on you," Keel said. "The only consistently smart creatures I've met are dogs and hogs, and sometimes horses and crows. People? If they're smart, it is only about how to get more. And that is what Governor Davis and all those people I just mentioned will be smart about. Getting more power. More land. More wealth." He shook his head. "The governor will not want those things either. Most of them. He will unhappily accept a death certificate that is attached to your resignation."

Gannon definitely felt the way Sketch must have felt in the last moments of his life. Disbelief and rising defiance.

"I won't do it, sir. I won't resign."

"You will or I will have you arrested here and now," Keel replied.

"Why, to impress a mob? The governor?"

"No, Gannon. For disobeying an order. The other charges—those'll come later unless you get out now. Hank, I'm doing you a favor." He threw a thick finger down the row of stables. "I'll have Bosley ready your saddlebred. Don't shave. Piss when you're gone. Just get your effects and come see me about your wages." He looked at his gold pocket watch. "It's 10:03. You've got till the half-hour. Do you understand?"

"By my clean soul, Captain, not a damn word."

"Doesn't matter. I'll have a paper ready for you to sign. Affix your name and go home to Florida, if you'll take my advice."

Keel turned his bulk around effortlessly and walked toward the doors. Gannon remained planted, like he himself was in one of those stalls. He could not believe that his life had just been upended for doing his job. He tracked a killer, attempted to bring him in, the man assaulted his horse, was trampled, died—and now a decorated veteran with an unblemished service record in war and peace was being asked to resign.

His inclination was not to. This was an outrage, and the officer felt that by giving in he dishonored his parents and their parents. Three generations of Gannons owned a farm in Florida where they raised cattle and pigs. One branch established a fishery on the Atlantic coast. The Gannons helped feed a nation and, when the nation was divided, those who did not fight continued to send pork, beef, and fish to the Confederate troops. Hank Gannon had remained in Texas after the war because his parents had urged him to bring the Gannon name and values west, to the Pacific seaboard. To raise a family.

Thinking of that brought Constance front and center. What would she think about all of this? If he were to run? There wasn't even time to find out.

Make time, he told himself.

There was a rickety back door, behind the stalls, and Gannon took it. He ran past the twin troughs, past the back of the feed store, and reached the Breen home. Constance's mother was in the kitchen, baking the apple pies she sold to tourists as well as to town folk. Gannon rapped on the sill above two cooling pies. With a little gasp of surprise, followed at once by a scowl of disapproval, Mrs. Breen looked down in thought before leaving to get her daughter. Constance entered the kitchen hurriedly, with pained eyes creasing her flawless skin. She went to the open window.

"Hank!" she cried. "I was just in the street seeing what was going on—"

"The man I was chasing was killed," Gannon cut her off.

"What?"

"It was an accident, an issue between him and my horse," Gannon said. "But the captain wants me to leave."

"Leave—the force? Town?"

"Both."

It took her a moment to digest the information. "Dear Lord, *Why*? You said it was an accident—"

"Being the only living witness, what I say doesn't hold water," Gannon told her. "It *was* an accident, but Keel doesn't think people will believe that."

"What people, the black police?"

"Maybe them, but he's mostly worried about the governor," Gannon told her, refusing to believe that the men of all colors and nationalities that he had worked so closely with, camped with, fought alongside, would turn on him. But then, Keel had done just that.

"You took an oath," Constance said. "An oath to protect all citizens of Texas. If the captain backs you—"

"The captain is not convinced I acted as carefully as I should have."

Constance hesitated. "Did you?"

Gannon took several seconds to answer. "I think so. Truth told, I also wanted to get back to you. Maybe I was sloppy. Maybe. But whatever the reason, a man died."

"I don't believe this," she said. "You should rest. Talk to the captain again when you're clearheaded. You've been up all night—"

"Won't budge him," Gannon said. "No, I've got to leave town while I sort this out," he went on. "But I didn't want to go without a farewell."

Constance shook her head, said firmly, "Hank, you have to stand up for yourself!"

"I agree, but not today. Not with everyone riled up or washing their hands of me." He leaned carefully over the pies, took Constance's shoulders gently, and kissed her on the forehead. He had intended to kiss her mouth until he saw her mother and father—a carpenter with strong hands—watching them from the living room. Maybe it was the shadows, but his expression seemed dark and disapproving.

"Hank?" Constance asked.

Gannon took a step back. "I will find a way to let you know where I am and what I'm doing."

"Find a way—how?"

"I don't know," Gannon admitted. "Homing pigeon, if I have to," he joked. "Would you get my wages from the captain? I don't particularly want to see him again. Buy yourself somethin' pretty."

"I'll fight for you," she said, smiling through tears.

"Whatever happened, I believe in my heart that you mean no man harm."

Gannon smiled tightly as he took another step back then ran off to the barracks on the other side of the stable. He did not look back when Constance was not correct. During the war he had inflicted a great deal of injury, and he meant every wound of it.

Martha Breen reentered the kitchen. She was a narrow-faced woman with an upturned nose and alert eyes beneath a bun of gray hair. Constance made a point of not looking at her. The younger woman turned to leave the room. Martha touched her shoulder as she passed.

"I believe we should discuss this," the older woman said.

"Were you listening?"

"I'm your mother."

"To what end should we 'discuss this,' Mother?"

"That man has dishonored himself," the older woman said. "Yet you have just promised to see him again, to speak up for him."

Constance stepped from under her mother's hand. She paused in the doorway. "Hank was wrongly accused and pursued, just like the slaves you and father once championed," she said.

"No, *not* like them," Martha snapped. She pulled at the underside of her floral sleeve, a habit she had to calm herself. "The situations are nothing alike. This man has admitted to a crime."

"An *accident*, not a crime," Constance corrected her.

"Murder no less," Martha replied.

"What of the man he was chasing? *He* killed."

"He had cause."

"I don't wish to discuss this further," Constance said and turned to go.

This time her mother grabbed her arm. She had strong fingers, equal to her will. "I do not wish to discuss this murderer either," she said. "I have no doubt he *will* desire to see you at some point. When he does, you will not see him."

"Would you say that, Mother, if the victim in question were a white Confederate and not a black man?"

"Men are innocent in this country until a jury declares otherwise—"

"Men other than Hank," her daughter said.

"—unless they have admitted their guilt. If Hank were innocent of a crime, he would not have been dismissed from the police force."

"You know that isn't true," Constance said. "His 'crime,' as you well know from eavesdropping, is having created a political hot potato."

Martha's lined expression hardened even more. "If that is true, Constance, then consider what this 'hot potato' would do to your career and to your future."

"My future with that gelding from the legislature?" she asked.

"You are impertinent! That *gentleman* has a name, Senator Daniel Delacorte, and you refuse even to talk with him!"

"Because I love Hank—"

"Your 'vision of manhood.'"

"Not *just* a vision," Constance protested. She felt betrayed by that. The young woman had come home

and told her mother about their first meeting;
Martha never let her forget the word she had used.

"It's only infatuation," the older woman per-
sisted. "I was a girl once. I recognize the malady."

"Even if that were true, and it is not, what of
Delacorte? He is the opposite of holding me in *any*
kind of thrall. The very look of him bores me,
Mother." The emphasis was Constance's dismissal
not just of Martha but of what the older woman felt
for Hank. "That man you would push on me—"

"For your own welfare, child!"

"—I would bear children and he would *bore* our
children, unless he made them just like him. And
that I could not have. I would not."

Martha was silent for a moment, regrouping to
resume this familiar attack.

"But you are educated," the older woman said.
"You read about history and science. How can a
former slaveholder from a swamp hold *any* lasting
interest?"

"Hank has *lived* life, outside of Texas. Outside of
fancy halls. Besides, I do not seek a scholar or social
position." She gently removed her arm from the
woman's grip. "I will be late for giving Mr. Jones his
reading lesson. And frankly, Mother, I am more
concerned about the future of an illiterate black
man than I am about my own."

With that, the young woman left the room. She
brushed past her father Albert, a slope-shouldered
man with a round face, curly gray hair, and a bit
of a belly stuffed behind his overalls. He stood with
his lunch pail ready to return to work. He had not
tried to push another man on her the way her
mother had. He had actually seemed to like Hank;

he cottoned to any man who had worked with his
hands, who rode hard, who was bold in his actions—
even one who had fought for the South during
the War.

Albert did not speak. There were no tears from
Constance, only a haze of anger at Captain Keel
and disbelief at the way fate had thrown her for
sacrifice on an altar her own family had taken part
in building.

Gannon's grip was packed and waiting outside
the barracks. Keel would not have ordered that;
had that been his intention, he would have said so.
It was a final indignity, a spit in the eye from one or
more of his fellow officers. It would not have been
Sgt. Calvin, who had no patience for petty vendet-
tas; and it would not have been Officer Hernando
Garcia, a Tejano who was too easygoing to want to
hurt anyone but Comanche. Not that it mattered.
It had been done.

Gannon wanted to go inside and see who was
there. But that would have given the captain another reason to arrest him. It also would have
delayed his departure, something that Gannon
suddenly wanted very much.

The Texas police officer slung the seaman's
canvas duffel bag over his shoulder. It had been a
gift from his fisherman uncle Maple. For now, the
love of his family and the love of Constance sustained him as Gannon returned to the stable,
mounted the saddlebred, and was beyond the town
center by 10:30.

PART TWO
Blood and War

CHAPTER ONE

October 16, 1871

It was a sky dark as a coal mine and sprayed with stars, each one proudly brilliant in the still night. A pair of Appaloosas stood obediently beyond the glow of a campfire. Grease from the two spitted hares caused the blaze to crackle and sputter, the aroma enticing the youth to lean farther out from under his woven blanket and into the cloudy gray smoke.

"Treasure all, not just some," said the older man sitting cross-legged behind him.

Puzzled, the younger man looked over. "What have I missed?"

"It is not just the cooking meat you celebrate," the brave informed him. "It is the spirit of the rabbits you inhale. Just as, in battle, you take the heart or hair or eyes of the fallen, so it is with the death of every living thing." He thumped his bare chest. "We become stronger with every deed."

His name was Roving Wolf. His long black hair was braided, he wore a long white neckerchief damp with sweat, and he sat in his own blanket with his sister's son Soon to Be a Man at the bottom of Cedar Valley. His knee boots sat beside him, drying from an earlier creek crossing. On the back of his right forearm was a blue cactus ink tattoo of a knife, warning all of the strength in his arm. The hair of both men was worn in braids, and around the older man's head was a beaded band with an eagle feather at back; below it was the tail of a wolf. Around the ankles of both men were leather bindings that were used to rub the sides of horses, for control, without abrading the skin of the ride.

The slope was gentle here, almost like a river that had gone dry. It was where Roving Wolf used to hunt as a boy, a place he knew well. The insects, the birds, the rodents were all known to him. The trees were larger, but the stones were familiar. It had been easy making his way through here, even in the dark. It was safer to travel, then; there was a war against the Comanche and the soldiers who made that war preferred the sun. Not so their Tonkawa scouts, who knew the territory well and had lifetimes of hate for the Comanche. But there was a saying, "*Unknown dangers are as harmful as known dangers—and more plentiful.*" One could not prepare for everything, and Roving Wolf was not one to live his life in hiding. The young man beside him must learn that, as Roving Wolf did when he was young.

The name Soon to Be a Man had caused the young man some embarrassment over his twelve years. Roving Wolf had brought him here to tell of the past week's events, to present him with a special gift, and to explain why even the elder Comanche, at more than thirty years, was still becoming a man.

The gift was first, something the boy's mother had expressly wished. Before he and the boy sat, Roving Wolf had gone to his horse and removed a bear hide that had been carefully bound in sinew from the animal. The elder Comanche held the parcel respectfully in both hands. The boy had not been expecting anything and seemed unsure what to do.

"This is yours," Roving Wolf explained. "It belonged to Great Bear and now it is yours."

"My father?" the youth said reverently.

"It was his dying wish that you have this," Roving Wolf told him. "And as the white man may come to our teepees for blood, you must be able to protect your mother, your people."

The boy accepted the package. Eager fingers tugged at the lacings. He collected them carefully and set them aside before he lifted the flaps of the skin. The light of the campfire revealed the most magnificent weapon he had ever seen. It was a bone the size of his own forearm. It was sharpened, at the end, to a knife point. At the other end, set in the base of the knobby hilt, were three large claws.

"Your father earned his name at your age," Roving Wolf said. "Tell his story as your mother told it to you."

"It . . . it was a time of drought and my father . . . he and a friend were fishing," Soon to Be a Man said. "They were attacked by a starving bear for their fish. The friend was mauled . . . and my father came between them, with a torch from their campfire." His eyes drifted almost reverently to their own campfire. The wood they had used was barely the size of his foot. "Was it a large torch?" the young man asked. "Was he very close to the bear?"

"Only the Big Father knows," Roving Wolf said. "But he protected his friend, who was thereafter called the Ugly One, and your father was no longer Running Fox but Great Bear." The brave pointed to the weapon. "With but one eye, Ugly One made this from the leg of the bear. He became a maker of totems, and your father fell in battle with the Tonkawa. It was his dying wish that you possess this weapon . . . and, with it, earn his name. When you have spilled blood, you shall be known as Great Bear."

The boy was overwhelmed—by the weapon, by the honor. He took a moment to raise the weapon in both hands, utter words of thanks to the spirit of his father. The flickering of the fire cast a shadow of the weapon on the rock behind them, made the bear seem to live once more. The spirit of the animal was present. To Roving Wolf, the young man seemed older, stronger, greater when his arms came back to his lap.

"The bear is very powerful," Soon to Be a Man remarked.

"He is."

"But my father defeated it," the boy said.

"That day," Roving Wolf said. He raised a cautioning finger. "Each bear is a new challenge. It may not behave as its kin."

"And the wolf? Tell me of your name."

"A she-wolf let a babe live while he was yet in the belly of his mother," Roving Wolf replied.

"You?"

Roving Wolf nodded. "My mother was gathering

nuts, and the wolf met her eyes from the brush. My
mother did not flee but met the eyes of the wolf,
equal to equal." The brave held his hands palms
down, fingertips to fingertips. "The wolf came forward and walked by. Her spirit remained."

"Is the wolf more powerful than the bear?"

"It is different, like the eagle is different from the
crow or the snake from the toad."

"But in a pack, the wolf *is* more powerful?"

"In some ways," Roving Wolf answered. "When
you rely on others, your strength is wider but that is
not the same as greater. In some ways, the pack di-
minishes the one because the hunting and killing
are shared."

"A war party is the same?"

"In very many ways it is," the elder brave said.
"My father, Swift Hawk, once sat where I sit and told
me of the day he went to the ancient lands to find
his spirit." Roving Wolf held his hand, palm up,
toward the lowlands unseen in the dark. "There
had been a sickness, and the tribe had suffered
greatly. Even the medicine man was unable to help."

"Your father?" the youth asked eagerly.

Roving Wolf smiled. "No. *His* father. Swift Hawk
wished to help him. So he went to the place where,
tradition tells us, fire once belched from the earth
and smoke covered the land and death touched all
things. He sat on a hard, hard ridge and prayed to
the Big Father to speak to him through that place"—
Roving Wolf grinned—"but with a quieter voice, if
the god would not mind."

The young man laughed at that.

"Sitting there, at night, Fire Hawk had a vision.
Our people in a field with no teepees. The sun caring

for them. He went back to the settlement and told his father what he had seen. Comanche helped Comanche, old helped young, mother helped father, and the vision was made real. The tribe recovered. There was a thing that was done in part by one, in part by the many."

"I like tradition," Soon to Be a Man decided. "I understand what it says."

Roving Wolf lay a hand on the boy's forearm and added, "But it is not to be decided as being 'good' or 'bad.' A woman and a man are different, each does different things, yet each is essential in their own way. Ask yourself if a baby is good or bad. It cannot hunt but it can suckle. There is a place for all things in the tribe."

"Did Blanco Canyon make you stronger?" the lanky youth asked, sitting back and pulling the blanket tighter. His voice was wary, tentative. He knew what had happened there.

Roving Wolf peered through the smoke as though he were looking directly into the past. A past that was just six days old, not yet shadow, still vivid and alive. He watched as the images of horses, riders, guns, arrows became increasingly vivid. So did the sounds: the crack of firearms, the cries of men and horses, the dull, dead *whump* of bodies dropping.

"It did," the brave replied. "The force of soldiers was greater than the number of us defending it. And a heroic death, protecting your lands and families, serves your life. Your spirit and those who follow grow greater in honor and in power."

"Can a victory be a loss?" Soon to Be a Man asked.

The elder man smiled. "That is very wise. Yes," he said. "The soldiers lost in the way a thunderstorm loses. It is here, fierce and great, but it passes. A force so large as the soldiers cannot be sustained. But the land remains. The Kotsoteka and Quahadi tribes who perished live on." He fell silent. "They were an offense to our people, the first white force to enter the *Sookobit*," he continued thoughtfully, using the word for the Comancheria, the "Comanche land." "We came for them in the dark. Only a few of us, led by Wild Buck."

"He is very brave."

"We were brothers in blood," Roving Wolf said. "We drove off their horses and the soldiers, roused, gave pursuit. They followed us to the top of the canyon where our party was waiting. The encounter was a victory for our people—but the only one, as the white men would not be fooled again. We divided in all directions of the wind. The soldiers," he said with a hint of sadness, "they are still out there, hunting us. Before long, they will be here. I tell you this because you must be ready."

Soon to Be a Man leaned forward again to put his face in the smoke, closing his eyes and inhaling deeply to accept the full gift of the rabbits.

"I will learn to—"

He had stopped speaking before the echoing crack of the weapon reached the ears of his companion. The youth was knocked back, his arms pinwheeling, his head turning slightly as the bullet pierced his forehead just off center. The weapon of his father flew, clattered, vanished in the dark. Blood fountained from the brow of his dead body as Roving Wolf simultaneously flung himself across the young man and away from the light of the campfire.

"Soon to Be a Man!" he said, more in mourning

than in an effort to rouse the boy. Even in the dark he could see the small wound, feel the blood. With a guttural sound that was more vulpine than human, the Comanche simultaneously drew his bowie knife from its sheath and scuttled farther into the dark, leaving the boy to commune with their ancestors as his own spirit rose like clear smoke.

The shot had come from the north. The gunman was not far, since the initial sound had been quite loud and the shot precise. The Comanche had no way of knowing if the man were alone, or how long he had been there. He and the boy—a *boy*, never to become a man—had arrived after dark. They would not have seen clouds of dust or the glint of the setting sun on metal, heard the sounds of horses or men. But it did not matter to Roving Wolf how many there were. Tonight, all would die.

He moved from the fire and, shrouded in dark, knelt to feel around. He knifed the ground, tucked something in his belt, and when he was well clear of the campsite he began padding in the direction from which the sound had come. He asked the Great Spirit to use fang and claw to protect the remains of the boy until he could return. He promised the land that the coyote and the gray wolf would soon have bones on which to gnaw.

"Bang-up job," the young black man said mockingly. "First cabin. Now the Injun is comin' fer sure."

The other man, Joseph Williams, a Tonkawa scout from the Oklahoma Territory, lay stretched out behind a large, flat boulder. The air still smelled faintly of gunpowder from the single shot of the lever action "Yellow Boy" Winchester.

"Good he comes," Williams grunted. "Save me trouble of going after him."

"Just make sure that when you hear someone, you make sure it ain't Ahrens and Hawthorne," the black man said.

"They not near," Williams said, touching his nose. "And they never travel alone. Four feet sound different than two. Horse sound different than man."

"I'm not an idiot, Joseph," the other said.

"Nor I, Rufus."

The other man, Rufus Long, an officer of the Texas Special Police, had been referring to the other party that had left Austin the night before, Kurt Ahrens and his scout Moses Hawthorne, a former fur trapper. Worse than killing a pair of Comanche would be shooting two of their own men. Especially Ahrens, who regarded the Texas State Police as the only sanity on this frontier. It was a responsibility he took so seriously that he had packed Gannon's grip and set it on the stoop rather than let a careless, undisciplined officer set foot among them ever again.

Long was sprawled on his belly beside but slightly behind the scout. His last smoke had been just before sundown, at least six hours before, and he wanted one badly. He also wanted to wring some of the stiff-necked, baked-in, rooster-proud arrogance out of the redskin. No matter how many times Captain Keel gave them instructions, no matter what the situation in the field, if Williams saw a way to bend an order to "bring the smile of his ancestors upon him" through some Tonkawa deed, he did it.

"The orders were to find them and report back, not to engage," Long said. "The word the captain used was 'reconnoiter.'"

Long's tone was not frightened but angry. A veteran of the Underground Railroad and the narrow survivor of a lynching by Rebels retreating from Gettysburg—which was interrupted when a Union spy put life above mission—Long did not scare easily. But he believed in following orders. Without them, organization crumbled and lives were lost.

Williams half-turned and thrust an index finger toward Long, who recoiled slightly. "Find now, engage later," the Tonkawa brave hissed, then turned the index finger toward himself. "Find now, engage now." The warrior's dark eyes seemed to pull his head around, back to the rocky field ahead. Even sharper than his eyes were his ears. Even in the dark, Williams could tell the footfall of a field mouse from a chipmunk. And though he couldn't know for sure, he believed his nose just might be as good as that of any dog. He could tell if a buffalo or bear was sick at a half-mile downwind. That was why they were out here now, he and his green partner who was supposed to be watching and learning as they listened for Comanche warriors who preferred to move about in the dark.

"Dammit, this was not in the mission talk," Long muttered on, seeing in his mind the big face of Captain Keel as he told the force what they were to do. He had rallied them from across the state specifically to observe the Comanche. "A two-man nighttime *huntin'* party was not part of his plan."

The Indian hushed him with a gesture. That was

the problem with many of the scouts Keel engaged. They had jobs for which they accepted pay, but they also had blood feuds. Most of the time, the two complemented each other. But not tonight.

The brave continued to face forward. He emptied himself of all but the present. He also knew when the creatures of the night were still, as they were now. It meant that danger was near—for them but also most likely for the two men. Williams did not like assuming a defensive posture, but after spilling Comanche blood that was the wisest course.

There was a whiff of something musky on the wind. It preceded by an instant an animal flying toward them. At first Williams thought it was a squirrel that had fallen from a nearby tree. It wasn't. The rabbit pelt landed on the Tonkawa, who flinched but did not fire. Long yelped as the Indian swatted it aside with his left arm. The bloody fur landed between them, and Williams raised the rifle barrel from the rock, listened. He heard nothing.

The skin hadn't flown far; the Comanche had to be near. Williams could smell him now but he couldn't see him.

"Jesus!"

Long screamed involuntarily as scorpions began to sting him. Williams felt a bite too, in his neck, where the pelt had landed. He swore like a white man as he involuntarily slapped at the creature and knew that he was as good as dead.

After hurling the rabbit pelt with an arcing swing, Roving Wolf had dug his toes into a layer of rock to give himself purchase. As soon as he heard the officer's cry, the slap of hand on flesh, he vaulted through the air like a human puma. He had smelled the remains of the shot that had killed his companion, heard the two men speak, knew where they were and how low to the ground. His right arm was raised and his mouth was filled with a silent war cry as he landed flat on the other side of the boulder. Only when the blade pierced sinew in the back of the gunman did the Comanche give voice to a raging scream. That was as much to freeze the white man as it was to vent his fury.

The blade struck bone before sliding into a lung. The Tonkawa wheezed and tried to turn over but Roving Wolf held tight to the sleeve of his victim's police jacket. His weight was too much. The knife came down again, this time into the man's side. Then again in the same bloody spot. The death rattle in the man's throat began to fade.

The Comanche scrabbled off to the man's right, ducking behind his moaning body, using it as a shield in case the other man came for him or fired into the dark. He did neither. Though Roving Wolf heard movement, saw shadows shift in the darkness nearby, the man was backing away—and also, if he had a raindrop of sense, afraid of hitting his partner.

Except for the bubbling wheeze in the throat of the brave whose blood was rising, there was suddenly no sound. Until a shot cracked from not far behind the two Indians, striking nothing. It was followed by a low, sonorous voice.

"Anybody move, he gets shot." After allowing a moment for that to register, the speaker said, "'Cept Long, if that's you."

Rufus Long didn't answer immediately. The man's confusion was evident in his silence.

"*Are* you Rufus Long?" the voice repeated. "Munitions man for the Texas Special Police? Who smokes that armpit-grown tobacco from Canada because it's cheap?"

"I am," he said after a moment. "Hey, who'n hell are you?"

"Someone who could smell that tobacco stink on your uniform from a good distance away," the speaker said. "Strike one o' your police-issue matches. Let's put some light on what's what. And you with the knife?" he added. "My gun's on you, Comanche. Flinch and you die."

Long turned and fumbled in his saddlebag, which sat against a cactus a few paces behind him. The horses were several yards beyond that, standing in a clearing amidst the bunchgrasses, tied to what was left of a lightning-struck elm. The officer scratched a match and extended it arm's length. There was no wind, no need to cup it in his hands. All he saw were the two tangled forms of the Indians and the silhouette of a man standing several yards distant. Long took a rolled cigarette from the pocket of his black shirt, used the match to light it. The move was practical as well as satisfying: the lighted cigarette would save him having to light another match.

The flame died, but the officer had already spotted dry tufts of blackseed needlegrass. He uprooted several with a fist, pressed the soil together as a common base, and ignited the clumps with the smoke. They burned bright enough for him to find and toss several twigs on the fire, washed into the valley by a June rain. The gurgling of the man beside him was impetus to move quickly, but as the Texas Special Police officer had told every runaway slave he had ever met, "Hound dogs love careless men." Like breaking a wild horse, he had to stay on top of the human instinct to bolt in the opposite direction from danger.

One way to stay calm was to stay focused on a task. Long avoided looking up until the fire was not only lit but sustained. On his knees now, he turned his eyes and perspiring brow toward the most recent arrival.

"Shit me a large stone," was all he said, but it was heartfelt.

Hank Gannon looked at Long from the other side of the entangled Indians. The young growth of scruffy beard made the former officer look ten years older. Over what was left of his vest and white shirt he wore what looked like a patchwork cloak of pelts that reached to his knees. A pocket on the inside held flint for a fire and several dried tendons from deer he'd eaten. These tough lengths of string were used to attach pelts or food to the horse or to tie off wounds, if it came to that. His dirty hat was behind his neck, held there by the loosely knotted string; his light brown hair, slicked back from a river-water washing, was no longer carefully parted in the middle. The dark eyes looked a little hollow but no less alert for that.

Those eyes shifted from the black man to the Indians.

"You on top," Gannon said. "Comanche!"

Roving Wolf turned his head slightly without lifting

it. His expression, what Gannon could see of it, was locked and feral, like a totem. He was lying flat on his victim, his torso athwart the man's waist, at an angle. The knife was still in Joseph Williams's side, blood running around the blade. The wheeze had dwindled to a whisper.

"You understand me, Indian?" Gannon asked.

The Comanche grunted through his teeth, which were like glistening little opals in the match light. Gannon was not surprised that the Comanche could speak English. Whatever the tribe, braves found the skill useful in dealing with traders, especially gun dealers.

"What's your name?" Gannon asked.

The Indian was defiantly silent.

Gannon shrugged, the flints in his pocket clattering. "I'll just call you Pale Rabbit," he said, thinking of two insults he did not think the Indian would allow to stand.

The Comanche spoke up proudly. "Roving Wolf."

"Fitting," Gannon said, looking at the man's teeth. "Roving Wolf, leave the knife on the ground and make your way to the fire," the man went on. "Slow. I won't ask you to crawl, but if you move too fast you die. Understand?"

The Comanche's expression seemed to relax in the honor that was shown to him—not to be made a creature of the dirt. Even so, in response to the command, Roving Wolf moved forward in a way that was surprisingly like a reptile, his toes pushing, fingers flat at his sides and also pushing, his entire body moving without apparent effort. While that was going on, Rufus Long knee-walked back several paces, reached for his sidearm.

Gannon half-turned on him. "Uh-uh, Long," he said. "Hands up and open."

"Hank? Dammit, he killed—"

"Yeah, I know. Hands. Show 'em."

The Texas Special Police officer raised them as slow as a sunrise, palms out. The cigarette was still between his lips, smoke curling up his nose. When he seemed disinclined to move again, Gannon turned his attention back on the Indian.

"You, Roving Wolf—that's far enough."

The Indian stopped. He did not put his face down but rested on his chin, peering into the darkness. Like his namesake, lying in wait behind a bush.

"Now what you can do," Gannon said to Long, "is get some more sticks for the fire. Then come and see if there's anything to be done for poor Joe. Sounds like there's still some breath left."

Long nodded, scuttling for kindling then moving around the fire and kneeling beside the wounded scout. He was within body-heat range of the Comanche. He could feel the radiant hate. The officer's head ducked around as he looked at the wound. His knees were soaking with blood and he noticed, now, how far the pool had spread. Almost at the same time, Williams stopped breathing. Long exhaled with him. The officer did not realize how taut his shoulders were until they relaxed.

"Cover him with something that ain't another Indian," Gannon said.

"Can I get up?" Long asked.

"Sure. I won't kill you if you don't give me cause. That was my horse."

"What? What was your horse?" Long asked, confused.

"Whatever else you heard from my brothers-in-arms, my loyal friends, my commander, it's my horse kills people, not me," Gannon told him. "An' said animal is a good quarter mile elsewhere." He took a step forward. "I'm assumin' the captain did tell people what happened with Sketch Lively, yes?"

"He did," Long said. "But he didn't tell us why you chose to run instead of tellin' your side at an inquiry."

"Did anyone ask him?"

"No."

"Why not?" Gannon asked.

"You had orientation," Long said. "You know commanders can't discuss legal matters that pertain to others."

Gannon shook his head. Keel could have told them, unofficially. He probably did not want to create factions of white versus black, Northerner versus Southerner, by revealing just how flimsy the evidence was against the man.

"I did not 'run,'" Gannon said.

"What do you call clearin' out of town like it was a whorehouse raid?"

"I call it bein' pushed out the window. There wasn't gonna be any 'inquiry,'" Gannon said, practically spitting the word.

"Why? If you had a case—"

"I had a corpse instead of a prisoner," Gannon said. "Keel made it clear there was no way I got out of this clean. He probably thought he was being

generous, letting me avoid dismissal and jail time."
He shook his head, the matter as raw as if he were
still standing in the stable. "You know that railroad
they're buildin'? Brother, I took that ride, straight
into exile."

Long considered this. "I don't care anything
about politics, but you been a good man to me. I
woulda said so."

"I'm gratified," Gannon replied insincerely.

Long got up, feeling the soaked blood run down
the inside of his trousers. He yipped. There was a
scorpion in the pant leg too, crawling on the inside
of his right thigh. He shook it out as he walked to
Williams's horse. Recovering the bundled blanket,
he returned and lay it over him. "I assume you came
here on account o' the shot?"

"Long-range rifle at night? Yeah, I wanted to
know about that."

"That was Williams," Long said. "He fired."

"At *boy*," Roving Wolf said hotly. He jabbed a
finger at his own forehead. "Shot kill him."

"I'm sorry," Gannon said sincerely. "Bastard
always was a good shot." He looked at Long, who
was just rising from the body. "By what authority
did he shoot?"

The officer finally drew on his cigarette. He knew
he was in trouble here; Negroes ranked higher
than Indians. In the field, the command was his.

"Joe did this on his own cussed authority," Long
said. "I—I didn't tell him to. He just did it. We were
only s'posed to watch for Comanche."

"Why?"

"Battle out west," Long said. "Army all tied up

there. Captain Keel figgered some'd come this way, so he sent a pair of teams out."

"Soldiers came to our land, many soldiers," the Indian said. He thumped his chest. "We defend."

"I thought something like that when I heard horses movin' through the other day," Gannon said. His eyes dropped to Williams. "Williams here had his own feud, yeah?"

"That's a likelihood," Long said, then added, "or maybe he was bored or itchy or he just got stupid. People get that way out here, Gannon."

Gannon got the point, right in his windpipe. He spit. "Talk less, Long. You may make me get stupid."

Roving Wolf was looking down at the dead man, shaking his head. "Northern tribes—hate. Kill Comanche. They always want *here*." He lifted an arm, made a large, horizontal, smearing gesture with one hand. "Great water."

"Right," Gannon said. The sea offered a ready supply of food and access to trade. Oklahoma tribes with historic rivalries to the south had only one route to the Gulf of Mexico: war.

"Long, me and this fella are gonna leave you," Gannon said. "You stay put, smoke all your butts till morning, and then take Williams back to the cap'n."

"Hank, this man murdered a scout," Long said. "He has to answer for that."

"He just did," Gannon said. The former officer came forward now, stopping beside the Comanche. His personal .12-gauge scattergun tucked under his right arm, he toed Roving Wolf gently in the side. "You may get up."

The Comanche rose, dead grass and leaves falling from him as if from a ghoul departing his grave.

"You cannot do this," Long warned.

"It's done."

Long shook his head firmly, casting big shadows on the ground behind him. "You got away once. This time the captain *will* come after you."

"For what? Saving your skin?"

Long's eyes drifted to the Comanche. In the firelight, his tattoo seemed to write. His shadow also seemed alive. "This Indian is a murdering renegade. He killed my partner, flung a pelt fulla scorpions at us—he is dirt and he must be brought in. Listen, Hank," he added with a whisper of softness. "Maybe if you do it, Captain Keel will rethink what he did. You can see Miss Constance."

The mention of her name seemed to harden the man unexpectedly. "Don't you remind me what I've lost," he warned. "I've been livin' off snake and quail out here, thinkin' of very little except Keel an' what he did. It was wrong, to think first about appeasin' the gov'nor and his fellow roosters . . . just like bringin' in this Comanche would be wrong. You already took from him—his lands and his travelin' companion."

"You're mixing things up," Long said. "I didn't do anything. *We* didn't. The action in Blanco Canyon was military. It was ordered by the Indian agent—"

"Long, just shut your mouth up. We're leavin'."

The officer did not move and then, suddenly, he did, reaching for his holstered Remington. A loud report from the rifle, fired from the hip, chewed up the earth a foot to Long's right. Dirt landed on the fire, dulling it.

"Next one is in your arm," Gannon threatened.

He took a step forward. Long retreated very slightly but enough to let him know the warning was taken seriously. "Do not test me. Don't even talk. Keel took my life from me, an' I don't want t'hear his name again." Gannon stood quietly, everyone remained still for a long moment. "But you can do something for me, man-to-man. You can tell Constance I will see her again."

Long nodded once but otherwise remained frozen, praying that there were no more scorpions under his clothes to make him jump. He had always liked Gannon and wished they had met in some other fashion. He wanted to know where Gannon had been, what he was planning. But his lips were pressed shut. Smoke trailed up his nostrils from the dying fire and from the cigarette. He coughed inside his mouth.

"Hank?" the Indian said, and pointed to the knife that was still on the ground.

"Okay," Gannon said.

"You just armed the enemy," Long said with open disbelief.

"Yeah," Gannon agreed. "But you're the one gave him reason to kill."

The Comanche bent and recovered his knife. He did not wipe the blade on the blanket but on the grasses. It was a show of respect to Gannon, not to further defile the dead man.

Slipping the blade into its doeskin sheath, Roving Wolf led the way into the darkness, Gannon following. Their footsteps faded before the small, dim fire had died. Only then did Rufus Long consider what he would have to do next: sit up with the dead man until morning, making sure his remains were not defiled. Come the dawn, he would put him on his horse and they would ride into Austin. He was not eager for those labors—or to face Captain Keel with the news that it might not have been the best idea to let Hank Gannon simply ride out of town . . .

CHAPTER TWO

October 17, 1871

Hank Gannon was usually not surprised by what God had up His big, white sleeve. Most times, God didn't have to do much but move the world along like a shepherd staffing his sheep. But then there were moments like this that mystified Gannon with their very specific nature.

After leaving Austin, his heart heavy and his prospects thin, the suddenly rootless lawman did not feel as though God had a plan for him. Gannon had intended to go to Houston or San Antonio for work. He wasn't prepared to return to Florida, like a cowed dog; but working on a ranch or farm or fishing seemed to make sense. For the moment, he didn't care what he did as long as it wasn't law enforcement, bounty hunting, soldiering, or anything else that required tracking. No God there.

But as that dark day had grown old and night settled on his aimless southern ride, something else settled too—the realization that Gannon loved the art of tracking, of challenging and honing his survival and sensory skills. He found himself thinking back to the trackers who worked with his unit during the war, with the Texas Special Police. Indians, all of them. Was the skill born into them or acquired? Or was it just dormant in everyone but the Indian, who used it every day? Gannon had no idea. He didn't know if he could become as good as Chea Sequa, "Red Bird," who had stayed behind when the men of the 2nd Cherokee Mounted Rifles quit the Confederate cause. But he did know this. "Chi," as they called him, liked long odds. He said they made him better. And if a Cherokee could become a better tracker, so could a white man.

Captain Keel had spoiled that. And Gannon wasn't sure what kind of law work he could get anyway, given that this unjust stain would follow him wherever he went. During the war, when his survival depended on it, he heard the refrain, "*Go home to Florida.*"

Gannon had received letters from home. Florida was no longer Florida. It had been blockaded by Union gunboats during the war, to prevent it from shipping much-needed cattle and salt to Confederate troops. He had learned only recently that his cousin Clementine had become a smuggler, carrying those goods southward, to Cuba, in exchange for gold. Both of those industries were crushed. Many Floridians, blacks included, had run to the North to serve in the Union army and had not returned. Countless others died of battle wounds and starvation. The state was invaded in 1864, Reconstructionists took over in 1865, and now Florida was run by northern business concerns and freed slaves.

"*Home.*"

It had died a brave death, the body profaned, the spirit bottled and smothered.

No, Keel's words had not been advice, as the captain himself had surely realized. It had been a dismissal. Keel liked things orderly, with the politics kept off the stove. Get out of *my* way, don't cause *me* trouble. The more Gannon had listened to those words in his head, the less settled he became. He stopped riding with a destination in mind. Instead, he rode with a goal forming somewhere behind his eyes. Fuzzy at first, like foothills creeping with morning mist. Then sharper, finally gleaming as a single word: redemption.

But a goal is always easy. That distant hill, that remote horizon—easy to see, less so to reach. So he had ridden, thought, camped, thought, trapped, and while he thought some more he used pelt and sinew to fashion his sleeping cape, a wide bedroll that he also wore on his shoulders to smell like something other than a man. It brought prey to him. It shielded him from trackers like the Comanche. It made Gannon feel more than just man, as a Seminole who tended pigs once told him. Maybe that, too, would help him track. His thought had been: give it time.

Now, this. God's handiwork seemed very present, of a sudden. But leading to what end?

Gannon and the Comanche recovered the white man's horse before walking toward the site where Soon to Be a Man had fallen. They did not speak. Roving Wolf had no questions and Gannon did not want to intrude on the Indian's grief. Different tribes and different members of those tribes each had their own way of honoring the dead. There was no chanting, no gesturing. Gannon knew, however, that they were taking a different path than the way Roving Wolf had come. Not because he had seen the Indian moving but because it was a very still night and the Comanche would have left his scent along the trail. By now, nighttime predators would have picked it up and gone there. One did not want to startle a pack of coyotes in the dark. They might attack and the horse would panic, for sure.

When they reached the campsite, Gannon collected the two horses while Roving Wolf knelt over the dead man. It was too dark to see very much, but he could see the Comanche kneeling silently beside the body, his hands cupped and rising up several times as though he were making an offering. Gannon guessed he was ushering the spirit to its guardian. It was a common enough gesture among all the tribes he had ever encountered. When he was done, Roving Wolf gathered the boy in his blanket and lifted him onto his horse. The animal tried to step away but Gannon was ready for that, gripping the mane firmly.

The frame-style saddle was made of cottonwood and covered with rawhide, attached by a single cinch cut from the same hide. It had a low arched pommel and an elk-horn cantle that held a lariat. The other horse was similarly outfitted. The Comanche removed his rope and used it to secure the dead man into burial position before the warmth had departed his body; the knees were bent upward to rest against the chest, the legs were lashed back to the thighs, the head was bent forward, and the arms were bent and tied to either side of the chest. The binding was done quickly, skillfully, even in the dark, the Comanche having practiced it many times in his life. The women of the tribe and the medicine man Green Snake practiced healing arts; the braves trained for death. When he was finished, the bundle was placed upright in the natural curve of the saddle. It was a precarious seat for a long journey but Roving Wolf would take the journey slowly. There might yet be other police in the valley, or trappers, or cowboys at camp. If they presented no threat, he would let them be.

For now.

Throughout the process Gannon stood respectfully, seeing little but knowing what the brave was doing. When Roving Wolf was finished, he took the two sets of reins from Gannon.

"You have no home," Roving Wolf said.

"Not here," Gannon said. Then he added, "Not anymore."

"You are welcome," he said, inclining his head toward the west.

Gannon heard that and choked up a little. "Driven out by my own kind, offered refuge by a Comanche." He exhaled. "It's a temptin' offer but when you ride in with your—who was he, anyway?"

"Soon to Be a Man, the only son of my sister. A great heart and a great curiosity."

"I wish I'd gotten to meet him," Gannon replied.

"I think if I went with you there would be great anger at me, at my skin."

"There are always rabid foxes," the Comanche replied.

Gannon smiled at him. "True. But if you can't shoot 'em, best to go wide around them."

Roving Wolf nodded once. Then he squatted, felt the ground around the camp.

"What is it?" Gannon asked.

The brave replied, "Bones that have been returned to the earth."

Standing and looping a hand through both reins, the Comanche raised both index fingers and put them side by side, facing Gannon. Even in the dark, he knew that the Comanche had made the symbol for "union." The white man did the same. Mounting his horse and tugging the other pony behind, Roving Wolf moved slowly along the canyon to the west.

"Shit."

The man who swore, Moses Hawthorne, was squatting on a scrub-covered bluff some fifty feet above a plain at the western edge of Cedar Valley. Below him was an encampment of Comanche braves. He was squinting into a spyglass that had once belonged to his mentor, trapper Jim Bridger. The collapsible brass tube moved slowly up, down, left, right as he tried to pick out details. There were no campfires, no teepees, but the scout roughly numbered the Indians at fifteen to twenty based on the shadowy horses he could discern moving in the darkness. What concerned him as much as the Indians was the fact that there was a steep but straight path from where they were to where he was. And just below his position he had spotted what looked like the shape of a human foot. It was difficult to be certain in the dark, but it was like an Indian to explore every avenue of offense, defense, and escape from a place. This ridge was both.

Hawthorne shared that information, and his assessment of their situation, with his fellow Texas Special Police officer. Austrian émigré Kurt Ahrens stood several paces behind him, chewing tobacco, spitting, and soothing the horses from the sounds of the night.

"We still got a bunch o' night," Hawthorne half-turned and whispered through a mouth of few teeth. "I say we git. Sun finds us here, we in a fight."

Ahrens spit again. "We stay with them," he said.

"Yeah. More like they stay with us. Then they spit-roast our dicks for starters."

"I knew a soldier, in the Old Country, shot his own head," Ahrens said casually. "Better than be caught by Gypsies."

"Fine story. Makes my case, don't it?"

"His job was track Gypsies," Ahrens said. "Our job is track Comanche."

Hawthorne hated the Austrian's logic because he was right. But being right and "shooting your own head" was not a skill he had learned from Bridger. The legendary trapper had taught him survival. Dogging the trail of savages who had just put up a wild-dog fight in Blanco Canyon was not how he wanted to die.

"You so eager, why don't you stay an' I ride back to Austin, get men," Hawthorne suggested.

"We have to know where they go, what are their arms, and how many are wounded," Ahrens told him. "*Then* you go. With information."

That was logical, too, and equally villainous. Hawthorne was not a fearful man, but he tried to be a sensible one. You don't go up a mountain in a snowstorm. You don't try to ford a swollen river. And you don't pit two men against a much larger party of Indian braves.

"They are not like bison," Hawthorne muttered as he folded his spyglass. "You shoot, they do not run."

"That is why buffalo will outlive them," Ahrens said.

Damn the man, Hawthorne thought. His logic was like those snakes Hank Gannon used to talk about, big ones that could crush a man. There was just no getting away from it.

Hawthorne slid the spyglass into its leather loop on his belt then looked out at the camp.

"You rest now," Ahrens said. "I wake you for your turn to watch."

There was finally some logic he could sign on for. Creeping from the ledge, he lay his shoulders against a half-rotted pecan log, crossed his arms across the front of his buckskin jacket, and was quickly asleep. It was the one talent Bridger had told him all trappers needed, the ability to stay awake for extended treks through dangerous territory, and to sleep whenever the opportunity presented—like a sudden gully washer that forced you under a ledge.

"Waste not," was the old trapper's saying for pretty much everything, which included sucking the marrow from bear bones and eating their eyes. Pan roasted, they were actually okay.

* * *

Hawthorne was awakened when a gloved hand clapped over his mouth. He gasped into the glove, which was the point. Ahrens's face loomed over him in the darkness.

"Shhh."

It was barely more than the sound of blowing out a candle. The Austrian removed his hand and, fully awake, Hawthorne rolled onto his left side. His Remington was in his hand and his ears had pinpointed what Ahrens had also heard. There were two sets of hoof-falls coming toward them. They were about thirty or forty feet distant; it was still too dark to see anything, but white men typically did not travel in the dark.

Their own horses snorted and clip-clopped suddenly, briefly, as they became aware of the other animals. Whoever was approaching stopped.

Ahrens tapped Hawthorne, motioned right in front of his face so he could see. He pointed north and indicated that the tracker should go south. Hawthorne nodded. However unlikely, if someone opened fire it was a bad idea to be bunched together.

The sound had been coming from the front end of the log, where Hawthorne was facing. He straddled the pecan, taking care not to bang anything on the bark or crush a rotted old nut on the other side. He continued moving sideways while Ahrens crept in the opposite direction. Every now and then, the tethered horses would renew their nervous sounds.

It had to be a Redman, Hawthorne thought. *No white pony would be so still and silent.* Police, troopers, hunters, trappers—they just sat on their mounts. Even Jim Bridger, who knew bear and deer better than any man, and who wore their skins, was still only Jim Bridger. Indians became one with their animals, spiritually. They were almost like those old man-horses he had once seen a drawing of in a book. Even if an Indian was just leading his animal, there was a bond.

There was a loud sound of an owl that wasn't an owl because Hawthorne had not seen any of the birds about. Neither of the white men moved. The identical cry came again from a slightly different position.

Owls stood still on their perches.

Shit.

There were sounds behind them, distant, low— from the Comanche camp. As Hawthorne had watched them through the spyglass, he did what he always did with quarry, calculated how long it would take them to sneak, walk, run, or gallop to where he was. The Comanche had done the same. On foot, without relying on the uncertain step of a horse in the dark, and able to ascend two abreast, the entire party could reach this position in about two minutes.

Hawthorne had told that to Ahrens, and the Austrian had apparently reached the same conclusion he had. It was time to leave, and not by going down into the valley.

Ahrens's gun lit up to Hawthorne's right, sending a shot in the direction of the sound. Before the loud pop had died, Hawthorne was already up and leaping the log, racing toward his horse. The "owl" screeched again, this time from higher up. He had mounted his horse.

Hawthorne paused to fire but the Comanche horses had already wheeled away, racing back in the direction they had come.

"They're setting up a catchall!" Ahrens yelled from the saddle. "Go the way we were going! Don't fire!"

"Catchall" was Keel's term for a funnel, where one force forced another force into a bunch, then herded that bunch into a shooting gallery. He wanted Hawthorne to go wide around but not shoot at the Comanche in the middle lest they hit each other.

Ahrens screamed, his cry swallowed in a large, thudding crash. It was either a gopher hole or—

Shit.

There were grunts, an oath, the sounds of a struggle. Hawthorne dismounted and ran toward them. He tripped over a rope pulled taut between two tree boles. That was what the Indian had been doing when he was silent. Acting, not just stupidly standing there.

Hawthorne holstered the gun, drew his knife, and scrabbled toward the sounds of the fighting. He held the bison-bone hilt tight in his right hand, moved with the fingers of his left stretched toward the struggle. He made contact with braids. Instinct closed his fingers like a bear trap, and he clutched a knot of hair tight. The owner swung on him like an eagle on a field mouse, and Hawthorne immediately found his right arm pinned against his chest by the weight of the Indian. That weight lessened almost immediately as Ahrens growled, slapped his hands on the attacker's back, and pulled him away.

"*Get the other one!*" he shouted at Hawthorne.

The tracker got on his feet and charged. He knew where the Indians' horses were and came at them from the side, his knife slashing from side to side in case the Indians were waiting.

The knife cut horseflesh. The animal reared and cried out and something slid from its back, half-hanging on its side. At that same moment the Indian fighting with Ahrens let out a cry the likes of which Hawthorne had never heard, not even from a wounded wolf. Ahrens screamed, there was movement on the ground, and Hawthorne heard someone rushing toward him. It wasn't his partner, who lay moaning on the ground.

There was a confusion of sound, but the war cry told Hawthorne where the danger was. It wasn't from the bundle hanging inches from him. A quick brush of his fingers before the wounded horse bolted away told him it was carrying a body. That was reinforced by the metallic smell of death that wafted on the air stirred by the horse.

Hawthorne did not know how badly Ahrens was wounded, but that didn't matter right now. There was a mad Indian up here, and he could hear the rest making their way up the slope. His own horse was ahead, and he dashed for it with every lick of speed his churning legs could get him. He ran into the rear of the horse, grabbed its tail, and swung around to the other side to put the animal between him and the Indian. The horse turned with him and he released the tail, jumped into the saddle, and kicked the horse to a gallop. He heard the brave scream behind him, something ancient and animal, and then Ahrens's horse was galloping hard in pursuit. The tracker swapped out gun for knife and craned around, firing blindly into the night. One shot, then another, then a third in a spread.

The horse kept coming. He decided not to waste any more bullets. He would not be stopping to reload. And if he were caught, he would need at least one for himself. It occurred to him, only now, that he should have shot the poor Austrian. God only know what the Comanche would do to him. Hopefully, he had thought of that himself. He listened for a shot—

It didn't come, and then he was down in a dry arroyo, the walls blocking sound from the outside, thundering his own hoofbeats back at him. The Indian was still behind him, though the pursuit ended as the first rays of dawn broke ahead. The Comanche had taken an unfamiliar horse with a police saddle; he would not be able to keep up with his quarry.

Unless he's riding over me, alongside the damn gully— Hawthorne did not slow until the horse decided it was time. And even then, the tracker listened to what was going on beyond the arroyo, watching for clouds of dust, waiting for an attack that did not come . . .

CHAPTER THREE

October 18, 1871

Realizing that he could not catch the white man, Roving Wolf had left the horse lashed to a large stone and had gone ahead on foot. It would soon be light, and he would be able to follow the hoof prints.

The Comanche from the encampment would care for the body of Soon to Be a Man. They would undo the great indignity that had been done to it. One or two braves, no more, would walk the young man's pony back to the settlement to the west and excavate a burial pit for it, in the presence of the mother. While that was being done the other Comanche would follow Roving Wolf, collecting his horse and following his trail. They would also bring the other white man, alive or dead. He would capture this one—alive, if possible. And then it would be for Buffalo Eyes to say what would be done. The war chief had been appointed by the tribal chief and granted full authority to answer the cavalry invasion. He was the keeper of the Medicine Bag, which was on his person at all times. It was a flat pouch containing items sacred to the tribe. So long as he did not make war on a fellow Comanche, he would retain the title. Even Peace Chief Running Cloud did not object to the decision of Buffalo Eyes. Both men held with the plan set out by their ancestors, in these very lands: follow the animals, not the fight. Slay them and the fight vanished like storm clouds.

As he moved quickly through the breaking light, Roving Wolf hoped that the decision would be to burn the captives front and back, harming nothing vital until their cries had overflowed the valley and reached the ears of other white men. That would flush them from their town and barracks, bring them to the field where they, too, would die.

The arroyo deepened, the river cut becoming a valley with walls as tall as four or five men. The new day was slightly overcast, throwing no sharp shadows but casting a gray mood upon the rocks and sand. Not more than a shallow creek had run here during the past many seasons, judging by the rocks and a few boulders precariously jutting from the walls; there had been no erosion to speak of. Climbing the walls would have been difficult if not impossible without causing a landslide. The few rivulets he spotted were old and baked. The river-bed was still, any wind blowing across the top; dry vegetation offered nothing for small animals, and the Comanche saw only lizards waiting patiently for a sliver of sunlight and more scorpions down here.

There were two wood rats that had apparently died of dehydration, and recently.

He moved at a slow run, looking for stones and pebbles that had been overturned, watching for the prints or partial impressions of a horseshoe, looking for a splash of water from a deerskin. The man Roving Wolf had left behind was not a tracker, so this one must be. And a good one he was; so far, only a crushed spider, still damp, was the only mark of passage. Farther on, a few hardy dandelions were broken. He had no doubt passed here when it was still dark; an alert tracker would have avoided those, as the Comanche was doing. With the wiry Red Snake in the lead, those who came after would notice the same things he had.

A bobcat peered over the edge of the arroyo, having smelled the Indian. He looked somewhat emaciated, his demonic eyes peering from a white, celestial face. Roving Wolf had his knife out and swung it up and down, signifying a bite. Whether cowed or unwilling to tackle larger prey, the hungry cat followed its head in another direction.

Roving Wolf drank sparingly and kept up his steady run by imagining war drums being struck, his lips playing out the beat. Before the sun was fully up, he was rewarded with the first whiff of his prey: the smell of the horse hanging in the still air. He quickened the run. He did not know when and where the gently curving valley opened but he wanted to try and catch the man before then, before he could see all around him.

Roving Wolf smelled the horse more strongly

and stopped to judge its distance. It was an action that saved his life.

Bobcats didn't like horses. That was because horses didn't like bobcats. Many cats met their end chasing a ground squirrel or rabbit, failing to steer wide enough of a horse, and getting his back snapped or his skull caved-in.

When Moses Hawthorne saw the "scrawny tawny" nosing along the edge of the arroyo, he knew it wasn't for him. He also knew it wasn't for another animal because he had not seen any, save for some dead rodents a piece away. And there was no mistaking the smell of death for the smell of live prey.

That meant something else had entered the chasm. Something not on horseback. Hawthorne had an idea what—or who—it was.

The dirt wall was high and uninviting here, but there was a solid-looking projection of flat limestone that looked like it was part of a much larger slab. It was about two-of-him high, but there might be a way to reach it. And above that, the slope was gentle enough so that he could claw himself from the arroyo.

Hawthorne anchored the reins to a large rock at the foot of the wall then side-walked the horse over, flat up against the steep dirt incline. Using the caked wall for support, he eased himself into a standing position on the saddle. That was nearly enough to reach the limestone; a little jump, from bent knees, and he had it. Hawthorne was able to swing his elbows up, haul himself to the flat surface, and then climb just like a newt on the side of a tree.

Reaching the surface, he knelt and dulled the barrel of his gun with dirt. Farther ahead, about thirty yards, he saw the bobcat scurrying off. That was where the critter probably saw that what he thought was prey, wasn't. Hawthorne crept just a few feet farther, to where a turn in the arroyo gave him a clear, straight view for at least fifteen yards. He did not want to go too far lest he step on loose dirt that went sliding down the side and gave away his position. He stayed back from the ledge just far enough to see the turn in the riverbed without being seen.

The silence out here was like being in a bucket without sides. Just *that* still. So when Hawthorne heard the gentle padding ahead and below, he knew it was most likely deerskin moccasins on stone. Raising his left arm and crooking it in front of his chest, Hawthorne lay the barrel of the Remington across it. He did not hold his breath but breathed slowly, his tongue pressed to the roof of his mouth so he didn't get woozy.

Hawthorne did not know how much time had passed but he finally saw the head of the Comanche coming around the turn. That was how it worked with animals: you saw the target, you led it a step, you fired. Otherwise, it was a missed opportunity.

The .44 boomed, sand exploded in a rush, but the Indian was not struck; he had stopped.

Shit.

Hawthorne did not know if the Comanche had a handgun, but he knew it would take a moment for him to draw and fire. There wasn't time to find out.

The tracker scrambled toward the edge of the arroyo, aimed down, prepared to fire. But the Indian wasn't there. He was—

Shit.

Hawthorne turned around, toward the northwest, the direction from which he'd come. Arms pumping, the Comanche was racing in that direction, ducking and swaying. He couldn't afford to shoot wild; the ammunition was in a box in his saddlebag and he had only two shots left. Instead, the tracker jumped to his feet and ran in the same direction, but the Indian had too big a head start. In one fluid move, the Comanche reached the horse, placed two hands on its rump, and vaulted onto its back. In the same move, a hard tug on the reins pulled them free of the rock; the Indian snapped the loop of the reins downward, whipping the flank of the horse. It bolted forward, the Comanche leaning low on the animal's neck as he rode along the wall.

Hawthorne did not have a shot as the Indian rounded a turn.

Shit.

It would have taken the rest of the day to reach Austin. On foot, with a mounted Comanche eager for his scalp, and the entire canyon and lowlands beyond where he could hide—

There was a thumping sound coming toward him; hooves.

The horse came charging back. The Indian had wheeled it around and was squatting on its back, having figured out how his quarry escaped the arroyo. The Comanche sprang to the limestone ledge, landed uncertainly on top, and without breaking momentum stumbled forward. He slammed into the wall, his hand digging into the dry, hard earth. Hawthorne leaned over, prepared to fire, and got a face full of dirt. The shot went wild and the Indian used the distraction to claw to the surface.

Roving Wolf charged, running low like a bull, and Hawthorne discharged his last shot. With the instincts and skills of a seasoned hand-to-hand combatant, the Comanche had been watching the man's footing, his eyes, his right arm, the hand with the weapon. Each had a function to perform before firing. A strong stance, eyes on the target, arm moving into position, fingers of the hand tightening on the grip. It developed as slowly as an approaching storm cloud to the Indian. An instant before the white man fired, the Indian turned to his side and threw his left shoulder into the man's chest. The Remington thundered across the Comanche's back, scraping his flesh across the spine as the men made contact. The impact sent the tracker flying backward, off his feet, over the edge of the arroyo. He landed on the rocky riverbed with a snap of leg bone and rib as he landed on his back.

Standing on the lip of the crevice, breathing hard and looking down, Roving Wolf spit down at the man who had defiled the body of his flesh. Sheathing his knife, he walked back to the limestone outcrop and made his way down.

"What the hell is it now?"

Hank Gannon woke stubbornly a little after dawn. The sun was persistent out here, like a dance-hall girl who did not want to leave your side.

"How? Why?" his fellow officer Eli "Skunk" Reynolds had once asked, before Hank had started wooing Constance Breen. As if the nickname given him by the girls had not been explanation enough as to why they shied from him.

"It's my diet," Gannon had informed him as they sat at the bar.

"That requires explaining," Skunk had replied.

"The apple I have, before lights-out. Cleans the teeth. Freshens up the breath. Also a bath every few days in the river—not just wetting my legs to the knees in a horse-crossing."

Gannon did not miss Skunk, a marksman who was lucky to have eagle eyes, because he was ignorant as a flapjack. In fact, the former officer was finding out here that he did not miss anyone except Constance. He wondered how long she would continue to hold a candle for him. Another month? Another week? That was the only burn in his gut, the thought that her parents just might impose on her to allow some other man to call on her. Like that weasel Steven Bard, the bank teller, son of Thor Bard, the swamp-snake bank owner. The more time he spent out here as a plainsman, the more Gannon started thinking in pretty basic terms like: I really should've sunk my teeth in the throat of that paleskinned coin-counter and put an end to him. At night, in the dark, chewing on bark instead of an apple to retain some semblance of hygiene, he would lie on his pelts and think about his life and habits, which was what he had stayed out here to do. He would stare at the sky and wonder if the coating of civilization was really so thin that his animal self could come out after just a month or so? Apparently so, since he felt closer to his horse and his fellow predators and his skins than he did to human beings. Even measuring days in the unpopulated wilderness did not seem quite so essential. It wasn't payday, it wasn't church day, it wasn't mail day or a birthday or a barn dance. Why keep track? And though it was liberating not to have to consider nonessentials, Gannon also found himself pondering things less and, more and more, just snarling at things like a mad dog—

Like when gunfire intruded, as it did now—a mechanical, tinny imitation of thunder. A grunt of displeasure had burbled in his throat before the words formed in his head.

Gannon rose and urinated on the campfire to make sure it was out, then talked to himself as he went to his horse. He did that to make sure he didn't forget *how* to use language.

"Can't say for sure because of it rolling over a lot of territory," he said, "but those shots don't sound organized, like hunting."

The horse stood mute and facing the sun, as if in silent prayer. Maybe it was, for all Gannon knew.

"I don't really want to see," he said, "but here's the thing. I start running from my own kind, I will become more like a rabbit or rodent and less like a hunter. That make sense to you?"

The horse continued to stare. Gannon patted its neck.

"You're right," he said thoughtfully. "You're always a horse. You do horse things. I'm still a man. To hold onto that, I have to do man things."

As he broke camp—which consisted of putting the saddle on the horse and checking the map he made to keep track of water—Gannon noticed an odd double dust storm in the distance, to the south. It was moving from west to east, and he could not make out what was causing it. That alone was reason to investigate. But there was another reason to go, one that stirred him to something bordering on haste.

The sky was beginning to fill with buzzards, which joined the shrikes that hunted the early-morning skies. That meant someone was dying—or already meat.

Constance dressed quickly and entered the small sitting room of the modest Breen home. She made a point not to rush; as anxious as she was for word about Hank, she did not want to appear in a hurry. Her mother was already displeased that she refused to allow other men to call, and eagerness in this instance would only increase the tension.

So she walked. Heart thumping, breath short, but her feet moving just-so like a proper lady. Her slippered feet shuffled quietly under her blue cotton morning dress, with a darker blue ribbon attached to the low neckline and a larger matching bow at the back of her waist.

Officer Rufus Long rose from one of two armchairs when she entered the room. Her parents were Philadelphia-born and had been Union loyalists during the War. Their stand on the rights of Negroes was a large part of that. So Constance was not surprised to see the black man being treated as a welcome guest by Martha, with coffee poured from the breakfast table. The man stood incongruously with his china cup and saucer, not knowing whether to keep it or set it on the coffee table.

Martha Breen graciously took it from him, set it down, and also rose. She simultaneously excused herself. That she did not feel the need to chaperone spoke of her racial advocacy, which trumped her social attitudes. Had the caller been Hank Gannon, the older woman would have left, but not at once and not with a smile.

"Officer Long," Constance said with a melodious voice and a little incline of the head.

"Miss Breen," he replied.

"Please sit," she said as she tucked herself into the other armchair, at the opposite end of the oblong coffee table.

Long waited until she was settled before resuming his seat. There was a faint smell of gunpowder about the arms maintenance man, residue on even his cleanly laundered uniform.

"My mother tells me you have been with Hank Gannon," she said in what was also a pointedly unhurried manner.

"Out on the plain, miss, yes," he said. "East of Cedar Valley."

"Is he well?"

"He's all right, I think," Long said. "He's been living out there since he left here."

"In the wild?"

"Yes'm," Long said. "North of the arroyo—Snake Water. He even made himself a kind of officer's cloak out of animal skins."

The idea was alarming to her, but Constance said, "I'm sure it gets cold at night."

Long smiled. "Yes, miss. I was out there. It does." His smile become something else, something reflective. His eyes looked past his outwardly serene hostess, whose small white hands were folded tightly in her lap. "In fact, I was out last night and the only reason I'm alive is *because* of Hank Gannon."

"You were in some danger?" she asked to break the silence that followed.

Long nodded. "Mad Indian. Killed my partner. Was aimin' to kill me, I suspect. Hank showed up an' took him away."

Her heart fluttered with expectation. "He arrested the redskin?"

"No, Miss Breen." Long's eyes dropped. "He went off with him."

Constance had to struggle not to show her surprise. "With a murdering renegade?" she said.

Now Constance was confused, and it registered openly on her face. "Let me understand. The redskin killed a police officer and Hank did nothing?"

"The dead man was a scout, but that is exactly so," Long replied. "As I said, miss, he has been livin' out there in sort of a renegade way himself." His eyes came back up. "But not so much that he failed to bid me tell you that he would be back."

Constance was touched and not surprised by that. Hank loved her, and she loved him. But there was another more urgent matter as she eyed the man's clean shirt, trousers, and jacket. He had already come back, made his report, washed his face, and come here.

"What—" she started, breathed to open her throat, started again. "What does Captain Keel intend?"

"Miss Constance, you can imagine the captain was not pleased by this," Long said. "He said—and I'd told Hank this—he said that if he'd come in with the renegade things might've been fixed for him. But he chose otherwise. I believe he will be pursued and arrested. Tried."

"What was he thinking?" she asked, wondering that herself but not expecting an answer.

"Miss, like I was saying, there was something different about him," Long told her. "Sometimes, three, four days out there, a man's mind loses a little polish. A couple weeks? A month?" He didn't have to finish.

Constance was angry, though the only sign of it was a hardening in her voice. "Did Mr. Gannon indicate anything else of his plans? Anything specific?" Her soul, her heart, had already begun to shift. The sudden wall of formality was the first step; he was no longer "Hank." *How could a red man mean more to him than she did?*

"There was no specifics," Long said, "nor when he would *be* back. But honestly, I don't see how that's possible unless in irons. He 'abetted an enemy,' is how the captain worded it."

"Of course." Constance felt that inner wall fall when she pictured Hank in chains, in a police cart. She rose, forced a tight smile. "Thank you for bringing this news to me, Officer."

Long shot to his feet, as if coming to attention. "I'm sorry it wasn't happier, Miss Constance."

She smiled tightly. "News is what it is. You have reported it fairly."

"I've tried to, ma'am. He—he was my friend, too."

Long did not see the tears in her eyes as she turned to go back to her room. He showed himself out, passing Martha, who was outside talking with her husband, who was repairing a loose runner on the patio rocker.

Constance shut the door to her room and leaned against it, her slender shoulders heaving with a mix of sadness and rage. She composed herself quickly, not wishing her mother to see her like this. But her mind was anything but free. Hank had saved this man's life. He had also spared the life of an Indian. He had said he would return. All of those were good and honorable things, yet she was angry!

Though she had forced herself to swallow her tears, the young woman's belly burned with upset. There was a throbbing behind her eyes, and her throat was once again tight. She prayed her mother did not come in now. The older woman had never liked Hank because of his strong Southern leanings, and this news would only validate her beliefs.

What does it do to mine? Constance asked herself.

The answer was in the struggle itself. She still loved him. She still wanted to love him. What she did not know was how that fit with his status, his life, as a fugitive plainsman.

There was nothing in the young woman's heart but agony, and there were only two ways she knew to settle that. One was unthinkable. The other—

"Snake Water Valley," she ruminated.

Without hesitation, she ran to her small wardrobe, pulled open the door her father had just re-hinged and trued, and went digging through the contents.

CHAPTER FOUR

October 19, 1871

The dust clouds had a strange, flattened shape. It wasn't until Gannon closed in on the moving target that he realized why. They were rising from below ground level, from an arroyo that wound its way toward the ancient volcano, Pilot Knob. The arroyo was Kwasinabóo Paa to the Comanche, literally "snake water" from the way the seasonal river wound sinuously through a mesa that unofficially marked the end of Comanche lands in the west and the Austin lowlands to the east. It was distinguished by limestone escarpments that looked like God had stacked jagged slabs one atop the other when He was trying to figure out just what to do with Texas. Unlike the other creeks that ran through the region—Williamson, Slaughter, Bear—Snake Water Creek was now dry bed populated only by the hardiest plants and critters. The mesa itself was cut in two by the north-south-ranging Roche Valley, named for the Austin surveyor who found out that rattlesnakes lived there in plenitude. Locals had argued that it wasn't so much a valley as a half-mile-long cleft in the mesa, one that was shaped like an S, but no one particularly liked the appellation Roche Cleft.

Before the drought—which had become more permanent than seasonal for reasons no one understood, but the Indians blamed on the spirit that lived beneath the plains—the creeks as well as the tributary of the Pedernales River, itself formed by the mighty Colorado, were more or less neutral territory shared by Indian and white hunters. When the Comanche moved on, patrols from Austin moved in to keep the region Indian-free. Though the Texas Special Police were spread throughout the state, with rarely more than a handful in Austin, the area was viewed by the governor and others as a source of revenue growth by allowing access to the entire Southwest and, thus, was of singular interest to Captain Keel. The governor also regarded the capital as a model city for racial harmony—which included Indians as long as they were not Comanche.

None of the men liked drawing duty in this territory since, now and then, what Keel called "rascals" from the tribe came back to cause trouble. That wasn't so much to keep the whites out but to keep them from pushing westward. Which was precisely what they did in Blanco Canyon after too many hunters, surveyors, and weekend riders recounted too many Comanche showing up to steal horses, provisions, and weapons. The Indians were careful not to seriously injure anyone lest they draw the wrath of the military.

Well, they should've realized that was coming anyway, Gannon thought as he rode toward the dust. All the

Comanche had to do to incur a war was to exist.
Not that he blamed Austin or Washington either.
There was too little water aboveground and thus
too little arable land. A nation needed to be fed,
fueled, clothed. Cattle, sheep, crops, horses—the
rivers to the east were accounted for. That left only
one direction.

Gannon was still puzzled by the dust, which seemed
to glow of its own as the sun was high enough to reach
it. The clouds were like something caused by a
horse in front, a mule in the back. But a pack
animal would not be moving that fast. He had been
approaching at an angle and, when he arrived at
the edge, he straightened his ride to run alongside
the deep gully. What he saw through the straw-
colored haze made him sick and angry.

The Indian he had met the night before, the
man he had freed, was riding a police horse,
marked with the intermingled TSP brand. It was a
large mustang, roughly sixteen hands high at the
withers. Behind it, tied to the animal by his ankle,
was Moses Hawthorne. He was on his back, being
dragged, the one-foot attachment causing him to
swing from side to side. His buckskin jacket was still
intact in front and on the arms, but ripped through
beneath him, the scraps flying like tattered butterfly
wings all around him. The arms danced as though
he were a marionette, bobbing and jumping every
time they hit a rock. A trail of blood followed his
every move, painting the ground with a winding
narrative of his death. There was no doubt that the
former trapper *was* dead: somewhere along the
way the back of his head had come off. Fingers of

blood-dampened hair followed him, waving through the dust.

The sun threw Gannon's shadow behind him, and the Indian was unaware of his presence. Pacing the baleful scene, Gannon waited until there was a straightaway. Drawing his shotgun from its saddle-mounted holster, Gannon reined to a stop, held the horse firm, swung the scattergun into position, and blasted the rope that held the tracker to the animal. He aimed as far from the horse as possible so it wouldn't be clipped by any ricochet off the stones. It was an ugly separation as the horse bolted ahead at the shot while Hawthorne bounced and flopped, front to back, spraying blood and bits of bone in all direction. He came to a stop at right angles to himself, his spine having snapped somewhere along the way.

Roving Wolf reined hard and spun the horse around while it was still rearing in alarm. Gannon had the shotgun leveled at the Indian. Roving Wolf did not try to run.

"I liked Moses Hawthorne," Gannon said. "I'm sorry I let you live."

The brave did not explain himself. It was arrogance, Gannon suspected. Comanche pride. The former lawman nudged his horse ahead without losing his target.

"Dismount and put your knife in the saddle sheath, then gather up the body," Gannon said. "Put him on the horse before the buzzards light and walk ahead o' me till the walls are low enough to climb from."

Gannon suspected the horse wouldn't give him any trouble about carrying the dead man. Horses used smell to mate, to sense out upstart stallions, to recognize their own foal in a mess of young. The mustang would know Hawthorne, even with his lungs half torn out in the back.

The Comanche went about his task without delay or complaint. That seemed strange until Gannon caught something to his left, something he had not seen before now. He allowed himself a brief look before turning back to the Indian. There was a bigger dust storm, one that seemed normal. But there was no wind, no flight of insects from that direction.

And he realized, then, that it was not a natural occurrence. Roving Wolf was cooperating because Roving Wolf was expecting reinforcements.

"You are one dog of a Comanche," Gannon said.

Gannon half expected the Indian to stop, slap his breast, and invite the man to exact vengeance while he could. But Roving Wolf continued his labors. He was clearly not one for grand, hair-on-your-chest gestures. Gannon also didn't think he was cooperating to stay alive. More likely he wanted to die in battle, perhaps trying to escape.

"Mount and ride slowly," Gannon ordered when he was done.

Without a word or delay, the Comanche was on the back of the mustang. Gannon stayed right behind him with one eye on the Indian, the other on the canyon. He did not want to stand and fight a war party of Comanche, but he could not just ride off. Moses Hawthorne was not a hero. He had no beef with the local natives and he would not have attacked first. His death and desecration were a cruel statement of some kind. This time, the Indian had to stand trial. Leaving that undone, Gannon knew he would be riding into a future that had no moral polestar, no meaning. Even if he went back to Florida, shame would dog everything he ever did.

With the chill night departing under the glare of the sun, Gannon felt much warmer under his cloak than he should have. It was fear. He recognized it from the war, when the body moved because the brain said so, in contradiction to its own best interests. But those were the cards, and he would play them . . . even as he turned an eye to the west and saw the dust storm surging closer.

Amos Keel sat on his horse in front of a stationary line of ten members of the Texas Special Police. To his right, Colonel Roger Piedmont Nightingale took his place in front of a company of twenty-four members of his own newly formed Texas State Guard.

Keel was not especially fond of Nightingale. The feeling was no doubt mutual, though it could be said that Nightingale regarded with barely concealed impatience everyone who wasn't a brigadier general or higher. Keel understood the man and his kind. During the war, there had been opportunities to rise through initiative and bold action. Now, the normal order of growth had been restored to its previous seasons. One put in his time and hoped to be noticed. Men like Nightingale felt some kind of urgency on the back of their neck, frustrated to be in an outfit that was widely spread across a vast state. By the time one's deeds reached headquarters, the actions were an echo.

The Guard was an outgrowth of the militia the revered Stephen Austin had formed in 1823 to keep the peace throughout the land—then on behalf of the Mexican Emperor Agustín de Iturbide. In addition to maintaining order, Lt. Col. Austin was instructed to subdue hostile Indians as well as settlers who wished to make Texas independent of Mexico. When the Republic of Texas was formed in 1836, President Sam Houston merged the scattered local forces into the Army of the Republic of Texas. That was absorbed by the United States Army in 1845, though many of the companies retained their charters to help patrol the vastness of the new state. These and other newly formed militias served with the Confederacy during the War and were parceled into a State Guard in the aftermath. Within that reorganization, Keel's team was formed expressly to fight local crime.

If the tall, flashy Colonel Nightingale understood the purpose of the organization, it was subsumed by his quest for personal aggrandizement. His desire for glory had won many campaigns for the Confederacy during the War, but that lost cause weighed heavily on him. His battles were no longer about causes first, but about the rise and legend of the officer himself. A reporter from Houston's *Daily Telegraph* accompanied him on his major excursions; that journalist, Lee Bates, who wore eyeglasses and a bowler hat imported from London, had begun his career in Beadle's Dime Novels. Some said he still wrote for them; the heroic Colonel Archer Barrington of the West bore a substantial resemblance to

Nightingale, down to his trim goatee and pale blue eyes.

Nightingale's company had bivouacked at the U.S. Arsenal on Street Avenue by Waller Creek on the morning of October 16 with orders to protect the city from Comanche reprisals. Their orders gave them territorial jurisdiction that would have conflicted with that of the United States Army had they been present. Nightingale's command was not to attack; making war was the job of the army, which was already in the field doing just that. The colonel established a picket line to the south, stretching for a half-mile along the river. The leeway Col. Nightingale had—and Keel saw, in the man's eyes, an eagerness to use it—was that he could extend the defensive perimeter "as far as he judged necessary beyond the Colorado River." Attacks were not expected, since the Indians had their own lands to protect. Nonetheless, Nightingale had instructed Keel to field small teams to watch for them. Though the colonel had no authority to make such a command, Keel obliged because his men knew the territory and the Guard did not.

The arrival of Rufus Long with the body of the Tonkawa scout Joseph Williams had changed the plan.

"It was a renegade, not a raiding party," Long had told Keel and Col. Nightingale at a meeting that had been called at once in the captain's office where the men were having breakfast. "One of our men—one of our former men—stopped him."

Keel had told a perplexed colonel who Hank Gannon was and explained that he had resigned and departed. Long did not add to the captain's sketchy account. The colonel had left to arrange a march across the Colorado River, while Keel had asked his officer to stay.

"What is Gannon doing out there?" the captain had asked.

"Livin' off the land," Long said. "He didn't say much." The black man did not reveal the message he was supposed to deliver to Miss Breen. It was an unwritten law among the men that anything that wasn't police business wasn't Keel's business.

Nightingale's men were perfectly regimented in their brown uniforms and matching peaked campaign hats with wide brims to keep out the sun. The high collars were buttoned and their hands were bare. One man in the two-man line directly behind the colonel was the standard-bearer, who carried the thirty-seven-star flag of the nation. The man to his left carried the flag of Texas. The whites in Keel's group could count on half of one hand the number of times they had ridden behind an American flag since the end of the War. Many of those men had to swallow their visceral resentment at being partnered with the banner. They were still Texicans first, Southerners second.

Compared to the white, crisply dressed members of the guard, Keel's men were a careless mix of skin colors and casual appearance. Except for Dr. Zachary, who rode in a compact, two-wheel, one-horse ambulance wagon in the rear, all the men wore dark vests, white shirts, and badges, but some were bareheaded, and not all had shaved that day. It was not a question of respect, or Keel would have disciplined them. It was a matter of priorities. Some had just arrived from other posts, two were trackers who needed flexibility, and others did not expect to have time for grooming in the field so didn't bother with it. If it bothered Nightingale, he did not show it. The police reflected on Keel, not on him. The citizenry who came out to see the muster were clustered mostly behind the men in uniform. Even the governor came by to see the militia off.

A parade where the parade is the honoree, Keel thought with displeasure. He remembered events like these from the War, rallies that kept fighting men from the front, where they were needed, to calm anxiety at home and in the halls of power.

But as soon as they had crossed the river bridge at the end of Brazos Street, and were away from the city, the mission took charge. The orders the colonel had given to his men were to expand the picket line to a point where the Texas Special Police would be safe to perform their duties. That meant he could go all the way to the nearest Comanche settlement without infracting his own orders.

"Commanding well is what makes a George Custer triumph at Gettysburg and a Joseph Hooker fail at Chancellorsville," the New Jersey–born colonel had been telling Keel over lunch. "Forward thinking is essential to victory. Major General Meaney issues all of my orders with room for initiative."

"Does that, in your judgment, mean commanding well or commanding boldly?" Keel had asked.

"They need not be exclusive, one to the other," Nightingale had replied. "The question you should be asking, Captain, is what is the relationship between commanding well in the field or commanding well from an office?"

"And your answer to that would be?"

"They are bound together," he had said, knitting his fingers for emphasis.

"The general in an armchair—and I use the term with no disrespect—must believe in the judgments he makes thereupon. He must trust absolutely his commanders or he has no business fielding them. That means he must know them absolutely, as well as the challenges they are apt to face—because he has faced them himself."

"Sadly," Keel had replied, "the armchair general does not base everything upon experience or field reports."

"You mean political exigency," Nightingale had said. "And the so-called fourth estate, the gentlemen of the press. The opinion makers." He had waved a hand. "In the end, as an idealist, I believe that men in uniform will not willingly do harm to other men in uniform."

Keel had said, "Uriah must have thought the same before King David sent him to battle to be killed."

"I have no wife Bathsheba," Nightingale had remarked, smirking, just before Long arrived.

Keel believed the man had quite missed his point. It was not the reason for David's action but the complete trust Uriah had placed in his leader that caused his demise. A credible commander will convince a good soldier to follow him anywhere, be it George Washington across the Delaware or Colonel Travis into the ill-fortified Alamo. The trick, for any man—and Keel did not exempt himself from this—was to know the leaders who, like David, would play on patriotism and loyalty to gain their own ends. In that respect, he greatly respected

and also feared the Comanche. They were not a
hodgepodge of nationalities and ethnicities but
a unified people of countless centuries' standing.
They were bound above all by tradition, which was
where King David truly broke faith and earned a
place in infamy.

Nightingale's company followed the map; Keel's
officers rode alongside but followed their instincts.
The two coincided until Pilot Knob came into view
some seven miles south of the city. The crusty old
rock complex of knolls was a place Keel liked to
visit when he had the time; it was black, gray basalt
with which his crusty old self felt kinship. It consisted of a quartet of hills sprawling across two
miles, mounds of traprock towering above a low-
land comprised of millennia-old ash and rock and
Cottonmouth Creek. The ragged old volcanic cone
was the largest of the projections, as well as the
home of the demon who had been blamed for
the drought. To its west was hilly terrain that once
spilled rainwater into the Snake Water Creek, dry
these last three years. The Houston and Texas
Central Railway had conducted extensive blasting
in the region before routing their rails another way.
The railroad was the main reason for the army's
push into Comanche territory: it was due to open in
two months, on Christmas Day, and Washington—
not to mention local cattle ranchers, lumber mills,
and other mercantile interests—wanted the expansion to continue to Dallas and then to Red River
City, where it could connect with the Missouri,
Kansas and Texas Railroad. That would join Texas,
by rail, to St. Louis, Missouri, and the East.

Keel thought, *If securing that extension took the*

scalp of "Uriah" Nightingale, then Major General Meaney would offer it to his *God, President Grant.* With self-awareness but without regret, he thought, *All you have to do is ask Hank Gannon about that.*

"Sir?"

The speaker was Andrew Whitestraw, a Tonkawa scout who had come in from Haskell, well to the north. He had broken ranks after the river crossing to ride several yards to the west of the column. The men continued at their steady pace.

"I smell dirt," the man said as he pulled up on the captain's right. He pointed toward the horizon in the direction of the dead Snake Water Creek.

Keel inhaled, did not pick up any dust in the still air. "Dust devils?" he asked.

"It'd have to be a twister to smell this far, sir," he replied.

"Thank you," Keel said.

The captain reined his mount to the right, rode up alongside Nightingale. He told the colonel what Whitestraw had reported.

"Your recommendation, Captain?" the officer asked.

"Whitestraw thought enough to mention it," Keel said. "That's enough for me."

"Very well," Nightingale replied.

The colonel raised his right arm so the column could see it, then leveled it at his chest and swept it laterally to the right, signaling for the command to move in that direction. Kicking up their own sandy cloud, the two groups turned due west, toward the parched arroyo.

* * *

Roving Wolf was leading the horse across the increasingly rocky terrain—large, dull-edged stones from a long-ago landslide in the valley to the east—when he stopped suddenly. Still riding a few paces to the rear, Gannon stopped with him.

"Feel." It was the first word the Indian had spoken.

Gannon did not ask what the Indian meant. He saw the man's moccasins curl at the toe very slightly, knew he was "gripping" the stones. Feeling vibrations. Gannon knew it wasn't the Comanche party to their rear; their presence was known. The Indian was looking ahead, toward the end of the arroyo and the lowlands beyond. Gannon's eyes were also facing northeast. He had been planning to head in that direction and make his way back to Austin with his prisoner. If someone were approaching from that direction, it was most likely a military force, either a routine United States Army patrol or reinforcements headed toward the Comancheria. But it could also be a small unit sent by Keel to investigate Rufus Long's report of a murdering Comanche. If that were true, the Texas Special Police would not be aware of the approaching Indian party. By the time they saw the dust, all they would be able to do would be to dig in.

Roving Wolf had reached those same conclusions and resumed walking at his previous pace. Gannon started up after him, still considering his options. It was imperative that he warn whoever was coming. A fire with signals would also alert the Comanche. He had to do it in person.

Suddenly but without haste, the Indian turned to the leather sheath on the saddle, retrieved his knife, and started walking. He left the horse, he left the body, and he left with his back facing Gannon.

The former officer raised his rifle, then lowered it. He was a step behind the Indian in everything and didn't like that. A shot would bring everyone to this spot at a gallop, the braves arriving first. They would have time to array themselves behind whatever cover the landscape offered. Fresh from battle, the Indians would have guns; mounted horsemen would stand little chance against them.

There was no time to go down and collect the horse . . . or the Indian. Pulling his kerchief up to his eyes and tilting his hat forward, Gannon rode ahead to intercept whoever was headed west.

"Lone rider approaching!" Andrew Whitestraw shouted. "And he's in a hurry."

Whitestraw had assumed point position and was several hundred yards from the main columns. He had risen in his saddle, half-turned, and shouted the update, simultaneously pointing to the southwest.

Captain Keel halted his men, and Nightingale did the same. He retrieved his binoculars, and a moment later the captain saw the dust and sent Sgt. Calvin forward. The former Union marksman was the unit's best shot and also their best boxer. Whether on horseback or on foot, he would stop whoever was charging toward them.

Keel turned to his left. "Colonel, I suggest forming a skirmish line."

"Who do you think it is?"

"Could be Moses Hawthorne or Kurt Ahrens,"

Keel said. There was thickness in his voice as he added, "Doesn't look like either."

The colonel turned his horse around, lifted his arm to his side, and crossed his chest. The men remained on horseback but formed a single line. He drew his revolver, rode to the right of the line, and gave the "ready" order. The men drew their rifles from their holsters and held them angled at the right side, prepared to go to shoulder when ordered.

By now, Whitestraw and Keel could see that the rider was neither Hawthorne nor Ahrens. But it was Rufus Long, two rows behind the captain, who saw the billowing fur cloak, "Sir—that's Hank Gannon."

"Your former officer?" Nightingale asked the captain.

"Yes, Colonel."

Nightingale ordered his men to remain as they were.

The figure materialized quickly, like a knobby plant erupting from the plain. He did not slow as he neared, only swung toward the police side of the formation which remained in a column. Recognizing the figure, Sgt. Calvin had lowered his rifle and ridden in at his side. The two men stopped between Keel and Nightingale, Gannon beside his former captain. The horses of the two commanders shied, dirt swirled, but Gannon just yanked down his kerchief and fixed his dark eyes on Captain Keel.

"There's a force of Comanche behind me," he said without preamble. "I do not know the size but they are coming fast."

"How do you know this?" Keel demanded.

"One of 'em was my prisoner for killing Moses

Hawthorne," Gannon replied. His eyes shifted to Long. "Same one killed Joseph Williams."

"The one you left with?" Long said accusingly.

Gannon replied to Long, "We recovered the Comanche boy that Williams shot, unprovoked, then we parted," Gannon said. He backed his horse from between Captain Keel and Sgt. Calvin, addressed the former. "I'm goin' back to get the Indian in Roche Valley. I promise to bring him in."

Nightingale had been watching the exchange with mounting displeasure. "Captain, this traitor should not be permitted his freedom."

"He risked that freedom to warn us," Keel said. The captain regarded Gannon. "God willing, we will see you back in Austin."

"Thank you, sir."

The former officer threw his erstwhile commander a quick salute as he wheeled his horse and rode off.

The hostility he left behind was thick. Like twin suns, the antagonism of both Long and Nightingale beat down on Keel, silent but fierce. Without taking his eyes from Gannon, Keel felt in his vest pocket for a cigarette. He lit it, snuffing the match with his fingers and putting it back in his pocket. It was a habit of his, not to leave a trail that winds would not cover.

"Before anybody says anything I won't like hearing," Keel said to no one in particular—careful not to insult a superior, "keep in mind that the last thing you want when facing a Comanche force in front is one of their braves in back." Now he looked at the colonel. "I assume we are continuing?"

"We are going to meet those renegades and stop them, if necessary," Nightingale announced.

"We'll be going, too, at a walk," Keel said, blowing a cloud from the side of his mouth. "No sense tiring the horses. Sergeant, you ride along with White-straw. You see anything, report back. I want it quiet." He pointed ahead with his smoke. "Sound carries in some of those rock formations."

"Yes, sir," Calvin said and turned to rejoin the scout on point.

Nightingale reformed the column, and both officers moved their men ahead.

CHAPTER FIVE

October 19, 1871

The long cart was painted black with the name *Breen Carpentry* lettered emphatically in white block letters on the back gate and on the slats of both sides. The sturdy cart was suitable for hauling sections of lumber and the tools used to transform raw planks into homes, shelves, patios. The seat, resting on high well-oiled springs, was fit for a man in overalls, the threadbare cushion having long ago conformed to the contours of the owner's bottom. The draft horse was brown and on the smaller side, but what it lacked in muscle it made up for with relative speed. That was important to Albert Breen, who often had to be at a farm well outside of town to repair a loft in the morning and then show up at a church in Austin to fix a spire in the afternoon. The horse was a favorite of Gary Bosley, who felt a certain kinship with any animal who was asked to do a lot, fast. Constance was also a favorite of the stableboy, which she put to good if selfish use this particular day.

Constance was not concerned with comfort or with commerce. Haste was all that mattered, not just the need to find Hank Gannon but to be well away from Austin before her father—who was still working on the house—came looking for his cart. She had hoped to buy one of her own using her own savings and the money she had tried to collect from Captain Keel that was owed to Hank. But the commander would not pay her, saying that she had no legal standing. He advised her to have Hank write from wherever he ended up and the money would be sent.

She slowed impatiently when a large wagon loaded with dented railroad track was in front of her, drawn to the ironworks by two slow Clydesdales. She crossed the bridge in excess of the posted speed restrictions, since the rails on the side were not sufficiently solid to stop a horse from going over. And then she took a jostling that even her tightly pinned bustle could not absorb as she drove the horse west across the lumpy field. Behind her, she could hear the distant sounds of a trumpet. No doubt the guard or the police or both were being organized for a search.

She had to reach Hank first.

Constance knew the terrain around Austin for a mile or two from excursions of the Young Ladies' Pioneer Society at church. They brought women from the bosom of the city into the wilds for the stated goal of appreciating the hardship of their forebears—but also, and more accurately, to dissuade them from leaving home themselves. Austin in particular and Texas in general needed population, and they did not wish to lose their young women to gold rushes, homesteaders, Pacific Ocean mariners, Barbary Coast gamblers, railroad surveyors, or adventurous easterners en route to Alaska, the South Pacific, or Australia. The warnings from old Miss Smith ran together in Constance's mind. The only real lesson the girls learned was that Carol Smith— piano teacher and church organist—would leave with any one of those gentlemen she had mentioned if one were ever to ask.

However heartfelt the warnings, the girls who went on these forays were stimulated by seeing the world outside their too-familiar streets. But now that she was out here alone, even the Smith & Wesson revolver she had taken from her father's dresser provided only slight comfort. She had learned how to use it years before, as had her mother, when Austin was less tame. The handgun was loosely bundled in a cushioning horse blanket sitting beside her; she did not know if the jostling could cause it to discharge but did not want to take that chance and kept it tightly padded.

As the landscape became increasingly unfamiliar, Constance began to doubt the wisdom of what she was doing. It was vaster and more intimidating than she had remembered, though she knew that if she followed the sun it would take her where she needed to go. The sun was also what Hank would have called "adversarial," as he sometimes described her father; it was warmer than it was in the city, and with no eaves for shade. But she did not doubt the depth of her passion for Hank Gannon, despite his curious actions, and her complete and overwhelming desire to share with him anything he might face out here or in the future.

It is only his gallant nature that prohibited him from asking me to leave the comfort of my family home, she had decided. And then she thought with a touch of rancor, *He must not have thought I would want to leave the loving bosom of my parents.* Constance believed they did love her, of course. But she also knew that the Breens were a controlling family, set in their Old World ways of obedient daughters and social ascension. She would have thought that the clan, having been here since the Catholics landed in the Massachusetts colony and were promptly told to leave, nearly two centuries earlier, she would have *thought* the Breens would have assimilated better to the class-free ways of America. *Perhaps they had, except where single daughters were concerned.*

Her love and admiration drove her on. That and the fact that her father would probably throw her out anyway for borrowing his cart. Constance hoped the family's personal horse and buggy would suffice until she returned. She didn't have a plan but she only expected to be out here as long as it took to reach the arroyo, find Hank, and convince him to come back with her.

Or take me away, she thought daringly. In that case, the cart could be her dowry.

Constance was glad she was riding away from the sun, though the collar of her old riding blouse kept falling and she wished she had brought a scarf for the back of her neck. She had water in a canteen her father kept in the cart, but she wanted to conserve that in case she ended up staying out here more—

The horse stopped suddenly and shook its head. Constance jerked forward but braced herself with the heels of her laced-up boots. Before she had settled back she saw the problem: there was a rattlesnake under the shadowy lip of a flat rock. The horse bucked and the snake coiled into a defensive S-shape, its rattle erect, and the horse whinnied fearfully. Constance tugged the animal back, hoping to get out of striking range. The snake moved forward and only now Constance noticed a nest of young deeper under the slab.

The horse was refusing to settle, and that only antagonized the snake more. Without time to consider her options, Constance removed the gun from the blanket and fired two shots in front of the rattler. She did not intend to hit it, and didn't; the snake withdrew, the shots caused the horse to bolt, and the cart flew past the danger in a moment. The escape was unplanned, but it had worked. Constance allowed the horse to run out its fear for a dozen or so yards, then *whoaed* it to a slow walk. Only then did she pay attention to her own accelerated heartbeat.

This venture was seeming like a poorer idea by the minute. She stopped the cart and looked out at the sloping mesa with the arroyo somewhere in its midst. And somewhere in that was Hank Gannon.

"Go on a little further," she said aloud. "Maybe he heard the shots and will come to investigate." That was what a mountain man who used to be a police officer *would* do, she reasoned.

Clicking inside her cheek and shaking the reins, she resumed her westward journey.

* * *

Buffalo Eyes, War Chief of the Comanche, was at the head of the war party when he raised a hand for the loose formation of riders to stop. He heard the shots over the drumbeat of the hooves and listened for the echo to die.

It was a quick death, originating not far to the east. He motioned for two of his braves to find out who was out there. He signaled the rest of the Comanche to continue along the arroyo until they found Roving Wolf. Eager to rejoin the party and driving their ponies hard, the two warriors charged across the plain into the noon sun.

Gannon heard gunfire, but it was not in the direction of the men he'd left or the Comanche. Two shots could be anything from target practice to bad hunting, none of which concerned him. He was riding hard to reach the eastern edge of the arroyo before the Comanche could vanish.

Moses Hawthorne had explained to Gannon that disappearing was a trait the Indians preferred over flight. It was governed by art, not fear. It was a skill mastered by the cleverest reptiles and insects but lost to prey like rabbits and deer. The pursued were eventually captured; the hidden, rarely. When he thought back on it, during the War, his nighttime tracking rarely involved Rebels in flight but in concealment.

Still, Gannon couldn't be sure that's what the Comanche would do. The man was not easy to read.

He might have doubled back to meet the war party. Or he might have climbed to a place where he would be visible to Gannon—but which would also make the white man visible to the Indians. No brave was afraid to sacrifice his life for the good of the tribe . . . and for the benefit of his own honored afterlife.

The valley that cut through the mesa had a massive rockfall at the southern entrance, the collapse of some ancient wall that probably followed the Snake Water Creek. When he had arrived, Keel had given him a short history and geography lesson. This region was originally mapped by Spanish explorers who called sections like this *"los Balcones,"* describing the sharp, imposing terrain arranged like a series of balconies. Gannon wondered if that could have happened when the old volcanoes erupted. He had heard stories during the War of active volcanoes in Mexico causing earthquakes that caused the collapse of hills and plateaus miles distant.

He stopped and dismounted. The Indian could have gone back along the arroyo, climbed the rockslide, or entered the valley. If he had gone back to the arroyo, he might have taken the horse, exited here, and turned west to join the party. Buzzards continued to circle, but that was no evidence of anything except that the body of Moses Hawthorne was still there. Gannon saw no hoof prints or trampled scrub, so that scenario was unlikely. Going back for the horse was pointless, then. It would only hinder him in the narrow valley. Gannon walked his horse forward, looking at the ground for signs of the Indian's passage. He saw none and looked ahead for flies; the Indian might have paused to relieve himself. There were no flies. He reached the portal of boulders framing the valley. Those at the base were shoulder-high and twice as large around. There were cracks and weatherworn edges where a man could grab on to hoist himself up. He knelt and looked for particles of limestone that might have been dislodged. There was nothing on the surface of either side. Not even the most skilled climber could have avoided cracking some of the fragile rock, especially the slabs that were marl— limestone that had been infused with clay.

Gannon rose, adjusted his hat to block the sun that was now angled toward the east.

"So you went ahead," he decided.

That's what Gannon would have done, too. The area was known to be spotted with underground caves, sinkholes, subterranean pools and rivers, and other geologic formations. The good news was that while the Comanche had a head start, chances were good he did not know this area any better than Gannon.

Rather than tire his horse and in order to stay close to the ground, Gannon decided to stay on foot, watching for clues of the Indian's passage. He did not underestimate the danger of what he was doing. This was not like a showdown, where the parties were more or less equal. Or a battle, where there were maps or a superiority of arms or men. Every tracker knew that he was always playing catch-up. The quarry had the lead, the advantage, the ability to surprise. And in the case of the Comanche, he had the kind of instincts and innate familiarity with the land that Gannon lacked. He did not take that disadvantage casually.

A warbler welcomed him from a nest somewhere on *los Balcones* to his right. It was safe there from ground-based predators. A tuft of golden fluff blowing in the wind suggested that a hatchling from a nest somewhere in the valley had fallen victim to one of the shrikes Gannon had noticed earlier.

The position of the sun wiped clean any shadows that would exist in the valley during the morning and afternoon. It was now just stark, vertical rock wall, layer upon layer of sand-colored or ivory slabs piled high, all of it tinged with streaks of green. At times, it had the appearance of velvet. The sun regularly flashed on particles of crystal and mineral embedded in the limestone; they could just as easily be the shiny metal of a gun. Only their position on the face of the valley suggested their true nature. At the top, in a nook, he would have to pay closer attention. In an hour or so, when the sun moved west, there would be no illumination at all to Gannon's left. And in another two hours, the mesa would block all direct sunlight. Spread out below were the smooth stones, large and small, deposited in the old creek bed. Here and there was the occasional hardy vegetation that fed on the noonday sun and sparse moisture. It would not be enough to watch for the Indian. Gannon also had to keep his eye on spots of shade that might conceal a venomous snake . . . or might afford him immediate cover if the Indian attacked. He was especially alert for caves, though the ringing gunshots that would produce was sure to cost him his hearing.

Gannon did not take the Comanche's abilities lightly. He might be unarmed but that was relative to the white man's way of thinking. He could have made a snare, he could drop a noose made from roots or his own clothing, he could drop a rock or start a landslide or toss a rattler or another skin full of scorpions.

Then there was a lesson Gannon had learned during the war, when it was dark or uniforms were so dirty or tattered it was difficult to tell one side from the other without an accent. He could not assume that whoever came at him was the bloody renegade. It was also possible that if anyone was out here, they might be used as a hostage . . . or worse. When Gannon had first arrived, he had been briefed about how, for a score of years, geologists had come and gone looking for underground petroleum for use in the manufacture of kerosene for lights. Drills were being used up north, in Pennsylvania, but Texas rock was tougher than that. The mechanisms broke. Even getting water from the ground was a chore. Nonetheless, scientists kept coming. A couple of months ago, one of them had been caught and gutted and left like a scarecrow at the edge of Kiowa territory in the north. To a white, that was enough to start a war. To an Indian, it was the equivalent of filing a paper at the assayer's office. Still, it was impetus to get the Comanche before he got anyone else. That much of a special police officer was still alive in Hank Gannon.

He had gone roughly an eighth of a mile into the valley when he heard, then felt, the approaching horses. It was the wrong direction to be his own

people. The Comanche had found the horse and
were coming this way. He stopped, squatted between his horse and the western wall of the valley—
affording him some protection from a surprise
attack by his quarry—and looked back. The horses
were coming at a steady gait but he could not be
sure why.

Gannon had his answer when the hoofbeats
stopped with a sudden, dusty finality.

They were sealing one end of the valley.

Roving Wolf had entered the valley and immediately sought high ground. His war with the white
man did not need to be hurried by ambush. The
war party would know to block one entrance to
the valley and let him have the man. They would
not enter the chasm themselves as they would certainly have their own fight soon enough. It would
be too easy for the white men to seal both ends and
lay siege or use brush fires to squeeze them slowly
toward a central killing field.

The Comanche's idea was an ancient Indian
tactic, but new to the invaders from the east: to turn
the tracker into the tracked. Roving Wolf had
scaled the wall to a ledge about twice head-high,
where there was a shadowed nook in which he could
crouch and hide. As the day grew old, the darkness
there would only deepen. And it had. All Roving
Wolf had to do was watch and make sure he did not
brush off a lizard or swat at a curious crow that
could attract the man's attention. That, and he
had to give his enemy a name. The man had freed
him, once. Then held him captive. He had two

faces, like a rock that was sun-baked on top, damp and infested with insects underneath. And he had his pelts—

Gray Stone.

Roving Wolf nodded once with satisfaction. It lacked the spiritual core of an animal name, but it was not dishonorable. Now the enemy was fixed as an idea, not just flesh to be killed but a being whose moves and thoughts could be more easily predicted. Solid but with hazy ideals. He was the opposite of most white men, who were fierce in their minds but flimsy of body. Without an army or a horse or a firearm, they were weak. That was why they required Indians to scout for them. They did not know how to read or face a world, only how to pummel and remake it.

The newly named enemy came before long, walking beside his horse. He was not stupid. From where Roving Wolf sat, he could only see head and shoulders. A handmade spear or slingshot would only harm the horse. Even a gun or bow and arrow, if he had one, would likely miss its target.

The Indian watched, waiting for the white man to reach and then pass him. Then he would descend and track the slow-moving man. The horse's hooves would make just enough noise to disguise the sound of any stones Roving Wolf might dislodge.

And then he heard the approach of the war party. It had taken them somewhat longer than he had expected, and he was surprised when they stopped by the valley entrance. War Chief Buffalo Eyes was not a warrior of tactic but of fierce faith: he believed in the grace of the animal spirits that watched over the Comanche. White enemies moved in columns;

Buffalo Eyes preferred to attack in a wide crescent, drawing their attention every which way, out of range of their gunfire, until a circle had been formed around them. Had he stopped to wait for Roving Wolf? To ambush the whites? He had not done that at Blanco Canyon.

There had to be something else. Buffalo Eyes hated the white man with fire in his blood, and the only thing that would change his battle plan was the ability to inflict deep, lasting scars. He was a warrior who preferred to scalp and release a still-living enemy rather than to offer his screams and raw heart to a campfire. Acts of horror instilled fear in settlers and soldiers or caused an immediate, unreasoning response of flight or attack—both of which worked to the advantage of the Comanche.

Had they captured a prisoner whose screams could be used to frighten or draw out the white man?

None of that was Roving Wolf's concern. Gray Stone had heard the war party as well. After determining that none of its members were close by, he had resumed his passage, looking up and around for any sign of his prey.

When the man with the fur cape was sufficiently ahead, deeper in the winding valley, Roving Wolf made his descent. He did so quietly, by feel of fingers and toes, never taking his eyes off the enemy.

Buffalo Eyes was an older brave, having seen more than forty summers, but he was as powerful of arm as he was of hate, and still immensely keen of mind and eye. Though his ways had always served him and the Comanche, this latest advance of the white man had forced him to consider another approach to battle.

The war chief watched with keen interest as the two braves approached with their captive.

He felt deep satisfaction as they neared. He did not smile, but his spirit rose. The Big Father had given him the means to control and destroy the enemies of his people.

A woman.

CHAPTER SIX

October 19, 1871

"There's a war party stopped at the mouth o' the Snake Water Valley."

Andrew Whitestraw had ridden to the side of Captain Keel to make his report. The columns had halted again, and a sense of faraway lightning had settled on them. The enemy was in sight, and a battle, perhaps a charge, was likely imminent. Though Colonel Nightingale was on the other side of Whitestraw, the scout spoke entirely to his own commander.

"Numbers?" Keel asked.

"Lotta shadow this side, an' they're in it," the scout said. "But far as I can see about two dozen men on horse."

"We outnumber them," Nightingale observed. "Can we count on your former officer there?"

"I expect we can," Keel remarked.

"But Captain," Whitestraw went on, "riders came in a minute ago. They was leadin' a cart, slow and sorta easy. My guess is so's I'd see it."

"Who would be fool enough to go riding out here during an engagement?" Nightingale asked.

Keel had no answer and did not offer one. That was not his concern just now.

"The Comanche have a hostage," the captain said gravely. "Andy, go and find out what they want. Sergeant!"

Richard Calvin was still on point. He half-turned. "Sir?"

"Cover him!"

The sergeant shouldered his rifle as the scout pulled a white kerchief from his saddlebag, kept there for just such occasions. Whitestraw rode forward, the white flag in his teeth. When dealing with the Comanche, the Tonkawa liked to keep both hands free.

"What do you hope to get from this, Captain?" Nightingale asked. His tone was slightly critical; his posture and iron gaze were not suited to field parlays.

"Information," Keel answered. "The poor hostage out there? As good as in the grave."

"Then you don't intend to negotiate?"

"There's no negotiating," Keel said, almost snickering at the thought. "They'd want our horses or weapons or both. Then they'd leave us to walk away with the hostage and our shame."

"So we *will* be attacking."

The captain watched his two men riding forward across the quarter-mile or so that separated them from the Comanche. "That's what we're here for," Keel said. "But we have to do it on our timetable, not theirs. And the field of battle also has to be what we select."

"Meaning?"

"Let's wait and see what Whitestraw has to tell us."

Except for the occasional snort and stomp of horses up and down the columns, the men were silent. The wind had picked up slightly, blowing to the backs of the savage but into their faces. It was not enough to cause them to cover up, but it would be a hindrance to the horses in a charge.

Minutes crawled like the sun itself. Whitestraw's ivory palomino was a smudge against the darker horses of the Comanche—and the out-of-place draft horse that had been detached from the wagon. Sgt. Calvin was dismounted and standing with his rifle across the saddle of his horse. Neither he nor Keel expected trouble. But the captain did wonder where Hank Gannon was and what he might be doing or thinking. Apparently having entered the valley ahead of the Indians' arrival, he would be in possession of additional information as well.

It was a longer-than-expected visit, after which Whitestraw came galloping back, Sgt. Calvin falling in behind him. It was a courageous move on Calvin's part: if the Indians were going to take anyone down it would have been him, not the man bearing the message they wished to send. It was also a smart move: he was putting his life at risk to test the honor of the braves. They would have every reason for wanting to kill one of the unit's best shots, the kind of man who would be sent with the scout.

The scout galloped in so hard he had to draw hard on the reins to stop the horse.

"Shit, Captain. They got Constance Breen."

The answer to Nightingale's question unfolded with horrifying clarity. Behind him, Rufus Long also swore before his chin dropped to his chest.

"Aw dear Jesus," Long muttered.

"Our young schoolteacher," Keel informed Nightingale before he could ask. "She was probably out here looking for Gannon. Where was she?"

"Standing behind her cart," Whitestraw said. "One ankle tied to the axle."

The silence that followed struck at the soul of every man present.

"What do they want?" Keel asked.

"Everything we got," Whitestraw replied. "Boots included. Canteens, too."

"We have to go in," the colonel said angrily. "They'll kill her regardless."

"How many men will you peel off when they whip the horse to drag her off?" Keel asked. "The Comanche will kill most of them as they pass."

"No doubt," Whitestraw said. "They got men on the rocks t'the west already."

"We'd start the fight with casualties who haven't fired a shot," Keel said.

"What do you propose?" the colonel demanded. "That we let them defile her?"

"They'll make her scream," Keel agreed, his voice somber. "But she'll stay alive. Gannon will figure out what's happening. He won't let that go on."

"And in the meantime? What do we do?" Nightingale asked.

"Andy, go back and tell them we're leaving," Keel said. "Don't ask for the girl. We have to make like we know she's lost but don't want her dead." To Nightingale he added, "We'll go back north, turn west out of view, and come in at the other end of the valley."

"Nightfall," the colonel said with sudden understanding.

"Our best chance," Keel said. "Andy can scout us a path before then."

"What if the Comanche figure what we're planning?" Nightingale asked, nodding without subtlety at the scout.

"Then I won't be comin' back," Whitestraw said, already turning.

Sgt. Calvin's fist was still on his rifle, his expression resolute as he wheeled round to follow his comrade-in-arms.

Constance should have been terrified from the first.

The two Comanche had come up on either side of her buckboard, one of them arresting the horse from further movement, the other riding up to her side, leaning in, and grabbing her left wrist. She hadn't tried to run because the braves were armed. She didn't use the buggy whip on the horse and it wasn't in her hand; she might have used it if it were for the self-respect of it. She did not want to go docilely with these men. But that seemed, at the moment, the wisest course.

It had been told to her, by her father and others, that a generation ago it was preferable to take your own life rather than be captured by Indians. She did not know if that were true, still, but she was also a fighter. She came from strong Colonial Philadelphia stock; the Breens had defied the British in Ireland, then again in America. She would not shame that legacy.

She saw the men from Austin as they were riding west. No doubt they saw her, since the wagon was kicking up considerable dust. Upon reaching the valley, with the arroyo beyond, another brave came over, pulled her roughly from her seat, and proceeded to tie her hands behind her back and around her waist, her left leg to the wagon.

Then, she was afraid. The horse was not a runner, but even being dragged slowly across this terrain would be fatal. She stood in the hot sun, trying to stand with her head high and defiant, but shaking from the thighs down. Perhaps it was hidden by her riding outfit; she hoped so. She kept her jaw locked to keep her teeth from clattering. She felt her heart leap when the men from the Texas Special Police arrived under a flag of truce. She had no idea what they said in Comanche, but it was obvious that the man who had arrived with a white kerchief in his teeth had returned to the column to deliver a message.

Constance was hopeful, then. She could not help looking at the braves who were arrayed along the sharp-edged rocks. They were not looking at her lustfully, as they did in the magazines she confiscated from some of the boys in class. Most were watching the white men, some were moving into position along the rocks in the direction her horse was facing, and a few were looking at the valley. She was perspiring from forehead to ankle by the time the two police officers returned. Again, she did not know what had been discussed. But after a few exchanges one of the Indians came toward her with a knife. Her breathing stopped and her throat was suddenly too thick to swallow. He went behind her, his chest pressed to her back, and put the blade under her hairline.

"God, no!" she whimpered—more to the Almighty than to the brave.

One of the two men from the police column had a rifle. He turned it on the brave—

No, Constance thought with horror. *On me.*

Her heart was like an animal in a cage, throwing itself against the bars in a desperate effort to escape. Under her breath, she uttered the Lord's Prayer—all she could think of—and closed her eyes. The insides of her eyelids were red. She squeezed them harder until they went black, hoping that would somehow brace her for the arrival of a swift death.

Over the thunder in her chest and throat and ears Constance heard the two Indians were talking again. It sounded as if the one from Austin was reassuring the other. He said *miaru*. She remembered that much from what little, useful Comanche she had taught the children. It meant "I go" or "We go." The Comanche grunted in what sounded like an assent. The blade was lowered. She opened her eyes. She did not cry and hoped that the Indians did not mistake her perspiration for tears.

When the two departed, the young brave who had been prepared to scalp her untied the rope that lashed her to the axle. Then he picked her up and threw her without ceremony or respect into the wagon, on her chest, as though she were a sack of grain. What had the police agreed to do? Leave her here? Could that be?

No, she thought. *They would not.*

Captain Keel knew that Gannon was out here. Perhaps Hank had signaled him, either in person or from a perch above the Comanche. He would have a plan. All she had to do was wait.

The sun was glaring down at her, and after a few minutes she called out.

"Might I have water?"

There was muted conversation and a brave came over with a deerskin. He climbed beside her, turned her face roughly, poured a little between her lips.

"Thank you," she said, smiling.

He left without a word, taking his disinterested expression with him. Only now did the woman consider how close she had come to dying. But she had not, and life seemed sweetly precious at that moment, even though she was helpless as a fox in a trapper's dirt hole.

She felt a jerk. The cart was being moved. From the direction it had been facing, she knew she was being taken toward the mouth of the valley. She heard one of the braves whistle like a bird, the tone sounding shrill at first, then echoing more and more. The wagon stopped right where the man sat on horseback, still chirping.

The Comanche left the cart there.

Constance could not, at first, imagine what any of it meant until the brave looked down at her from the back of the stallion. He had a wicked look on him, not like a chickadee but like a cat.

And then, with a flash of horror, she realized that sound was intended to echo along the valley.

The activity at the mouth of the valley did not concern Gannon as long as it remained in the mouth of the valley. There was just over a mile to go, and Gannon was beginning to think the Indian wanted him to exhaust himself looking. Patience was a quality most tribes possessed that the white man did not.

He stopped and looked around. There were enough ledges that the Comanche could have used to go up or sideways without ever touching the ground. There were crags and nooks where a man could hide once the shadows were long enough. As he had half expected, this was likely to get him nowhere. The one thing he did not worry about was the Indian circling back and rejoining his fellows. This was a blood vendetta and he would want it ended, man-to-man.

The problem is, who can afford to outwait who? Gannon thought.

Unless he was on the valley floor, the Comanche would not have access to edible prey and water.

Maybe you do, too. Gannon turned and looked back. There had been a cool spot several yards back. A possible venting spot for an underground spring. Turning the horse around, he returned to the section where fallen rock had piled—

Or been piled.

He had missed that, the first time he passed. There were indentations in the ground nearby where the small slabs had been picked up and moved. He looked around to make sure the Indian wasn't close by, then crouched and hefted the stones aside. There was an opening, about the size of a rabbit warren. Cool air rose from within along with a faint trickling. There were slightly eroded areas in the lower rock where ropes had been lowered to collect water.

Gannon wondered if an underground stream was all that was down there. These waters could have cut a channel or even a cave system. If so, the Comanche could have known about it or found a way in. He might be there now, waiting to emerge at night.

Or he might be somewhere else entirely, Gannon knew. A man could lose his mind trying to anticipate another. Passing a command tent during the war, he had overheard an officer remark, "Plan your own attack. You can be defeated by what you don't anticipate as surely as by what you do anticipate." The best tactic, Gannon agreed, was to do what felt right to him. And what felt right to him was to learn more about hiding places and, if necessary, other ways out of the valley.

Gannon rose and began pulling dry scrub from between the rocks on the ground and whatever hung to the ledge low on the side of the valley. He bound them like wheat using a pelt he had tanned but not added to his cloak. Then he tied the bundle to his lariat and squatted beside the opening in the foot of the wall. He struck a match, lit the brush, and lowered it into the darkness. Then he let the rope play out about two or three feet, looped his end around a rock, and stood back.

Gannon watched along the rock wall. The pelt would smolder as all-hell.

Peering into the dark, where nothing but the flame was itself visible, he saw the fire and smoke swept instantly to the north. Gannon left the makeshift torch hanging there and stepped back, around the horse, so he could see the entire expanse of wall. He scanned the rock wall, looking for any kind of natural chimney. He listened while he looked, half-expecting to hear a pebble dislodged, and as he turned, see the Comanche—

And then a section of the wall vanished, sending the horse to the ground and Gannon into the air.

The north side of the valley was more of a ruin than the south side. There were no stepped rises, just a chaotic jumble of rock, much of it thrust inside, some of it scattered on the outside. It was as if a giant fist had punched a solid wall in, then spilled shards here and there as it withdrew.

That fist was water, a lot of it, sitting against the rock and causing it to crash inward. This side of the valley bore dry rills that were older than human habitation, wide and weatherworn but still showing evidence of once having flowed with life. Captain Keel also wondered, based on what he had read in Sutton's *Theory of the Earth*, whether the volcanoes had caused landslides when they shook the earth. There were images from other places around the globe where that had happened. It was at times like these that Keel wished he still possessed both of his eyes, since the scale of the distribution encompassed breadth more than height.

The men from Austin had heard the explosion shortly before making the turn to the west. It was too strong to be a gunshot, lacked the rise and fall of a rockslide, and he didn't think the Comanche had a cannon or explosives. It could have been a prospector, though he could not imagine why anyone would be blasting with Comanche at the door. The explosion could also have been methane gas, either intentionally or accidentally ignited by someone in the valley. Dust had risen in a thin, white cloud indicating the location of the blast not far from the mouth of the valley.

The day was well into dusk when the twin forces reached the opening.

Keel had his own ideas about how to deploy the men but deferred to Colonel Nightingale.

"I don't see the point of sending anyone up there." The officer gestured toward the mesa. "Out of effective firing range, and we'd hear the redskins coming most likely."

Keel agreed. He also wanted every man where he could be of use, if needed.

"We should stay out of the valley, lest the enemy cut us off from those men," Nightingale said, looking around. "I'll put my boys, in twos, on the rocks that offer a shooting range if the Comanche come through. We should have yours in reserve in case we need to mount a charge."

"That's how I would have arranged it," the captain said.

Nightingale thanked the captain for his support; it was good for the morale of the men when the officers did not disagree or have to confer in private.

"What do you propose about their captive?"

Nightingale asked, as Sgt. Calvin took over the task of disbursing the men. "Do you think they will harm her?"

"Most likely," Keel said. "Those braves get bored, a wagon wheel, a white woman, and a knife can provide amusement. Or they may test us." He regarded Nightingale pointedly. "You've been around, Colonel. You know that whatever it is, we are already too late to stop it."

Nightingale nodded unhappily and went off to survey the entrance to the valley before it was dark. Then he sat with the journalist Lee Bates, who tagged along in his civvies with a notepad that was also a sketchbook, chronicling the few facts he required to make his bigger, bolder yarns.

Calvin went about his work with quiet urgency. The men were told they could keep their blankets but were not to sleep. He had another task, which Keel had ordered silently, with just movements of his head: it was a job for Whitestraw. Despite what Keel had said when he agreed with Nightingale, the Comanche could well come around the mesa and attack from the sides. Andrew Whitestraw was to be sent to the top of the mesa to watch for just such movement. Before Calvin went to work with the men, he gave Whitestraw his orders. The scout left to find a way up; he returned with what he had seen in the fading light, an outside slope near this end of the valley, masses of fallen rock he could use to crawl to the top. He said he would leave at nightfall and signal with gunfire; Calvin instructed each team to be prepared for new orders, from him, should they be necessary.

There was no campfire and smoked jerky was

consumed as darkness settled in. With it came the chirps, hoots, and rustling of nocturnal hunters. The men knew that any of them could be a Comanche, which is why they had been stationed in pairs. A single, stalking Indian was unlikely to take two men down at the same time.

Sgt. Richard Calvin sat on the edge of a four-foot-high rock, his Springfield rifle lying beside him on a blanket to keep the action free of dirt. The marksman spent the time chewing dinner and then tobacco. He had offered some to Captain Keel, who was marching slowly around the encampment, anxious because he could not light a cigarette. Keel was grateful but did not accept; he didn't like the paste of it in his cheek, he explained.

Calvin understood that it was not decorous for a captain to spit. But missing several back teeth from a long-ago brawl, he tended to park the wad there. It wasn't much of a conversation, but Calvin's relationship with the captain was always reinforced by personal little moments like these. They were exchanges that did not cross the boundary of military propriety.

Keel leaned in toward his sergeant.

"You send Andy near or far?" Keel said quietly.

"I left it up to him," Calvin said. "Knowing Andy, he'll want to get as close as possible."

"Which is probably what the Comanche will do, to see if we continued north and where we made camp."

"It'll be an interestin' meetin'," Calvin said.

Keel answered with a quiet grunt, though neither man knew how such an encounter would go. Two scouts might let each other be; or, being from historically hostile tribes, they might try to kill one another on sight.

Though the men seemed relaxed, Calvin could not help chewing hard and running the tips of his fingers across the bare, particulate rock. It kept his skin raw and sensitive, useful for dealing with horse or gun. The big man had always been easygoing—until the war. Hunting in upstate New York to provide for his folks and three sisters wasn't the same as sitting in a tree or on a cliff or across a river, hunting Rebels. It wasn't that he minded the killing—the secessionists had started it, after all—but he minded the *when* of it. He had in his power the moment to end the life of a scout, an officer, a sentry. If they were smoking or shitting, he let them finish. If they were reading, he waited for them to turn a page. If they were doing anything military, like tending a horse or helping a wounded man, they died as quick as he could fire. Nothing that furthered the war effort should be allowed to continue.

That was all different than this, waiting for you-did-not-know-what-or-when. He would have loved to be on the mesa with Whitestraw, picking off Comanche, but he would be more useful here if they attacked. That was the main reason he liked serving under Amos Keel. The captain commanded with a clear mind, not with emotion. Considering he only had one eye, his ability to see ahead was formidable.

"Like bobbing for apples." That was how he had described one doomed Rebel charge through a canyon that was only slightly narrower than this valley. *Pop, pop, pop*—it wasn't just the clustering of the men but the way their chests or heads went bright red each time he fired.

It was not long after the half-moon had risen, giving the lowlands a ghostly complexion, that all of the men came alert as one. It was a faint, distant cry that might have been a word, they could not be sure.

That word was, *"No!"*

CHAPTER SEVEN

October 20, 1871

Hank Gannon awoke in darkness and in thick silence. The latter was due almost entirely, he knew, to the cottony pressure inside his ears; whatever had gone off had done so with pounding force. The blast had not only knocked him off his feet, it had left him hard of hearing.

Those realizations did not come immediately but over the course of time it took him to become fully conscious. It wasn't like waking up. His body came back well before his mind, which was simply a helpless, lost observer. He did not even realize, at first, that his eyes were open and he was looking up at black cliff and charcoal sky.

Where am I? Where was I? What was I doing?

Awareness and memory came back in fragments, shuffled together like a deck of cards.

Lying down . . . the valley . . . flowing water . . . ears throbbing . . . Indians . . .

And then the deck was whole and he remembered everything up to the explosion. No doubt caused—he realized now, stupidly—by lowering a lighted torch into a passage of water where odorless natural gases were no doubt also flowing.

He moved, but it came painfully—and it was then he realized he was not alone.

Roving Wolf was sitting beside him on the ground. His silhouette leaned over Gannon, dragging with it the distinctive scent of his animal-skin clothes. The Comanche held a waterskin and poured liquid into Gannon's mouth. The white man drank in cat-like sips.

"Thank . . . you," Gannon said.

Though the words sounded muffled, at least he heard them.

"Horse dead," the Comanche said casually. "You caused."

"Yes . . . I realize that."

Gannon braced his soul as he tried to move his hands and feet. To his relief, he felt them all. To his dismay, he realized that he was in his stocking feet. The Indian had taken his boots.

"Horse save you," the Indian went on. He made an up-and-down movement of his hand, which Gannon took to mean that the animal was between him and the blast. Now he remembered: he had stepped behind it to look up the cliff, watch for smoke from the embers. Now that he thought of it, he realized his head was resting on part of his saddle.

Though Gannon suspected he knew the answer, he asked anyway: "Why . . . why did you help me . . . Roving Wolf?"

"You save me, once," the Comanche replied. "And cannot kill dead man."

Gannon exhaled loudly. His back hurt, but he didn't think he had cracked any ribs. The cape had apparently cushioned his landing.

"Where were you when it happened?" Gannon asked. He rotated his jaw, which did very little to clear the stuffing in his ears.

"Other side," he said. "Long shadow."

"Too many damn crags to see clearly," Gannon said.

"You would not see . . . you did right." He touched his own head. "Think."

"Yeah," Gannon laughed weakly. "I guess . . . I was too busy thinkin' about you and not enough about gas."

"Big Father put his wind there. Keep white men away."

"Sensible and effective," Gannon said. He shook his head. "But white men will not learn. We will still come." He grabbed at the air, made a fist. "We are learning to trap the blood and breath of the Big Father."

"Not you," Roving Wolf observed. Gannon thought he detected a hint of mockery in the man's voice. He held up a hem of the cloak. "You more like Comanche."

"Lately, yes," Gannon agreed.

The former police officer began to think about events beyond the valley. It was night, which meant the men from Austin should have been here hours ago; any battle should have been long over.

"What is happening out there?" he asked, cocking his head to one side.

"There is noise both sides," Roving Wolf pointed

left and right. Then he shook his head. "Know nothing else."

"Your tribe is waiting for you," Gannon said.

"Yes."

"But they wouldn't stop their war for that."

"No."

That meant either Keel and his people were defeated or had left. He did not smell the residue of gunpowder in the air, not even the faintest trace. During the War, fields of combat stank for more than a day. So there had not been a battle, at least not nearby. And they wouldn't have gone home, leaving a war party less than a day's ride from the city.

His thoughts were interrupted by a scream. It was a woman, speaking English.

"No!"

Gannon's eyes shot toward Roving Wolf. As much as the white man could tell in the dark, the Indian seemed as surprised at the sound as he was.

"Your people have a prisoner . . . a hostage," Gannon said.

Roving Wolf did not respond. Gannon pushed up on an elbow, felt his upper arm wobble, and collapsed. He tried again, and Roving Wolf pushed him down.

"Stay!"

Gannon swept the Indian's hand away and grabbed the front of his fringed buckskin tunic. Roving Wolf pushed him back forcibly. Gannon reached up again, this time with just one hand. That was just a distraction; the other hand went to the Indian's breechcloth where they typically wore their knives. He only got as far as the hilt before the brave wrestled him back down. Roving Wolf pulled the knife and put it to his patient's throat.

"*Stay!*"

Gannon did as he was told, but only because if he died there might be no one to help the poor creature at the mouth of the canyon.

She screamed again, louder now.

"No! *Please!*"

Gannon pushed roughly at the Indian and simultaneously used his heels to scuttle back on the rock, away from the blade. Roving Wolf fell on the man, grabbing his hair with one hand and putting the knife blade back under his chin. This time he pressed hard enough to draw blood.

"Why won't you let me go?" Gannon demanded.

"They give you, me," he explained. "They not kill."

Gannon understood. If he reached the Comanche camp, they could not molest him. Therefore, Roving Wolf could not permit him to go there. Not unless he was dead. Releasing him, Roving Wolf would be a "nonhuman," something less than a creature, never again a Comanche.

Gannon's only consolation was that whatever they were doing, they would do it for a while. The woman would have to endure. He steeled himself with what little comfort this afforded: the knowledge that no woman out here was a frail, paltry thing.

Besides, the struggle with Roving Wolf had turned him slightly, and looking around, he had an idea about how to get free of the brave.

It was like another world up here.

Andrew Whitestraw took a good while getting his

bearings on top of the mesa. The occasional strong wind, the baking sun, and the gully-washer rain-storms all used this terrain as an anvil. Though there was barely any moonlight, he could see that the flat terrain was spotted with low cacti and a healthy array of stubby buckthorn and holly trees, many with exposed roots. He heard owls in the trees and mice on the ground and three times the two met in a flapping, squealing, bloody finish.

However, none of that was what preoccupied the scout. He was watching for movement that wasn't animal or tree but human. There was no breeze to carry a scent, though the still air carried sound for quite some distance.

There had never been a time in his life when Whitestraw did not hate Comanche. From the time he was a boy, over thirty summers before, his people had been allied with the settlers of Texas against the Comanche. It was the only way to preserve the peace in their northern territories; too many years of hate between Comanche and Tonkawa made it impossible for there to be any other alliance.

Before moving out, Whitestraw considered what to do when he encountered a Comanche. He did not doubt that they had put an observer here when there was still daylight, and that the man was prob-ably near. He would have been watching to see not when but how the white men broke their promise. There was no way they would leave a woman in Comanche hands; the distant cry he had heard was added inducement to draw them into the valley.

The scout was going to have to get from the out-side of the formation to the chasm, to see how far the Comanche had penetrated. He decided to do that by going forward along the outer rim; it was less likely the observer would have been deployed there where there was little to see.

Unless his task is to wait for you, Whitestraw thought. He could not discount the canniness of the Comanche.

Despite the ancient rockfall, the edge of the mesa was solid. He would move ahead, stop, watch, and listen for movement to the east, then continue. Nearly two hundred yards lay between his position and the valley itself, and there were times when he had an unobstructed view of the terrain. A night-hawk twittered songfully on a large oak stump, having feasted on insects at sundown and calling predators away from its nest.

He heard movement to his left, toward the valley, and turned; he had just enough time to face the enemy before the Comanche had risen from behind the stump where he had lashed the nighthawk—a distraction to cause Whitestraw to dismiss the site as a hiding place. The bare-chested brave, dressed in the skins of a buck, leaped over the stump and ran at him with a stone-headed club, held well back over his head. Two things were impossible for White-straw. First, the enemy was too close to use the rifle. He dropped it at his feet and reached for his knife. Second, he did not know how lengthy the club was until the heavy, tapered stone came down against his right shoulder.

There was an ugly crack followed by numbness down to his fingertips, and the scout lost the use of that arm at once; he adjusted quickly, reaching across his waist with his left hand to grab his knife.

Whitestraw swung the blade back in a slashing lateral cut as the Comanche's arm was still moving down from the force of his attack. The knife cut his left bicep, digging deep, then continued across his chest. Whitestraw immediately turned the blade in his hand for a return cut, but the Comanche moved in, dropping the club and grabbing the wrist of the knife hand with powerful fingers. The men struggled for possession, but the Comanche had two good hands and used them both to wrest the knife free. Whitestraw immediately jumped back, his arm hanging uselessly, and turned to retrieve the rifle with his left. But the Comanche was on him, thrusting the blade up at his belly. The scout jumped back, fell over a rock, and fought to bring the rifle stock against his shoulder so he could fire.

The Comanche kicked the gun away before it could discharge, then dropped with both knees on the chest of the other man. He dropped the blade and put his hands around the throat of the scout. Leaning forward, he closed his fingers and Whitestraw gurgled. Because of the cut to his arm, the Comanche attack was not immediately effective. He adjusted his posture, sat on the man's chest, leaned in with his good right arm, dug in with that hand. The Tonkawa native used his own good arm, his one fist, to pound at the rigid arm. But Whitestraw's counterattack was unavailing. Blood and air had stopped circulating, and his mind and senses started to swirl. He stopped punching the Comanche, felt on the ground for a rock, a stick, anything to hit or poke against him.

The last thing Andrew Whitestraw heard before

losing consciousness, and then his life, was the whistling of the nighthawk calling him to another world . . .

Angry at having permitted himself to be wounded by a scout—a *Tonkawa* scout—the fearless Wild Buck felt around for loose dirt to put on the wound. He scraped together a fistful, patted it into a paste, and gave it time to harden while he stripped the dead man.

It had felt good to choke his life from him. He was worse than a white man: he was a red man who had forsaken his own kind. His spirit could take comfort in the fact that soon he would be joined by the dogs he served.

Working quickly, Wild Buck donned the clothes of the dead man and pulled his hair into the same braids the man wore. The resemblance did not have to be exact in the dark, but it had to be close. He did not think there would be a signal of any kind: either gunfire or flame might attract unwanted attention. Perhaps the moonlight off the knife blade?

When he was finished, the Comanche picked up his club along with the dead man's rifle and knife and made his way to the north.

The horse was beginning to smell.

Not bad, but it had been lying in the sun, its side torn open, for the hot afternoon hours. Vermin were starting to find it, crawling over and around Gannon to get to it. The Indian did not shoo them;

he did not even seem aware of them. While he was up on the ledge, he had obviously noted a clutch of arrowwood and alyssum and had gone to gather the berries and flowers. He had offered some to Gannon, who declined. He had jerky in his cloak pocket and had that—which the Comanche declined.

Gannon had moved himself, tentatively, while Roving Wolf was gone. He was still in pain and wasn't sure he could get up and away without the Indian tackling him.

The occasional cry from the woman gave him a deep stab of guilt. He had to get to her, and as soon as possible. Not that he knew what he would do, could do, when he got there. The Comanche had absconded with all the weapons. In the dark, he had no idea where.

He wanted to ask the Indian why it didn't bother him, whatever torture they were inflicting. But there was no point. Comanche women and children had died as well, innocent victims of war. And Roving Wolf would not understand the evil of cruelty for its own sake. To the Comanche, to many Indians, the creation of suffering was a good thing. It unnerved an enemy—if not in the moment, then when word of the atrocity spread. And it enhanced the brave who asserted his virility, who undermined the superiority of the white man, who blighted the honor of their cherished women. Gannon understood it all. The police had been briefed on the primitive mind of the savage.

But it still knotted his gut and made him curse his inactivity. He knew he would not be able to wait until dawn, which would have been the sensible time to make his move.

Roving Wolf took a blanket from the dead horse and lay it on a seven-foot-high ledge where Gannon could not easily sneak up on him and split his head with a rock. The Comanche's attitude toward the injured man puzzled Gannon until he realized that the sooner the white man moved the sooner the hunt could be resumed and the sooner the Indian would be able to return to the war party.

Gannon shifted onto his right side. The pain was sharp but manageable. His neck did not particularly want to hold up his head, but he hoped that just moving around would help. That's how it was falling off a horse. If you could work the injury you'd be okay. If you couldn't, you were damaged too bad for anything to help.

He rolled farther, onto his belly. The rocks were not a comfortable place to rest, so he got onto his hands and knees. Roving Wolf had to know what he was doing and was simply letting him do it.

Gannon could live with that, these Indians and their strange damned code of ethics. Better to heal an enemy before killing him, rather than working with the man to prevent hostilities. Then again, he remembered that private in the War—he couldn't remember which battle it was, but it was loud, close-quarters, and terrifying—who deserted and was found a day later when Gannon was out looking for spies. The boy was wounded in the taking, nursed to health, then put in front of a firing squad. Gannon didn't suppose there was much difference.

He moved his arms, turned his torso this way and that, moved his head. Everything was working:

painfully but working just the same. He saw the spot he needed to go. It was on the other side of the festering horse.

The scream came again, this time lingering as a sob.

"You not well yet," Roving Wolf said.

Gannon looked over. He saw enough in the scant moonlight to know that the Indian had not moved.

"That doesn't matter," Gannon said. "I have to do something."

"You go, I come after you. Better for you with rest. And daylight."

For all his wisdom, it had not occurred to Roving Wolf that he was dealing with a night tracker. That strengthened Gannon's resolve to depart.

He put his hands on his knees as he acclimated his body to the vertical. Injured sinew adjusted to what he was asking it to do. As he rested there, Gannon looked into the dark toward the opening he had inadvertently expanded.

"The water I saw in there was flowing north," he said, "away from the Comanche encampment. And . . . if I judge right, it was no more than six or seven feet underground. Thing is, I have no idea how deep it is. What do you think about that, Roving Wolf?"

The Indian did not answer.

"I'm thinkin' if I go over and jump in, I could sure as hell break both legs and drown as I try to fight the current. But as I consider that, I have to admit those're about the same odds I'd face in the morning tryin' to get away from you."

Still, the Indian said nothing.

"If I wait, it also means hours more suffering for that poor woman," Gannon went on.

"You drown," the Comanche finally decided.

"Most likely. I have no idea where the underground stream goes, though there are several water holes scattered round the lowlands. The odds are pretty good they're connected to this waterway in some way. 'Course, that might not help me. To fill a waterskin out there—they all require a long rope. Good thing is, you'd get my cloak. I couldn't take that."

Gannon undid the hemp-and-bird-bone clasp from around his neck. He realized, doing it, that there was something almost ritualistic about that, as if he were preparing for a baptism.

What do you want to be reborn as, Hank Gannon? he asked himself. His answer was honest enough, probably because he was tired and in pain: *Myself, about a month ago.*

Gannon dropped the cloak to lighten his weight. Then, taking a deep, steadying breath, he pushed off against his knees and rose slowly. He felt wobbly and went right back down on the cloak.

"Maybe you die before you even reach water," Roving Wolf said. "Fall into horse."

The Indian was enjoying this. That was part of the game, gloating over the fallen. To many tribes, the misfortune of a captive being used to create humor, laughter, was the highest form of insult. This was little different from the old prospector who worked for the blacksmith in Austin, a man who hadn't been right at all since his capture by Kiowa. He was scarred all over his body, the result of being tied to a stake with a length of rope, surrounded by women with torches, and being burned as he darted this way or that. While he ran and screamed, the braves said things like, "We call you Little Sun" or "You smell like skunk soup." The Kiowa only let him go because his pain and shame might frighten others from coming into their lands.

Gannon rested a moment on the cloak and then, with effort, got back to his knees and stood. This time he remained standing.

"I'm leaving, Roving Wolf," he announced. "I have to help that girl."

The Indian swung from his ledge, landing carefully on his feet. "You stay."

"Let me go," Gannon said. "I will come back, you have my word."

The Indian slashed the air with his hand. "No. Strong enough to swim, strong enough to fight."

Gannon looked from the Indian toward the wall of the valley. Without any further discussion he started toward the wall. His leg hurt at the knee, but he wasn't going to let that stop him from what he needed to do.

With a huff of annoyance—probably because he had to kill a weakened opponent, winning no honor—Roving Wolf came briskly toward Gannon. The white man turned to face him. The Indian did not crouch, did not intend to tackle his opponent; he did not make a fist. His intent was apparently to strangle the former officer. Gannon found that ironic.

The Comanche lunged with a single war cry, letting his brothers know that the battle was engaged. Gannon did the same, ducking to his right at the last moment as if he were a prizefighter ducking a

roundhouse right. What Roving Wolf had not seen
was what Gannon had done when he was on the
ground, kneeling on his abandoned cloak. As a
result, the Comanche was caught off-guard when
Gannon straightened beside him and looped the
length of dried deer tendon around his exposed
throat. The duck-and-weave had cost Gannon some
strength as pain shot up his side. But he was able to
support himself on the back of the struggling native
as he pulled the cord tight.

The Comanche bucked, reached back over his
shoulders, dug his fingertips into his own throat.
Failing to dislodge Gannon or the cord, he dropped
to the ground to try and roll onto the man, arching
his back and pounding down with his head, shoulders, buttocks—writhing, wriggling, kicking, moving
any way he could to try and gain an advantage.

He failed.

All of that happened very quickly, as within a
very short time the Comanche, gasping, lost consciousness. The red man was bleeding from the
neck where the cord was still dug deep, his blood
coating Gannon's fingers warmly. He lay, a deadweight, on his attacker's chest. Only then did Gannon
realize that his own teeth were locked, his lips
drawn back in a feral snarl, a guttural sound like
that of a great cat rolling from his throat. He relaxed his face and, more cautiously, his grip.

The Indian was still breathing; that was how
Gannon wanted it. He did not wish to kill his adversary. Not now and not this way. His left side and
back hurting—that latter, more from having been
bashed against the rocks by the struggling native—
Gannon held the cord loosely in place as he rolled

out from under Roving Wolf. He wanted to make sure he was truly insensible before letting go. He shifted his grip on the ends of the cord to one fist then used his free hand to claim the man's knife. Only then did he finally let go.

Grunting in pain, Gannon started to drag the Comanche to the dead horse. He planned to use the cord to tie the man's wrist to one hind leg, then removed the Indian's belt to lash his other hand to the other leg. But pulling the man caused whatever was wrong with his side to get worse, so he just dropped him.

"I'll prob'ly be dead before you come to," Gannon said quietly, slowly working himself back to an upright position. "My consolation, Roving Wolf, is that your tribe will deny you my blood."

He went back to his cloak and put it on, then used the dim moonlight to find his boots. He sat, struggling into them because of the effort it took to bend his sore back. But there was a girl out there who needed him, and whatever her agonies, they were worse than his.

Within just a few minutes he was on his feet and headed, half-stumbling, toward the mouth of the valley. Thanks to the war cry, the Indians would be expecting *someone*. Now that he was mobile, he had to figure out his own next move.

CHAPTER EIGHT

October 20, 1871

The quiet tension in the camp was palpable to Richard Calvin.

Standing at the northern fringe of the deployment, where the horses were tied to trees and stones, Captain Keel and Colonel Nightingale kept vigil on the men and geography. The sergeant was not far from where the two men stood, Nightingale in a cloak to keep out the night chill, Keel with a blanket over his shoulders. Neither man sat nor walked. They simply watched and listened.

Most of the men here were white, and every one of them had both the advantage and disadvantage of having been in exactly this same situation during the War—somewhere, in some battle, at some date. Then, they would have been five, six, seven years younger . . . and greener. They had experience now. Virtually every man here had also fought Indians during the interim. They knew that the red man did not think like a Union or Rebel foe, that Christian values such as mercy and forgiveness were foreign concepts. Captain Keel had spent considerable time with new recruits reminding them that the Indian was a new kind of adversary. Not just ruthless but clever . . . especially when desperate and cornered, as they were now, in Southern Texas.

But there is no choice, Sgt. Calvin reflected as he stood watching for movement anywhere along the valley. *The expansion westward, perhaps southward, is inevitable.*

Calvin did not understand why Washington did not push harder to expand the southern border. With so many former Confederates having fled there, with poverty so widespread and foreign investment needed, it would be a relatively bloodless move to put the Rio Grande behind them.

Then you could circle the Indian and, with the help of hungry Mexicans, form a southern army to push the hostiles from the south and east.

Well, neither President Johnson or now President Grant had asked him, to their discredit. It was a wise commander-in-chief who took advice from outside the circle of career officers who were by nature also politicians. They said what they knew the President wanted to hear.

About Reconstruction, too, he thought. A lot of the government agents, appointed and elected, did not grasp the difference between "fixing" and "paying back." Calvin had always believed that if more leaders rode horses, they would know that give-and-take gets the best results.

"Identify yourself!"

The cry was like a rifle shot from the western side

of the camp. Everyone came instantly alert, like deer around an unprotected watering hole. Calvin turned and immediately began walking in that direction, peering into the near-black expanse. It was a solitary figure with a rifle—a figure increasingly familiar as he neared.

"Whitestraw!" Calvin called out.

The man raised his left arm. Calvin was immediately concerned not only because he was back prematurely, but he hadn't signaled from atop the mesa.

The figure lowered his arm, did something that was lost in the darkness, and then—

There was a bang from his location and a cry behind Calvin. Keel went down. Nightingale began to move in response, reaching for his own sidearm, and then a second shot knocked him backward as well.

A fusillade from the western picket spun the intruder like a top and he flopped to the side.

"*Everyone* hold your positions and watch for others!" Calvin shouted, his own rifle shouldered as he scanned the west side, the valley, and then the eastern perimeter. "If it moves, kill it!" Only when he was sure that there was no immediate threat did he call for a medic and send a trio of skirmishers out to where the attacker had fallen.

Calvin was angry for a number of reasons, all of which came rushing into his head. First, they had stupidly grouped their leaders in a position that all but announced who they were. That left him now the ranking man out here, meaning this was suddenly his mission. Second, their classic deployment had allowed the resourceful enemy to swap one man for two—a bad trade; three men, when he added Whitestraw; more men, if either Keel or Nightingale had survived and had to be taken back to Austin. Finally, the Comanche had revealed a tactic that had been anticipated but not adequately prepared for: the willingness to advance with no hope of retreat or even of survival.

The sergeant had to fight the urge to launch a surprise of his own: to mount up and charge his men through the valley. In the dark, half of them would never make it due to the broken terrain between those sloping walls. Every man in uniform had heard of the disastrous British light cavalry charge against Russian forces seventeen years before, in the Battle of Balaclava during the Crimean War. There was no room in the unforgiving American West for impulse.

It took a few minutes for the skirmishers to return with the body, two carrying, two covering the retreat. They brought it to Calvin, who knelt beside it. Other than three bullet holes in the chest, there was not a mark on Whitestraw's clothing. No cuts, no blood. The Comanche had not wanted to do anything that might be noticed before he got close enough to accomplish his mission.

"Whitestraw was a good man," one of the police officers remarked.

"We'll commemorate when we can," the sergeant said. "Strip this man," he said, then rose and walked to where the medic was bent beside the two leaders. He had lit a lantern. There might yet be another Indian sharpshooter out there, but he was unconcerned with revealing his position.

"The colonel is gone, the captain—well, he's

fighting," Dr. Zachary reported without looking up. The bespectacled medic was a veteran of two wars—the Texas Revolution and the Civil War. Calvin had always found him to be a skilled man and a straight talker. The arch in the sergeant's nose was the result of an unset break; Zachary had determined, correctly, that it actually improved his breathing and his facial character.

The medic had cut away Keel's vest and was busy probing a blood-pumping hole in his chest. The captain's eyes were open and staring. They shifted to Calvin when he walked into the light.

"I . . . stay . . ." Keel wheezed.

"Quiet, sir," Calvin said. "I ain't gonna send you back. Can't spare the men."

Keel nodded once approvingly.

"Stay still, sir," Dr. Zachary insisted.

"No!" the captain said. He used what little strength he had to push the doctor away.

Zachary frowned down at him. "Captain, you must let me—"

"Wait . . . *please*," Keel implored.

The doctor stayed where he had been shoved, but his disapproving expression indicated that he would not remain there for long.

Keel's eye sought Calvin. The sergeant squatted beside the officer.

"G—Gannon," Keel said.

"Yes, sir?"

"I want . . . hearing. Fair . . . hearing. Reinstatement . . ."

The sergeant lay a hand on the man's arm. "Yes, sir. I swear he will get one," the man said.

"Officer . . . should look . . . after . . . his men."

"You are, sir," the sergeant assured him.

Calvin did not want to distract the medic further. He rose and went to see to the dead Indian. The corpse lay in the dirt, Whitestraw's clothes piled in a heap beside it.

"What're we doing, Sergeant?" one of the police officers asked, a Tejano named Hernando Garcia who came from Jalapa. Though he was only twenty, Garcia was descended from several generations of Mexican officers; his grandfather, Lopez, was a member of the surrendering delegation at the signing of the Treaty of Guadalupe Hidalgo, which ended the Mexican-American War in 1848. His father Jesús had distinguished himself in the defense of the Constitutional government during the War of Reform.

"Wipe off that war paint on his chest," Calvin ordered with open disgust. "The Comanche'll have heard the shooting. They can count and they can time it out. They'll figure he prob'ly got one of our people, else he wouldn't't've took the first shot. From our volley, they'll know we got him." He glared down at the dead man. "I want to return him without his paint. Let them know he wasn't admitted into the presence of the Big Father."

"We can do worse," Garcia said.

"Tell me," Calvin said.

The officer explained and, without hesitation, Calvin nodded approvingly.

The sergeant picked up the club that the man had tucked in the back of his belt. He snapped it over his knee, tossed it aside, and looked at one of the other men. "Pepper, find our smallest pony, bring 'im over."

"That would be Little Link's," said the former army balloon operator.

"Good. Get it."

"Yes, sir," the police officer said.

Calvin then asked for a knife. Garcia gave him a *laguiole* pocketknife he carried in his vest pocket, a weapon with which he was inordinately skilled. The sergeant dropped beside the Indian. As he pulled the blade from its sheath, Calvin said, "However repugnant, it's time we give the Comanche something to think about."

It was not a long walk to the end of the valley, but it was a taxing one. Three times, Hank Gannon had to stop, lean against the rock wall he was closely following in the dark, and push his body back into an upright posture. Pain caused him to lean forward or to the side or to limp, depending on what started to ache.

What kept him moving were not the woman's cries but the moans he could now hear the closer he came. They were almost constant, like the sound the wind makes past a window that doesn't close quite right. There was no plan, as yet; he had to reconnoiter before he could conceive of a way to save her.

The mouth of the valley was like an earphone, magnifying sound as he went along. There was no sound from any of the braves. This wasn't a ritual, a celebration; it was bait, and he knew it. They would be waiting to see who bit.

Gannon had to work to remain separate from the suffering of the woman. She was not far from where he was; from his earlier passage, he knew that the valley curved here, toward the east, after which it was a short walk to the lowlands. He was now hugging the valley wall, shielded from even the half-moon, using the absolute shadow to move forward. Gannon actually found himself thanking the pain for keeping him alert. He felt, heard, smelled, saw everything.

The nearer he came, Gannon noticed a very faint glow. The bait had been illuminated, not for the savages but for any potential rescue attempt. The victim would be visible, as would the white men who sought to free her. All of them would then be slaughtered.

It was strange to be wrapped in animal skin, stalking at night. To track a man or hunt for food was different from taking on the personality of a predator. He found himself fully aware in a way he had not been at any time in his life—

The glow brightened as he neared the mouth of the valley. There was a cart, a small campfire burning on the other side so only its black outline was visible. As he had expected, the sound and the woman who made it were there. The back gate was down and he saw only a messy shape inside, between the center boards, part fabric, part leg, all blended together. The victim's arms were lashed to the slatted sides of the cart, forming a V-shape. The moans came with every breath. The open back was facing him, the seat on the other side. The horse stood docilely in front, tethered to a tree. He was not surprised to see it there: if they were attacked, the Indians would want to be able to move their captive quickly.

Gannon froze as an Indian came to the side of

the cart. The Comanche looked down at her and she cried out.

"No . . . *no more* . . . I beg you."

The brave leaned his rifle against a cactus and came around to the back of the cart. Gannon sunk a little further into the rock. The man climbed in and shut the gate behind him before releasing the woman's wrists. For a moment, the angle of the door, the illumination, revealed the lettering printed on the outside.

Breen Carpentry.

There was very little in Gannon's stomach, but he felt it rise in his throat. He had to bite his arm to keep it in, to keep from screaming, both of which would have given his presence away. The one brave he might have taken; but more and Constance would be on her own.

Dear God, he thought. *Christ Jesus.*

Constance was not reckless, nor was she a pioneer woman. She would not have come out here simply for a ride. Rufus Long must have delivered his message, and she came searching for him. That was the only explanation. And with the Texas Special Police already out here, there would have been no one to come searching for her, save her parents. And they would not have known what Long told her; they would have had no idea where to go.

All of that flashed through his tortured brain within the space of several heartbeats. He looked away, not wanting to witness what came next. But it was different from what came before. The Indian had let her free so she would struggle and make more noise. It was time to turn up the heat on the men at the other end of the valley.

Gannon bit until his arm bled. He cried into his sleeve, heaving as he could not escape the horror of what was transpiring. And then, without thought, without care, more animal than man, he drew the knife and turned toward the mouth of the valley and stalked forward.

The brown mustang had to be restrained by two men as the naked body was lashed to its back. The corpse lay faceup, tied on the bare animal with the billet strap from the saddle and additional lengths of rope. His neck was tied to the neck of the horse so that his face was looking backward. Defiling Comanche tradition, the man had not been bundled for interment but exposed to the world like carrion.

Nor did the insult stop there. In that face were two dark, bloody holes where the eyes had been. The Comanche believed in dying bravely and enjoying the rewards of smoking a pipe with ancestors and warriors in the presence of the Big Father. Sightless, the spirit of a dead Comanche could not find his way to this eternal tribe. As much as the suffering of the captive woman was meant to unnerve the white men, this would shock the Comanche. At least, it would tell them that their enemy was not new to the ways of the plain. As Governor Davis understood, drawing on different nationalities, different ethnicities, different tribes of many to create a new one, an American tribe, was the way to defeat these large pockets of resistance.

When everything was ready, Garcia walked the horse to the valley entrance and gave it a swat that started it running. Unhappy with its burden, it would venture in far enough so that the Indians would hear it and likely send another scout to the mesa, if they hadn't already. The cries of the woman, growing louder as the horse went along, would also cause it to run. Soon enough, the message would be received.

"Do we want to send another man up there?" the Tejano asked Calvin when he rejoined the camp.

"I don't know what happened up there with Whitestraw, but I don't want to lose another man," Calvin told him.

"Sergeant!"

It was Dr. Zachary. Calvin hurried over. The doctor was standing beside his patient, who was covered in a heavy wool blanket. Just beyond the lantern light, Nightingale had been covered with a white sheet.

"I know what the captain said, and I know what you said," Zachary drawled, "but his body temperature is very low. As risky as moving him in the wagon might be, leaving him out here, in the nighttime cold, and without proper surgical facilities, is almost certainly going to kill him."

"I'm . . . staying," Keel rasped.

Calvin put his hands on his hips, studied the ground. "You can't go at night," he said after considering the matter. "Comanche may have circled round, set up an ambush—and I can't spare any men. If we get that girl, she will need the wagon." He shook his head. "I have to go with the captain on this."

"Fine, fine," Zachary said. "I have done my best here and I leave it in God's hands now."

Calvin looked down at the officer, whose eyes were shut, his breathing strained. The sergeant decided not to tell him about Whitestraw. He lay a big, comforting hand on the man's shoulder and walked back to the men.

"What do we do if they do nothing?" Garcia asked.

"I've been considering that m'self," the sergeant replied. "Neither of us can afford to leave the other camped here. I've been thinkin' about maybe a small squad going around one side or the other, trying to pick off a few in the dark, draw 'em into a larger force waiting behind."

"I volunteer for that," Garcia said, adding, "It will have to be done, sometime. And before dawn."

"What if the Comanche had the same idea ten minutes ago?" Calvin asked.

Before the sergeant could decide, something unexpected draw the attention of every man to the valley.

Except for hate, there was not a human thought or feeling in the mind or body of Hank Gannon. Any pain he felt before was gone now, consumed by the flame that filled him from toe to skull. He did not care if his life ended, for it could never be the same. The stench of this deed would remain in his nostrils every minute he lived. Even as he moved toward the wagon, he was not sure what he would do, whether save Constance by trying to get her away or by killing her. This would never leave her, awake or asleep, even thousands of miles from here where once they had dreamt of being.

Just a few yards from the valley opening, there was enough of a military man and police officer still functioning in Gannon's mind and muscles to form a plan: stab the Indian, stab the girl, stab himself. He did not know where the rest of the war party was, but they would be nearby and they would see him in—

The fire.

They had given him the means to do more than stop the suffering of an innocent girl. The brake was not on; he could see that by the way it shifted as the brave moved.

Gannon pulled his fur cloak around his right shoulder to cushion the blow and ran forward. He hit the cart hard, driving it forward. It stopped on top of the fire the Comanche had lit. The Indian in the back got up on his straightened arms and looked back as Gannon tore down the back of the wagon and pulled himself in. He remained on his knees; the Indian only had time to turn his body as the knife was driven into the small of his back, then again. Gannon crawled forward, put the blade under his chin, and cut so hard and deep that the man's head listed to the right before the rest of him did. With his left hand, Gannon grabbed the brave's free-flowing hair, dragged him off the girl, and thrust him against the right side of the wagon.

The underside of the wagon was beginning to smolder as Gannon loomed over Constance. He saw the outline of her face, a shape he had seen and lightly touched so often in the dark, and he knew in that same instant that he could not kill her.

With a snarl, Gannon tore off his cloak and forced it on top of her. The camp was already stirring as war cries pierced the silent night. He rose as fire began to crawl up the sides of the wagon. It wouldn't be long before they were overcome with smoke or dropped through the weakened floor-boards.

The pain was catching up to Gannon as he bent and scooped up the cloak with its precious cargo. She was panting, sobbing, confused. He had a choice: to run uncertainly into the valley or to rush blindly out into the night.

He chose the shortest distance to armed sup-port. But not on foot.

Gannon stepped onto the toeboard below the seat just as the floorboards gave way. He dropped Constance onto the back of the horse then bent to slash the straps that held the animal to the hitch rail just as a pair of Indians rounded the burning wagon. They charged toward him. In that moment, Gannon saw the entire camp, lit and exposed. What he saw concerned him. More accurately, it was what he did not see that worried him.

The animal bucked and whinnied as the fire crawled up the neck of the wagon but wasn't able to get away.

He and the woman were not going to get away in time. If Gannon turned to face them, he would never get away. And Constance was in no condition to sit the horse, let alone guide it by herself. But that is exactly what they were going to have to try.

Wincing from the pain in his side, the exertion, Gannon jumped to the ground to cut the straps and free the horse.

"Constance, hold on to the reins!" Gannon cried. He was able to cut one strap, the one on the far side of the blaze, then turned to the nearer length of leather. His sleeve was on fire and he had to take a moment to slap it out.

The Indians had separated, one of them clearly intending to circle around the white man and pull the woman from the horse. Gannon had to stop him. Leaving the second strap half-cut, he rose, the knife across his chest, ready to slash the man to bloody ribbons.

Two shots banged out over the crackling fire and the two Indians fell in succession. Gannon looked in the direction from which the shots had come. He saw Constance standing on the other side of the horse, his cloak still hanging from her back, shouldering the rifle that her attacker had left against a cactus. There was no time to admire her courage or to chastise himself for having forgotten the weapon. The rest of the camp had been roused and was in motion, whooping.

Grabbing the hip strap above the intended cut, Gannon slashed down to free the animal from the burning wagon. The horse tried to get away, but Gannon was able to hold it long enough to pull himself to the side. Constance was standing on the other side, breathing hard, hunched like a woman four times her age. Swinging into the saddle, Gannon held the checkrein at the animal's neck and backed it up several paces.

He reached over to Constance. "Come!" he said urgently.

She stood frozen.

"Constance, take my hand!"

The woman looked at him. She threw the rifle down as if it were a viper, then took his extended arm with both hands. He swung her into the saddle, wheeled the draft horse around, and rode from the cone of light cast by the fire. Shots cracked, missing him in the dark. The Indians must have thought he was headed into the plains because they were spreading out in that direction, grabbing burning planks to use as makeshift torches. Only at the last possible moment did Gannon swing back around, briefly entering the outer extremities of the glow before galloping into the valley. The Comanche saw him and fired into the mouth of the valley, but their shots did nothing more than spark and ricochet wide of his position. He slowed only slightly so he could hear if the Indians would pursue. They did not; they could not be sure this rescue was not part of a larger ambush. More likely, they would send a scout to watch and see if the white men left or peeled off a small party to send the girl home. Gannon did not think they would do either. The men were here to stop a Comanche war party and would need to be at full strength.

The sudden, urgent desire to survive was a strange sensation for a man who had wanted only swift death for himself and his loved one just a few minutes before. He was too focused on escape to consider the matter, but he was not unaware of her slender arms holding his waist and, more than that, her cool poise saving their lives just moments before. He did not, could not, know what she was thinking and feeling or what the future might hold for them. But right now, he knew that he had never felt closer to a person in his entire life. The hope rooted in that feeling was as powerful and new as anything he had ever experienced.

He did not bother Constance as they rode. She would speak if and when it suited her. Gannon imagined that, right now, what she wanted was to feel safe and pray—for her deliverance and for her soul, should she be forced to surrender it this night.

CHAPTER NINE

October 20, 1871

Gannon's mind was drawn back to the moment by the sounds of rustling in some scrub ahead. Whoever it was made no effort to conceal himself. Gannon didn't think it could be an Indian, but he couldn't imagine why one of the soldiers would be moseying around the valley in the dark. From his experiences during the afternoon, he was relatively sure no one else was down here. Roving Wolf? If he were awake, he would not likely be rummaging around in the dark but resting from the loss of blood.

Gannon remained in the center of the valley; too far to either side, he would not be able to make out anyone or anything in the dark. Nearly abreast the sound, he finally saw the shape of a man spread on the ground.

"Look away, Constance," he said softly as he moved closer.

"What is it?" she asked.

"A dead Comanche," he replied.

She answered, "I will see it."

Gannon did not argue. He had not expected her to speak at all. His own mind was numb and he needed to focus on immediate matters.

His first thought was that Roving Wolf had come to, began making his way toward the Comanche camp, and passed out. But it was not Roving Wolf. In the dim light of the fire burning at the Comanche camp, he saw a relatively small man who had no clothing, no body hair—a brave. He appeared to have been shot in the chest and there was blood on the side of his face. There were ropes strewn about—none of it made sense.

Coyotes were pulling at the flesh of his thighs and a pair of rodents had their mouths in one of the chest wounds. His eyes had been cut out, but not by any of these; the blood around them was dried.

The eye-gouging was done by a man, a show of contempt for the enemy. It did not seem like something Captain Keel would do, give the Indians an earthbound spirit to assist and guide them. He knew from the captain's briefings that their belief in the power of the dead was strong and it made them a more aggressive, cohesive fighting force.

But then what is he doing out here? Gannon wondered. *And who brought him?*

"What is it?" Constance asked.

"An Indian," he said. "Dead."

"I'm glad," she replied.

There was clearly a reason for this mutilation, but Gannon had no mortal notion what it could possibly be. There was nothing he could do, save to ride over and use the horse to chase away the animals. It was a gesture, nothing more; as soon as he had gone, they would be back.

Shifting his attention from the Indians behind him, Gannon began to think about the one before him. He was angry he had left him free, yet his priorities had been so different a short time before.

You expected to die there, he reminded himself.

Come what may, Roving Wolf was a creature of honor. He might not care about the lady, but he would not take any action that might harm her.

The deeds done, the fire in the blood subsiding, Gannon's posture on horseback began taxing his ribs. There was no saddle, just a back pad, and the pain began to return.

"H-hold on to the checkreins," he said. Gannon stopped the horse and slid from its back. He landed with a jolt that caused him to gasp.

"How are you hurt?" Constance asked.

"Explosion knocked me back," he said. "I'll be okay. Horse took most of it." He gestured toward the other side of the valley. "We can't stop—Captain Keel is on the other side." Since they were talking now, he added apologetically, "I'm sorry I don't have any water—anything."

"Washing cannot help," she said.

He had been thinking about her being thirsty, not about her body or how she felt. Her remark cut like a scythe.

Gannon grabbed the throat latch with his right hand, as much for support as to guide the animal. He began to feel miserable again, stupidly helpless. If Constance were to have a child, it would be a half-breed. If she were to see a physician, she could suffer organ damage from the tansy oil, pennyroyal, and opium mix such doctors prescribed—or hemorrhage to death at worst, or give up forever her ability to have children, if the "female syringe" or a surgery were used. Gannon had seen it all in Florida, where slaves were routinely abused by their masters.

The question was not just for Constance, however. It was for him. What would *he* do if she gave birth to the child of a Comanche or were rendered sterile? He did not like any of the answers he gave himself.

But what man would, who is not a saint—and for whom the question would not, thus, be relevant?

As they neared the spot where Gannon had blown out the side wall of the valley, they were forced to move to the opposite side to avoid the extensive debris. Gannon did not realize he had done so much damage. He could not see if Roving Wolf were still there; if he had not bled to death, then he would be looking for a way to bind his wound. Either way, Gannon continued on.

"Hank—"

There was slight urgency in her voice. Gannon looked from Constance to where she was pointing.

Before him stood the brown pony of Officer Lincoln Leon Ames, one of the newest police recruits. On its back, however, was not the diminutive young man.

It was Roving Wolf.

Roving Wolf had awakened when he felt a horse nuzzle him. He wasn't sure which of them was more startled when he bolted upright and gagged. The horse backed off, and the Comanche immediately reached for his throat. He felt the blood, winced at the narrow wound, remembered what had happened.

Not every warrior had red skin. He had underestimated the white man and had paid the price.

Roving Wolf used the ropes strung strangely around the horse to help him get to his feet, and only then did he notice its cargo. He could not see it clearly but he saw enough to stagger back, fall over some of the rocks blown from the wall, and scrabble back in horror. He had recognized Wild Buck, his friend. This was another black day, and the white men had added to their bleak destiny with each murder.

The Comanche went to the wall of the valley, retrieved his blanket from the ledge, and used what was left of the harness of the dead horse to extend its reach. Then he felt his way to the opening in the wall, careful not to tumble in. He lowered the blanket, allowed it to soak up water, then retrieved it. He used one hand to wring it out, the other to wash his throat. The wound stung, and it was deeper than he had first thought. He could feel the soreness inside as well as out.

When he was finished, he tore the blanket at the edge and wrapped a length of it like a scarf around the bloody wound. Then he returned to the pony. He felt for and found the knots that held Wild Buck in place. Quickly undoing them, he gently cradled the dead man and carried him to the center of the valley. He would bind and bury him when there was light. For now, all he could do was cover him with rocks—

There was a flash to his right, at the mouth of the valley. Noise, followed by war whoops. Gunfire. Then more gunfire and a larger blaze.

The white man is dead, he thought bitterly.

The Comanche was still crouching on the ground when he heard the crack of the hooves on stone: one horse, headed into the valley, riding heavy— likely two on its back and not one of the Indian horses. There was no pursuit.

Roving Wolf stood, wavering slightly with the sud- denness of his move. As he slowly straightened, blood trickled down his chest and back. He waited for his head to stop swimming. Then, raising the arm tattooed with a knife, he pressed his palm to his breast, leaving a red impression of his hand, then drew himself onto the back of the pony. He had no weapon but his courage and his resolve that these riders would not pass.

Leaving Wild Buck as a sentry, Roving Wolf wheeled to take up a position deeper in the darkness.

Standing just yards apart, the men faced one another in the barely perceptible flutter of the orange flames from the camp. The fire was near death. The only sounds were the shallow breathing of the horses and the creep of the coyotes return- ing to their meal.

Roving Wolf walked the pony forward. His own chest was thrust proudly forward. Gannon saw the war mark before the light went out entirely. He did not know whether the blood of the palm print be- longed to Roving Wolf or to Officer Ames; there was no question whose strings of blood were running over it, from the neck down to the waist.

Gannon drew his knife, stood between Constance and the Indian. "Where is the rider?" he demanded.

The Indian angrily thrust his chin beyond Gannon. The officer was confused.

"The dead Comanche—was on this mount?" Gannon asked.

"You know!"

"Not of this," Gannon said.

"You—defiled my blood brother!"

"I did not. I would not," Gannon said. "You did not kill the white rider?"

"Only Wild Buck rider!"

Gannon was beginning to see that the two of them—the three of them now—were caught in a proxy war between the two sides. A war within a war. If God had a plan the day He sent Gannon after Sketch Lively, the officer was unable to make sense of it.

Holding tight to the mane of the pony, Roving Wolf threw a leg over the back of the animal and dismounted. The Comanche wavered as he hit the ground. He released his handhold with care, steadying himself with his right palm. The men were just feet apart now.

"You are injured, Roving Wolf," Gannon said. "Miss Breen is hurt. I'm—not so good m'self. It's a few hours to dawn. We won't fare so well in the dark, on these rocks. Shouldn't try if we don't have to. We know where there's water, a blanket, a place to rest. Let's—well, first, let's call a truce so you an' I can put some rocks on your fellow brave so the coyote don't get him. They can eat the rotting horse. Then we will see to everyone's injuries as best we can. You an' I don't need to settle things like this." Gannon held up the knife in emphasis.

Roving Wolf was not afraid of the blade in the man's hand, did not care about the disadvantage or about dying. Even if his body were mutilated, he would still be together with his brother.

This close to his enemy, Roving Wolf could smell the sweat of the white man. His stink was like a living venom, even under the stench of the smoke he carried from the fire. It was offensive to the red man's nostrils, to his lungs, to the very air of this land. He wanted to rip skin from the invader, even though his own death should follow. Nothing mattered but to raise his arms in defense of his people and their home.

But the loss of blood continued, the haziness in Roving Wolf's skull grew stronger, and soon the earth itself seemed to turn on end. He steadied himself against the animal. Sheathing his knife, Gannon came over and put his free arm across his shoulder.

Roving Wolf recoiled.

"Stop it, you savage!" Constance yelled from the horse. She wheeled the animal around so fast it startled Roving Wolf's pony. The brave would have fallen if Gannon had not been supporting him. "God help me from sinking to your level! Everyone has disgraced his race this day, but you can begin to atone by helping each other!"

There was no further discussion. Still supporting the Comanche despite his own injuries, Gannon started toward the spot where Roving Wolf had left the disfigured brave. Collecting the pony, Constance followed.

Still on horseback, Constance was strangely, she would almost say dangerously, awake . . . alert. There was a feral quality to her thoughts, something rooted in survival, she suspected. She did not think about what had happened, only that seeking blood and revenge would take her down a road from which she would never return.

The young woman felt like an animal, dirty and abused and feeling nothing except what she needed to do to survive. Yet as the men worked together, weakly, piling stones on the dead man, she felt some of her humanity return. She had been used but she was alive. She at least had a chance to try and understand the indignity of what had been done to her. She would, she hoped, not be alone in that.

Unless your father blames you for what happened, she thought. In which case this night would have cost her a parent, as well.

When the burial was finished, the Comanche knelt, leaning on the rocks for support, and said a few words to the Big Father. Then, with Gannon's help, the Indian walked to where the smell of the dead horse was noticeable but not yet oppressive. Another day in the sun and the carcass would make this part of the valley quite foul.

The air was cool and it was stirred slightly by the flow of the underground stream. Gannon sat Roving Wolf to the north of the opening, just south of the ledge where he had been resting a short while before.

"She will wash first," Gannon said.

"No," she replied. "Give me light."

Gannon recovered his flint from the cloak that still rested on the girl's shoulders. He struck it to a dry twig, shielded the glow with his body as he brought it near the Indian.

Constance removed the makeshift bandage and looked at the clean, fine slash. "You did this?" she asked Gannon.

"To get to you, yes."

"What did you use?"

"Dried deer tendon."

She rose and walked to the opening. It hurt to walk but she refused to cry out or show her discomfort to the Indian. Looking around, she saw the line that the Comanche had used to wet his neckerchief. She lowered the remains of the blanket into the water, dunked it several times, then hauled it up and carried it over. She knelt in front of the Indian and used an edge of the cover to dab at the cut.

This is not one of the men who attacked me . . .

"He should see a doctor," Constance said.

"We have one at the encampment," Gannon said, nodding toward the north.

The Indian shook his head once. As he did, blood surged onto the cloth.

"Sit still," she ordered.

The Comanche stopped moving.

"This is not a wound we can bind tightly," she said.

"Can we cauterize?" Gannon asked, still holding the burning ember.

"I don't know," she replied. "Most of my patients

have only had scraped knees. Where is the string you used to inflict this?"

"Back there," Gannon said, indicating the horse.

"Get it. We must sew this wound. I have read of catgut being used for that purpose—deergut should do."

"Don't you need a needle of some kind?"

"I have pins," she said vaguely.

Gannon jabbed the burning twig in the ground, picked up a few more, threw them around the small torch. He picked up one and walked back to find the thread. Locating it, he returned and handed it to Constance. In his absence, she had reached under her dress and removed a pin. Her ordeal had already caused the locking head to twist. She bent it back and forth until it broke away, then stuck the point through the makeshift thread. She briefly held the point in the fire so it would penetrate the flesh more easily. She tried not to consider whether it would cause more pain.

She leaned closer to the red man, his smell offending her, his proximity making her want to scream until she had no voice. But she could not give in to that or she knew she would never stop. Quickly deciding how close to make the stitches, she began sewing the wound shut.

The Indian flinched a little, then not again.

Standing there, holding the light, Gannon looked away from the bloody procedure toward the mouth of the valley.

"They not come," Roving Wolf told him.

The man turned. "How can you be sure?"

"Men be target. Not you and woman."

"Hold still, savage," she said, which was as far

as she would allow herself to go. "So now I am a woman," she said. "Just minutes ago, I was like the dog or pig you torture to upset the children of settlers."

"Yes," he answered honestly.

She pushed the pin hard through the flap of skin. Roving Wolf yelped, seemed to want to strike her. Gannon moved toward him; the Comanche relaxed. Roving Wolf continued to sit there, very still. Constance resumed her ministrations.

"I have become what I beheld," she said angrily. "I am like these animals. God help me, I do not want to be that."

Gannon came closer. He wanted to put his arm around her but resisted. "It's all right to be angry," he said.

"Does it help?"

He shrugged. "It does, me."

"It didn't," she said. "It made me feel even more shame."

She finished wiping blood and the flood slowed. She did not reapply the original swatch of cloth but tore the sleeve from her blouse. It came away easily, tattered as it already was. She put it gently around his throat, bunching it slightly under the chin where the deepest wound was.

"More blood on my clothing," she said to herself.

"Constance, don't think back—"

"Back? *Back?* This is now, Hank. I bleed, I *am* bleeding. I *hurt*. I am afraid for what may come of this."

"Whatever it is, I am with you," Gannon said without equivocation.

Constance laughed mirthlessly. "You say that here, without the looks of townspeople, the disdain of my parents, the children who do not show up for class should the worst come to pass. Will you study the ABCs with little Running Blood?"

"Constance, please!" he said, stamping out the fire so he could move his body. He crouched beside her just as her face crumpled into a tearful wail.

"And if you die here, and I live?" she asked through her sobs. "What then?"

"We will leave at first light," Gannon promised. "I will take you home."

"Home," she practically spat the word. "I lost that, too. Do you know what I thought—there?" she threw an arm in the direction of the valley mouth. "I thought . . . I almost laughed like a madwoman when I considered how all of this can be tracked back to a terrified black man who frightened a horse. An impulse, a moment!" she cried. "Something that had *nothing to do with me!*"

The woman fell onto Gannon and he held her gently. But his eyes were on Roving Wolf, who watched for a moment and then moved away, toward his ledge. He curled up under it, carefully holding the bandage in place with a hand. Gannon did not believe he was being insensitive, but respectful. He had to know his presence could in no way lessen the woman's pain.

Gannon did not know for how long they stayed bound and bonded, but the fire had died and the stars had come out in all their brilliance and his own eyes shut in welcome snatches of sleep . . .

CHAPTER TEN

October 20, 1871

"Either the girl's dead or she's safe," Garcia said to the two men standing across from him.

The Tejano and Officer Aloysius Pepper stood with Sgt. Calvin, who had a rock in his palm, running his fingertips across it, looking at the faint yellow-orange glow that gilt the top of the mesa. It was followed by the distant pops of gunfire. The camp came instantly alert.

"That fire says that someone tried, anyway," Pepper said.

"Do you think it could be Gannon?" asked Garcia.

"It was his lady out there," Calvin said.

Garcia shifted uneasily. "Sarge, he may need help."

"We're out here for Austin, not Officer Gannon," he said. "Where we are is a defensible position. We start peeling men off—"

"We bring Gannon here, we are back up a man," Garcia said.

Calvin's mouth twisted. There was no disputing

that logic—assuming it was Gannon and he had survived, uninjured. One was likely, the other less so.

"If it is Gannon, he'll make his way here," Calvin said. "We hold our positions for now."

The decision sat in the sergeant's gut like warm, flat ale. Command filled him with nothing he wanted inside: caution and an outward impression of cowardice, for one. A divided sense of loyalty, for another—the good of many men versus the needs of one. And there was a new one he really did not like: what would Keel do? Calvin could defend staying put, if Keel or someone higher up asked. He could not defend risking a man or two on the same kind of reconnoitering that had cost them Whitestraw and, as a result, Nightingale and possibly Captain Keel.

There is nothing good about this, nothing at all, Calvin thought. *Not if you want to continue being a man and having a clear sense of right and wrong.*

As the men watched, the rainbow of fire quieted and finally vanished. There had been no sounds after the initial shooting. The quiet around the valley suddenly seemed deeper than before.

"The night varmints have all left," Pepper observed.

"They're smarter than people," Garcia observed. "That'll make it tough for Injuns to signal by imitating 'em."

Calvin had just been considering that same point. A people who built their lives and culture in and around the land lived and died with that land. It was why they were fighting so hard for the Comancheria.

Problem for them is, no people on this continent love their land more than Texicans, he thought. Even misguided agents of federal policy could not change that.

The men listened for something to break the silence, other than their own breathing. Smoking had been forbidden, and some of those breaths were fast, anxious. Chewing tobacco was all that was allowed, but the men had gone through those supplies early in the evening.

"If they'd caught him alive, there'd be a party," Pepper suggested. His voice seemed to carry for a mile.

"I wonder if Gannon killed Miss Breen," Garcia said solemnly. "Maybe those were the shots we heard. If it was me, that's what I'd've done. Just came up and shot her."

"Then himself, mebbe," Pepper said.

"Awright, button it," Calvin ordered. On top of everything else, he was the last one to see them together before sending Gannon on his mission. That picture of them, together and happy, was not something he cared to contemplate now. It made him think of his own eldest sister, Susannah, writing to him about the death of her newly minted husband early in the war. West Point Lt. Cornelius Taylor of the 3rd Infantry Regiment had fallen outside of Big Bethel, just two months into the conflict, thrown by his horse and breaking his neck.

"War to me is needless," she had written, *"but this death is so much more a waste . . ."*

Her brother did not agree with Susannah about war, though he had not written her so in her grief. But of all the events of life that had seemed designed to confound and conspire, none was quite so maddening as this. Calvin was not a particularly religious man—people assumed from his name that he must be—but times like these, when random events triggered such deep pain, made him believe even less.

And yet . . . Calvin thought.

On nights like these, when the world was still and even the agents of carnivorous death were in hiding, and the atmosphere seemed ripe with the presence of the Devil himself, he had to wonder whether God or Satan had been responsible for the suffering of Hank Gannon. Had that officer, or his lady, or someone close to his lady, done something for which penance must be exacted?

Calvin did not know and he did not want to think of it too deeply. Doing so, he would inevitably go through the catalogue of his own life and create a ledger of the good and the bad and deeds for which he had not yet answered. The war—there had been so much in that for which his only justification was that he had been obliged to follow orders. The one misery in particular that stuck like a burr in his soul was shooting a scout who turned out to be a lost deserter, no more than a boy, who was trying to get home to his mama. Lying on his back, alone in a thicket, spitting blood, he talked to her as if he were in his bed at home in Georgia. If Calvin had known he was a frightened lad, shorter than the rifle he carried, he would not have shot him.

Yet allowing a Rebel to pass? Which would have been the greater sin?

The medic felt his way through the dark to Calvin's side.

"Captain Keel is asking for you," he reported.

Calvin dropped the stone, picked up his rifle, and followed Dr. Zachary to the rear of the encampment.

For Captain Amos Keel, the worst part of being incapacitated was that he was conscious. Even when his one good eye was closed, even when pain snapped it open before the doctor heard his moans and plied him with laudanum, his mind was awake.

Now it was thinking about tactics, by default. His professional life kept other worries away—such as having no children and a wife who had taken to Jesus Christ to fill the absence. Then it was thinking about his wife, who he worried about when he was away.

Then it was very specifically taking stock of a fateful conversation he had had with Governor Davis just a month before, about the function of the military garrison in Austin. Until the Blanco Canyon offensive, the army had been used mostly for elections, when they were sometimes required to keep order. They were also used for quieting the occasional uproar over a Reconstruction mandate that went against the nature of the Texas natives and Southern transplants. Primarily, the military contributed its skills and personnel to agricultural, mechanical, and construction endeavors.

Four weeks earlier, Captain Keel was enjoying his monthly lunch with the governor when Keel broached the subject of asking for troops from other states to man the Austin barracks while the main force remained well west.

"That is where they are needed," Davis had told him. "You will be reinforced by the State Guard only if it becomes necessary."

"I understand," Keel had replied. "But if it becomes necessary, will there be time for them to acclimate to our geography and the Comanche way?"

The governor had shrugged. "Unfamiliar terrain and adversaries were a constant challenge during the War," he had said. "This is no different."

Indeed it is not, Keel had thought of the time, though he did not broach the subject. *But Southern boys were fighting in the South and the Union simply threw body after body at any problem they could not win by tactic. We have neither luxury in our war with the Comanche.*

And so now they were pinned down here, with no one except a token force left to defend Austin should their own line fail. It seemed absurd, insane, but it was conceivable that with a victory here, a war party of Comanche could ride virtually unopposed into the streets of the state capital. Keel was so fond of his men during the War that he refused to consider the worth of the Prussians, the Bavarians, the Russians who populated the remaining force. He would have given his good eye to have them in the field with him now.

"Good evenin', Captain."

That good eye shifted to the speaker who was above him, looking down with a crooked smile.

"Sergeant, how many hours until the daybreak?" Keel asked.

"Four and a bit," he said. "Why, sir?"

"Not enough time," Keel said.

"For?"

"To send a rider to Austin . . . federal troops," he said. "I have been . . . thinking . . . we must stop . . . the Comanche here. *Must*," he said, with an emphasis that caused him to cough.

Dr. Zachary leaned in and rested his palms on his chest, applying very light pressure.

"Sir, speaking stops you from breathing, which stops from healing," the medic said. "'Less you got something urgent, keep it to yourself."

"Captain," Calvin said, "we believe that Gannon" —he paused, and added out of respect for the man's courage—"*Officer* Gannon has inflicted some injury on the enemy and possibly escaped with the girl. We are watching and listening for him now."

"Is . . . is it possible?" Keel said, drawing the displeasure of the doctor.

"There was a sudden, big fire in the camp," Calvin informed him. "Rifle fire. Whatever happened, sir, we think the Injuns are just sittin' tight till mornin'."

Keel was about to speak, saw the doctor's black shape over his good eye, simply nodded twice. That information was the best tonic he could have received.

"With your permission, sir, I will reinstate the officer upon his return."

Keel nodded again.

Calvin smiled thinly. "Will you rest now, Captain?"

Another nod, then the officer reached up, grabbed

Calvin's sleeve. The sergeant's smile broadened slightly.

"I will inform you, promptly, with any news," he promised.

Keel lay back, relaxed, and felt a wash of both pride and shame for everything Gannon had undergone this past season. It had started with that unfortunate argument begun by the girl's father Albert when Constance declined to dance with that state legislator at a social. The civil servant, who was both lawyer and dandy, invoked Hank Gannon's name with something just shy of contempt, a sentiment vouchsafed, with a look and a nod, by the elder Breen. None of that was what stuck with Keel—save his own reprehensible silence upon overhearing the dignity of one of his men derided. He did not want to insult a Democrat who was deeply in the governor's favor. Instead, he had dishonored himself.

Keel could imagine Hank Gannon, out in the lowlands, helplessly reliving that, and his dismissal, and many other, smaller injustices. Keel felt miserable for his part in what had brought them here and prayed to God for his life—at least long enough that he might see his wife again and also make amends to Gannon.

If Gannon survived.

If Constance Breen survived.

If any of them survived.

Roving Wolf had not slept.

Though weary of mind and limb, he would have been able to had he permitted himself to do so—

but he did not. He would not. It was not unlike his younger years, when he had first gone to the prairie to learn the spirit skills, starting with skin walking. Alone in the foothills above Wildhorse Creek, to the north, near Tonkawa territory to show his courage, Roving Wolf had earned his name by taking the Great Wolf as a spirit guide. In the dark, chewing the dried mushrooms given to him by the medicine man, he had let the animal enter his body and command his walk and movements and voice. He had padded across ledges that, in the dawn, he could not remember having crossed—and with no practical knowledge of how he might have crossed them, so thin and unforgiving were they. He knew that the Great Wolf had done it, and that it would never leave him. When needed, all he had to do was retire his human spirit and let the other in. That was what allowed him to stalk and track, to fight, to hunt, to become one with the land and the pack that was outside his vision—but through whose senses he could smell and listen and see.

Roving Wolf did not invoke that spirit or that pack now. He was still weak from loss of blood, and still wounded. He must rest his body if not his mind. It was also necessary for him to think like a man, to understand what this man and his fellow warriors would do. Only when it became time to fight.

How he yearned for the simplicity of combat. Even against the Tonkawa, questions and challenges were never complex. Loyalties were clear and goals equally so. If you did not defeat the enemy, and if you survived, you went home shamed and hungry. In either case, the tribe would move: away from lost

territory, or into more fertile lands. Combat itself
was not firepower but skill. How you rode, how you
fired your arrow, how you swung your hatchet or
club, how you worked your lasso, how you slashed
or thrust or parried with your blade when you and
your foe were no longer on horseback.

These were skills passed down by fathers and
their fathers, essentially unchanged since the earth
was new. Guns—he understood them for fighting
the white man. But then, during the conflict of
white brother against white brother, he learned of the
weapons that fired endless bursts of death. *Bullet,
bullet, bullet, bullet*, one after the next, as if they were
gold coins being counted from a sack, *ching, ching,
ching, ching*. The thunder and lightning that exploded after tracing a black rainbow through the
sky, killing all around it. That was not combat, that
was slaughter. This was not the spirit of the wolf or
eagle or snake, it was not something to give the children of your children. It was a means to demolish
flesh and land and spirit. That was what the white
man brought to the West. That willingness to destroy utterly and without honor was the enemy of
Roving Wolf and his people.

The Comanche had never before faced a dilemma
like this. The white man might not have realized it,
but he had assured his survival by not binding the
Indian. Perhaps the officer was too tired, too pained,
too protective of the lady to think beyond any of
that. The fact remained, it would be dishonorable
to kill him while he slept. That was where the wolf
ended and the man began; a brave had more than
food and drink to consider. That was why the animal

was merely a guide, not a conquering spirit. And the spirit did not free the Indian from his own human duties and loyalties.

This man could not have escaped without killing my brothers, Roving Wolf thought. *His own party butchered Wild Buck. Sparing my life does not pay any of those debts.*

Roving Wolf also had to rejoin the war party. That weighed on him as well, to fight and if need be die alongside his tribe.

Rising, his neck burning all along the wound—but not bleeding very much—he raised his arms to the Big Father to ask for guidance. He did not speak, not even in his mind. The vision would come, the future that was to be.

It was the rustling along the valley floor that caused Gannon to wake. He had become accustomed to the occasional stirring of the two horses, which were tethered side by side well north of the dead one. He had become familiar with, and relaxed by, Constance's breathing. She slept, and he could only hope that her dreams were of something other than this day.

What woke him was a sound he had heard before, the coyotes—only moving faster than before. To the north, away from the Indian encampment.

They are coming.

Probably not all, but some. He did not think the war party would commit their full number to a nighttime assault on trained, armed officers who

would have their weapons and manpower trained
on the valley bottleneck.

Gannon was sitting and Constance was resting
against him, surrounded by his arms and by his
cloak. He gently moved her to a reclining position,
causing her to stir and mutter but not to waken. He
noticed, as he did this, Roving Wolf standing by his
ledge, his arms upraised to the skies. He had no
weapons, he was wounded; he had to be praying, or
whatever Comanche did that was like prayer.

Gannon withdrew his knife and padded to the
valley wall, south of the dead horse and the upright
Comanche. If there were braves, he did not think
they were coming from above; that would not have
caused the coyotes to run. Perhaps they had seen
the fire or the smoke, despite his best efforts to
block it. Gannon knew that saving the damned redskin would come to no good end. In addition to
enemies to the south they had an enemy in their
midst. Constance had needed to redeem her sense
of dignity, he understood that. They should have
found another way, like cutting out Roving Wolf's
heart to pay for the sins of his people.

He considered where he was, where Constance
was, where the horses were. It might be possible to
get her out—if Roving Wolf did not intervene. That
would be his first thing to do.

But they know you have a horse, he thought. *They
have guns. That will be their first target.*

He had to wake her and get her out of here now,
before they arrived. If the worst should happen, if
he should be outnumbered, under no circumstances

could he allow the Comanche to take her again. If they were trapped here, getting to her would be his only priority. And getting to her, he would push his knife into her breast, into her heart—and then his own.

Still listening, he crept to the woman's side. Noise could not be helped. Rocks tumbled annoyingly, each of them a little rattle signaling just where he was. He reached the girl's side, and as gently as possible, he shook her. She came awake with a start and a small cry.

"It's Hank," he whispered urgently. "Hank!"

"What—?"

"Get up and go to the police pony," he interrupted with a whisper.

"Why?"

"The Comanche may be out there. You will have to risk a break for the other side of the valley. At least be ready for it."

"You will come!"

"I will hold them off," he said. "No argument, Constance. Please."

She had begun to get to her feet. Any disorientation she had felt a moment before was gone. "Where is the other one?"

She meant Roving Wolf, he presumed. "Behind us, where we left him. He is praying."

She nodded, looked into the dark for the pony. "The horse is near the brave."

"I know. I'll come with you."

Gannon took his cloak to lighten her load. Together, they began walking into the pitch black, feeling their way with sore feet, Constance stumbling several times, her dress cushioning her fall. Each time Gannon helped her with his left hand, he kept his right hand ready with the blade. He still did not see movement, either before him or from Roving Wolf. He wondered if the brave were in some kind of trance.

Gannon wished he could stop *thinking*. He had lost so much and gained so little. More than ever he felt detached from the society of men he once embraced, from the civilized man he once was. Like Constance, and regardless of Constance; like Florida and the rest of the South; he wondered if he could ever go back to what was, to what *he* was.

He also wondered if he should rush over and kill Roving Wolf. The Comanche's death would mean one less flank to worry about. He considered, then dismissed, the idea. She had said herself she did not want to be like her attackers. And Gannon still did not know for certain that anyone was out there. For all he knew he had dreamt the coyotes—

Rocks fell to the south. Softly, and just a few, but enough. The Comanche were out there.

"Hurry," Gannon urged, taking her small, fine hand and holding it tightly. It was as much an anchor for him as he was for her.

There were only about fifty feet between them and the pony. Even it was anxious now, tugging lightly on the rein lashed to the rock.

"You not leave."

Roving Wolf's voice broke the night like a blacksmith's mallet. He lowered his arms, scooped up a rock in his right hand.

"Let her go," Gannon demanded. "I'll stay."

"Both stay. She understand need. Say so."

"You are most vile," Constance hissed at him.

"Step away or die," Gannon told him.

"No die," the brave replied.

Just then, four Comanche ran at them from the center of the valley.

CHAPTER ELEVEN

October 21, 1871

"Sergeant Calvin?"

The high voice belonged to Corporal Evan Bosley, one of Nightingale's men. He was five-foot-six and had a round face with freckles that made him seem even younger than he was. The guardsman carried a sidearm, his collar was buttoned to the top, and he was permitted to not wear the regulation hat in order to keep his ears free of impediments. The young guardsman had run the few yards to where Calvin was sitting on a rock. It was the only spot that gave the temporary commander a clear view of both walls of the valley as well as the opening.

Bosley was a telegraph operator. During wartime, he had been skilled at cutting into wires on the trail and sending false information. He still tapped into wires to send messages when it was necessary; unfortunately, there were none out this way to summon reinforcements from the garrison. He had been positioned just inside the valley, it being the colonel's idea, and anyway, he had wanted one of his men on point.

"Yes, Corporal?"

Bosley still had an ear turned to the valley as they spoke. "There's voices coming from the other end of the valley," he said. "Not yelling . . . quiet. Can't say what they're talking. Could be English or Comanche."

"That is not a lot of information," Calvin replied.

"Regrettably," Bosley agreed.

"Male or female?"

"I heard male, but ladies talk soft."

The experience of young Bosley with women was obviously different from his own. But the point was well taken. It could be Gannon and the lady, if she were even capable of speaking now; it was unlikely the Comanche would be speaking. They tended to sign, even in the dark, to avoid being overheard.

"It could be Comanche trying to make us think they're not," said Garcia, who was listening nearby. "I once heard 'em blow a bugle they had captured, make us think it was cavalry."

"They are canny," Calvin agreed.

As far as the sergeant was concerned, nothing had changed sufficiently to warrant an expedition into the valley. He remained conflicted; no man could fail to be. But the mission was the Comanche, not a rogue officer and his lady.

"Report if you hear anything further," Calvin said.

Bosley hesitated.

"Was there something else?" the sergeant asked.

"Can I go in the valley, Sergeant? Get closer?"

"We cannot cover you in the dark, Corporal. I appreciate your enthusiasm, but I cannot allow it."

"Yes, sir. But it's like when I climb a telegraph pole—sometimes, I cannot do my job from where I'm stuck."

"Again, thank you—but go back to your post."

The young man hesitated. Then he nodded and left.

"He's saying what we all feel," Garcia remarked.

"Me, too," Calvin assured him. "You know I'm not a patient man. But that's why we have missions. Because men who join any force, police or military, are men of action."

"I suppose that's true," Garcia said. "Though wars'd be pretty short if we all just fought and got things over with. Maybe save some lives, too."

"You can put it in the suggestion box when we get back," Calvin told him.

"We have a suggestion box?" Garcia quipped.

Calvin ignored the remark. His eyes wandered, settled on young Bosley. Garcia caught his gaze.

"I'm thinking the kid lied about his age to get in," Garcia said. "He's sixteen if he's a day."

Calvin had no opinion about that, just a thought. He hoped the kid obeyed orders so he would make it to seventeen.

"Swine! *Animal!*" Constance screamed at Roving Wolf.

The Indian grabbed the reins of the two horses; all he needed to do was delay the departure of the two whites and they would be caught. This was not what he had desired; but as it was here, as the Big Father had sent it, the only course of action was to join his braves.

For his part, Gannon would have given a limb for the rifle Constance had tossed aside back at the encampment. Yet even possessing a gun, he would have saved the knife blade for Roving Wolf. He wanted that creature's blood.

The couple stood for a moment, Constance resolute and ready to follow Gannon, the white man considering what was best among two poor options: fighting for the horse or fighting the oncoming Comanche, whose numbers he still did not know for sure. If he was sure anyone would hear and could get here in time, he would have shouted for help and hoped Captain Keel and his men heard.

And then Gannon remembered that he had a fourth option.

"Come!" he said, tugging Constance toward the valley wall.

The woman half-ran, half-tripped where he was pulling. When they stopped, suddenly, and she realized where they were, he grabbed her about the waist.

"Oh, God," she said.

"No time to remove your dress," he said, pulling her forward. "The water is straight down, I've seen it. Lie back when you strike the surface. I will follow."

There was only enough time for the woman to draw breath before he carried her over the lip, still upright, and dropped her feetfirst into the darkness. She landed with a muffled splash, the sound absorbed by her torn dress. The garment and her underthings absorbed water rapidly, became immediately and almost unbearably heavy, and she had to throw herself back to keep her torso afloat. Even so, the dress wanted to drag her under.

Floating in water that was cold, numbingly so, she tried to tear at the lacings around her waist, but they were already sodden and adhering as a thick and expanding knot. Moments later there was a second splash, louder, well behind her; it was only then she realized how far the current had carried her from the opening in the wall. She was also, she noticed, pinwheeling . . . as well as sinking. It was all she could do to keep her mouth above water.

There were additional, softer splashes. The Indians following? She was probably well ahead of them, but what did that matter if she drowned?

Suddenly, she heard rending sounds and began to bob up and down, back and forth, and from side to side. Something pricked the outside of her thigh—a rock?

No, she realized as it stung on the other side now. *A knife.*

Gannon had been able to jump in after her and was cutting away her dress. She felt herself getting lighter as the garment fell away. She also was completely disoriented as the darkness above gave way to utter pitch below, with the sound of the water echoing and reverberating until it was a roar far greater than its actual size. At least the current wasn't strong; if she felt rock on either side, she was able to push off with a foot or hand without being dashed against it.

Her legs were finally free, and she was able to straighten them to help with floatation. It was not very long after that she bumped against a curve in the rock, one that slowed and redirected the river.

Constance inverted herself and felt flat surface above the ledge. Her clothing was too waterlogged for her to pull herself up, but she held on to it to keep from drifting farther. Moments later, Gannon flowed into her. Grasping the rock beside her, he stopped his own movement.

"I'm going up . . . will pull you!" he said.

There was suction in the water that swung her from side to side like a bell clapper, after which she felt strong fingers under both of her arms, dragging her forward. It wasn't a delicate move, sheer force, but by grunting, kicking her legs, and wriggling against the stone, she helped him to raise her. She was quickly out, lying with her cheek on flat, cold rock, and thanking God, with tiny gasps, for her deliverance. Not just from the current but from the red man.

In the dark, she felt herself lifted onto what felt like fur, was fur; Gannon's cloak. It was soaked. It was there that he placed her, shivering. He wrung out a corner of the garment and handed it to her.

"Place this in front of your mouth," he said. "There are gases here."

She nodded, while he removed his neckerchief and did the same.

"Wait there," he said through the fabric. "I want to see if there's a cave or a nook of some kind."

"Feel . . . on the ground," she said. "And watch your step."

"Why the ground?"

"Gravity," she said simply.

"Of course," Gannon replied. She heard him move away on the silty surface of the ledge.

It was too cold to stay still. Feeling above her,

Constance was able to stand with at least a foot to spare. She knew, from Sir Charles Lyell's book of geology, that not just the state but the entire southwest of the continent was ribboned with underground, freshwater aquifers such as this. There were more in fact belowground, in the clay of the earth, than there were aboveground. Some of those were caused by erosion, though she suspected that these tunnels—given their width and length—were probably cut eons before by the eruption of the Pilot Knob volcano.

She wished she could remove what was left of her clothes and beat the water from them, but she did not know where there might be a nearby opening—an opening the Indians could use. They might hear her slapping the garments on the rock. Thinking of the Indians, then, brought back the horror of the night. It did not seem possible that any of the day's events had happened to her.

They had.

And though she was relatively safe now, she knew that her life would never be the same. Not her life, her soul, whatever equanimity and charity she possessed. But she was also aware that if she did not find a way to go on without hate, there would be no going on at all.

Gannon returned and reported that he had found a break in the rock that would be large enough to sit in.

"And there is fresh air coming from an opening somewhere," he said. "If we find a way to fix the cloak in front of it, we may stay warm and dry and be able to breathe for a few hours," he said. "We won't have light but at least we'll have water."

Gannon picked up the cape, took Constance's hand, and walked her back to his discovery. She wanted to say, "Our first home," but the words wouldn't come. The dream seemed to have turned to ash.

He found outcroppings above the entrance and used the knife to make cuts in the cloak. It hung well enough and they sat inside. The small chamber had a salty, iron-like atmosphere—ancient minerals that were exposed to old air and the rising and falling of the underground flow.

"That's quite a river," Gannon said. "It must feed the wells and watering holes throughout the lowlands."

"I've read that there is plentiful underground water in Texas and each stream or lake nourishes hundreds of miles aboveground," Constance said.

"There are people who study only that, aren't there?" he said with some amazement. "How much knowledge must come from men who saw something as boys that they could not explain?"

"Some," she said. "So much comes from accidents, too. Mr. Newton and his apple. The spoon lying on a silver plate and leaving its shape behind to give us the daguerreotype—"

"I met *you* by accident," he said.

If the comment was meant to console her, to reassure her, it failed. Gannon's effort to invoke the past only heightened her sense of loss, and she was glad he couldn't see her eyes crinkle and tear. Nonetheless, it was a pleasanter thought than others that had taken control of her, and she allowed herself to be whisked back—

It had been the late winter of that year and she had taken the class to the river to find different kinds of stones for a building project that was also a lesson in erosion. They were going to construct nests for birds, outside the school, so they could study them throughout the spring. Gannon had ridden by on patrol, watching for Indians. They exchanged no words, only looks, and those looks were like nothing the young woman had ever experienced. And he tipped his hat as if he meant it. One of her pupils, a shoeless boy named Keith Cassidy, said, "Miss Breen has a boyfriend, Miss Breen has a boyfriend." None of the others joined in, and the chant died on the riverbank. But not the jolt that had made her forget where she was and who she was with until Keith spoke.

The next day was a Saturday, and Constance had gone back to the river to gather more stones—material that she did not need. Her heart thumped hard the entire time because she had decided, after a blissfully restless night, that if he came by and did not speak to her, then she would boldly address him. And if he did not come by, she would find some excuse to visit the stables. Or the Texas Special Police office. The phrase "school project" would open a great many doors to her.

But he did come by. And, seeing her, he did more than tip his hat. He doffed it and dismounted. Henry Gannon stood well over a head taller, and he had eyes that were simultaneously hard as granite and warm as sunshine. And it was true: her knees turned to water. And it was also true, they were true, every sonnet she had ever read, every sentimental line, every seemingly hyperbolic word—true, true, all of it true. Suddenly, no man, no person, no thing, mattered as much as this person who had not yet spoken a word to her. When he did, when she heard his voice lightly sprinkled with the sounds of Florida, she married him in her mind with the phrase "till death us do part" repeated over and over.

And then the magic was poisoned—not by Hank nor by her.

Almost at once, the fighting began at home. Her parents did not crave social standing. They were content with their lives, working with their hands. They were in fact proud of that life. It suited their view of the century-old nation as a slate for wiping clean the blight of European class. But they had a different vision for their daughter. Someone who could, through her education and poise, ironically use power to erase the barriers of caste. To them, every life event must be a pitched battle, an extension of the war so lately fought. They had even talked to Senator Delacorte about finding a means to place Indian representatives alongside the Northerners and blacks in the legislature as a means of ending the wars. Their daughter was to be their means of added pressure.

But a goal, however well-meant, did not justify the funneling of all resources to it. Constance had views, too, many of which differed from those of Martha and Albert Breen. She did not understand why men like Hank, who held with a different cultural tradition, should be shut down politically and socially. She had wanted his views heard, as well.

Poisoned, Constance thought, not of the battle fought through three seasons, but of today. *The magic was poisoned not by Hank. Not by me. By . . . savages.*

Here, surrounded by rock, insulated from all, there was something approaching clarity. Not clarity of answers, but of questions.

"Why did you come?"

Gannon's question surprised her. "Do you know how many times I ask my pupils questions about why they do things? Pull a girl's hair, hit a window with a slingshot, fight over marbles. They always muddle through an explanation, but the truth is they *had* to. Well, I had to."

Her voice was close, so close he could feel her breath. He felt sick about what had happened, and he wanted to be angry at her for having come out here. It was reckless, not in line with her sensible nature. But her commitment to him moved him in a way he had not felt before.

"How did you do it?" she asked him.

"What is that, Constance?"

"Forgive the Union, the looting, the destruction?"

"I haven't," Gannon answered.

"Do you live with hate?"

"I suppose I do," he said. "Maybe not hate. More like—sadness? I don't want to hurt anyone. Even when Captain Keel threw me to the dogs, I understood. I didn't like it, but one thing you learn working the earth the way I did in Florida—God doesn't order things to suit your preference. You adapt to His world."

"Even after what was done to your home?"

"I would have died protecting it, as many did."

"And if those perpetrators showed up here?"

"Are you asking if I'd do what Sketch Lively did?" Gannon asked.

"I suppose . . . yes."

"I've thought about him a lot while I've been out here," Gannon said. "Until today, there was nobody I would've kilt for what they did. If it was in my power, I'd kill the Comanche who hurt you."

"All of them?"

"I don't know. Probably."

"You didn't kill the one I stitched up."

"No," Gannon agreed. "I figured that if you had mercy in you, I should, too. But his and my fight is different. Those other Comanche are just soulless things."

Constance thought for a moment. "You always told me you weren't very religious."

"I'm not, in terms of churchgoing," he said. "But in terms of—" he stopped.

"What is it?"

"I was gonna say in terms of moral right or wrong, but Sketch had a moral right even though it was a legal wrong," Gannon said thoughtfully. "Christ, why is this all so confusin'? You never hurt anyone, I've tried not to—maybe the lesson is to *be* heartless. Protect your own self."

"That life cannot be very satisfying," she said.

"Is *this* satisfying? Our lives?" he asked. "We're hiding in an underground cave, both of us injured body and soul, each of us facing an uncertain future. How is that better?"

"I don't know," Constance answered truthfully. "Yet both of us just fought to survive."

"Instinct," he said.

"Was 'instinct' the reason you pushed me in?" she asked.

"No," Gannon admitted.

The two were silent then.

"Constance, ever since the War started I haven't known how to fix anything," he said. "That day I was riding along the river, I had been here three months, and I was still tryin' to figure out how to relate to Yankees, to black men. I told myself, 'Just treat 'em like the people they are.' But I also always asked myself if I could count on them. If there was a fight, would they see me as a Rebel, dispensable, repentant only 'cause I have to be? Would I help them only to prove I wasn't, not 'cause we had a job to do? I didn't have answers. Then I saw you and I was able to stop thinkin', start feelin'. I don't suppose I liked any of those other people any better, but I do know I stopped hatin' them in my heart." He drew a long breath. "So I guess, to answer your question, I started to see a way back."

Constance took a shuddering breath. The violence that had been done to her, the ruination of her romantic notions of love, did not seem to have a similar path to redemption. Right now, like Hank, she wanted to kill every Comanche in the camp.

Yet she had saved the one. And she had thrown the rifle down with disgust at having killed, even though it was to save her own life and the life of her affianced.

Perhaps there is hope, she thought, shivering and

moving closer to Gannon. Instinctively, he put an arm around her. She did not remove it. *If there is not, then I would prefer to stay here among things of stone.*

But it was not to be as they heard three loud plunks, followed by sloshing sounds, from where they had entered the underground world.

CHAPTER TWELVE

October 21, 1871

The three Comanche came crashing through the darkness, feeling their way as they rode the current, finding the same ledge Constance had discovered, and pulling themselves from the water. Roving Wolf had already told them not to bring a torch into the gas-tainted hollow. They had decided that the three of them would be sufficient to overpower a wounded white man and his woman. Each man carried a knife or club, and they came to the lip of rock with weapons probing the space ahead of them.

The cave with the fur cloak was straight ahead. Gannon could hear them already sniffing the pronounced smell of wet fur; they would be upon the couple in just seconds.

He put his lips against Constance's ear.

"Stay very close to the back of the cave," he spoke in a voice barely above breath as he gently urged her back.

The woman lay on her side and tucked herself against the wall with less than a yard behind them.

Gannon had no idea how the men were coming. They could be crouched or on their bellies, which was a favored way of attacking on the lowlands— hiding behind scrub and snaking forward. They could have sent one ahead with two still in the water or one in the water. They were unlikely to have brought guns; even if they kept them dry, firing in the dark would be a bad idea since the bullets could ricochet.

That did not stop someone from firing a weapon. Gannon recoiled against Constance from the noise as a flash and a deafening crack filled their hollow.

Corporal Evan Bosley was a patient and meticulous young man; his job required it. He could not afford to have shimmied up a large pole and then drop a wire or tool or his telegraph key from sloppiness.

Bosley was born in Bethel, Connecticut, the birthplace of showman P. T. Barnum. From his earliest youth, Bosley was enraptured by one of Barnum's attractions. It was not the diminutive General Tom Thumb or the Feejee Mermaid but the opera singer Jenny Lind whom he adored. He only heard her once, when his parents took him to New York City, and it nearly drove the six-year-old mad that he could not hear that voice again when he wished. And yet, he thought as they rode the train home, there were telegraph wires in New York and also in Bethel, and there had to be a way to make those sing.

There wasn't. At least, not that he could discover with his own homemade devices. He obtained discarded lengths of wire and metal from a hat factory near his home. He used nails to put the wire in trees, to see if they made noise. Apparently, they did not, though the wires vibrated in the wind and made sounds. That led him to read about telegraphs and about how sound traveled, how the Indians put their ears to the ground to hear distant hoofbeats, to the rails to listen to oncoming trains. Sound was not just Bosley's hobby, it was his life.

He was too young to enlist in the army, just fourteen, and he was too young to be on his own: when his parents were killed in a fire, he was sent to Oklahoma to live with his older brother, Gary, who had gone west in search of silver. The younger Bosley helped him as they lived in their tent near the Texas border until failure and poverty drove them both to seek employment. Gary's experience with a succession of packhorses and mules earned him a job in a stable with the U.S. Army. But Evan did not want to be in the tomb-silent dark. He lied about his age, joined the army, got himself assigned to a military telegraph-battery wagon, and resumed his passion. After the war, the Bosleys pursued their respective trades in Texas, where there was a need for manual laborers who spoke English and young men who had experience with electricity.

Corporal Evan Bosley was not an uncommonly brave young man, but he was an adventurous one when it came to his trade. And as he returned to his post at the northern end of the valley, he took a sip from his canteen and reflected on the encounter.

He was dissatisfied with the decision of Sgt. Calvin—
a man to whom he did not technically report.
Nightingale's own sergeant, a black man named
Fenster, did not know the area, did not know the
Comanche, and had yielded decision-making to
the police sergeant. The reporter Lee Bates had
switched his own attention to the articulate Negro,
perhaps wondering if the adventures of a black officer would make for popular dime-novel reading.

Bosley was determined to find out more about
what was going on to the south and used the rocks
to tell him. He moved along the valley wall by short
steps, putting his ear to the stones like a doctor
searching a man's chest for a heartbeat. He became
mesmerized by what he heard: voices, a man and a
woman. It was impossible to tell how far they were,
since there was considerable echo. But the tones
were improbably conversational.

It occurred to Bosley to take his fluted-cylinder
Colt from its holster. If he encountered a bobcat or
a Comanche, moments might matter. Feeling his
way with his right hand, the gun in his left, he sought
smooth spots among the ragged limestone edges
on which to place his ear.

He moved ahead, listened again. More often
than not, the voices were a muffled drone, like cello
strings of different lengths. The sound seemed to
originate from a point lower than where he was,
since it was slightly louder the lower to the ground
he placed his ear. Were the speakers underground?
In a cave? He continued creeping forward in the
dark. Though Bosley was exceeding his orders and
might very well end up dead or mucking out stalls

beside his brother in Austin, he decided not to turn back. He was doing what he was born to do.

He stopped when he heard a trio of splashing sounds, like big rocks tossed in water. They did not come from the rock, it came from somewhere ahead. But then he heard it echo through the rock.

An underground waterway, he realized. The police officer and the lady could well be down there . . . with Indians searching for them. The red men were no less adept than Bosley at listening when the earth "spoke."

He stopped listening for echoes, started listening for water—not through the rocks but through cracks in the rocks. He moved more rapidly now, head tilted slightly toward the wall, hand waving in front of his ear, as though he were wiping a window, feeling for air. He heard another whisper, this one very close. The young man stopped, allowed his inquisitive fingers to hover over the area from which the sound had come. He felt a patch of cool air.

His heart beat faster, and he looked back toward the camp. He had rounded a gentle bend, had come farther than he had imagined. There was no time to go back. The silence of the couple suggested they were in some jeopardy from whoever had made the splash. He lowered his palm toward the opening. There was bristly foliage—where there was moisture and evaporation that was to be expected—and he pulled the plant from where the bold roots had taken hold in the rock. The sloshing was very close.

Bosley knew what he had to do but he had no idea how it would play out, other than it would not go well for him. He had deserted his post. He did not know how Sgt. Calvin would interpret the gunshot he was about to fire. He did not know what the Indians would do. Bosley raised the gun and pointed it straight ahead, over the opening. He did not know anything of what would follow, only that he could not be here and do nothing—

The shot came from the north. Perhaps fired at Roving Wolf; there was no way of knowing. The Indians wouldn't know either. Something else that might not be known: that the air down here, and possibly close to the opening, was explosive. The shot gave the Indians and Gannon momentary pause.

His first thought was to charge them like a bull, with Constance on his back; push through them to the water and try to get away. But he might not make it through slashing knives—and he might not be able to help Constance. That left just one option.

Squatting, Gannon grabbed both ends of the suspended cloak. "Constance, grab my shoulders!" he said loudly, hoping whoever was on the surface had heard.

"Constance? Gannon, is that you?" said a nearby voice.

"There's gas here!" Gannon yelled back. "Set it on fire at once!"

"But you—"

"Do it and fall back!"

Gannon yanked hard on the cloak, tore it free,

bundled it around his shoulders, then turned and threw himself on top of Constance. She exhaled loudly as he hit, but he wrapped his arms around her and held her tight, shielding her. Even if the man fired in, striking him, she would be safe—

There was a pop, a whooshing sound, and a moment later the tunnel lit like a barn on fire. Gannon heard screams, knew that the Comanche had been caught in the conflagration, and heard them either fall or jump into the water within moments.

The pelts on top of him did not burn because they were wet, although the dry corner had gotten singed, and the air quickly became acrid. His arms were still around Constance and he bundled her tightly, simultaneously rising. He took a moment to give her the knife since he would need both hands.

"We're going back in the water!" he yelled, running with his back bent low, his sides stabbing him sharply. He half-ran, half-crumpled into the stream, pushing Constance ahead of him and shucking the cloak as he hit the water. The current carried them forward again, Gannon gasping as he drew breath against the will of his injured ribs. His biggest concern was that instead of remaining at this level, the flow took a downward turn. He had no idea if there were underground waterfalls and did not want to find out.

Constance remained in front, bumping against rock on both sides as the channel narrowed. The thought of being trapped in a too-narrow passage suddenly seemed very real. But then he saw something that made his racing heart throb with something other than fear: the vaguest hint of *visible* rock. Not phosphorescence, which he had seen in mineral samples at carnivals. This was light from outside the subterranean world.

Moments later he saw the vaguest hint of Constance's outline as she swam toward it, moving with the flow.

It was the last thing he saw before a hand grabbed his ankle and dragged him underwater.

Constance saw a large, flat rock ahead. It was part of the wall above it and sat under a jagged bit of light that was noticeable only because it was dark gray instead of black. She threw an arm onto the surface, pulled herself from the water, then turned to help Gannon up. She knew he was injured and could probably use a hand.

She saw him go under the instant she turned. Pushing her hair from her eyes she slid back in, swimming with one hand, her other hand holding the knife. But even the slight current was too strong for her to make much headway. Fortunately, that same flow carried Gannon and the Indian toward her. She got back on the rock and waited until she could make out the figure who was trying to get free and the one who was trying to hold him down. The men crashed against the rock and Constance could now tell them apart: even in the dark, she could discern the skin of the Indian, mottled and blistered in the flames. She stabbed down at the arm and shoulder that presented itself, saw the arms bend toward one another, blood washing down the spine. She stabbed at the backbone in the middle, and the Indian moaned, relaxed, went down. His flesh took the knife with him.

Gannon had gotten free and was clawing to find the rock. Constance grabbed his wrist but wasn't strong enough to pull him up. Instead, she placed his hand palm-down on the stone and let him pull himself from the water. As soon as he was enough ashore to speak, Gannon raised his face toward what appeared like a patch of dark sky.

"Whoever is up there!" he shouted. "Be careful! There's another Comanche!"

The officer did not reply for several seconds.

"Are you still there?" Gannon asked, anxiety in his voice.

"I am," he said. "The Indian has my gun."

Roving Wolf stood with one hand on the fabric around his throat, the other holding the gun on the youth.

"Gannon!" the Indian said, his voice raw from the wound.

"I hear you!" the officer shouted.

"You stay, boy and girl go!"

"I agree!" Gannon shouted eagerly.

It had not taken much skill to sneak up on the distracted boy and hit him with a rock. Nor would any honor have attached itself to the death of such a soft warrior, one who was—like so many white men—deployed with just one or two skills, like ants in a colony. If there had been time, Roving Wolf could have used fire and blade to remove the useless parts of this cub, reveal a screaming, angry manhood somewhere inside, one that was worth taking, however small. Each defeated enemy revealed more of the soul of his people, exposed shreds of strengths and tapestries of weaknesses. The attentive brave who guided them to their death became wiser. His spirit was enriched by the clinging shade of the dead man. As a result, combat with others of his kind was more precise.

That was why, despite his injuries—which even now made standing difficult—Roving Wolf was determined to meet Gannon in single combat. He believed that there was much to gain from the heart of that man.

Roving Wolf was standing just a few feet from the officer, but slightly below where he stood. There were muffled sounds of conversation from underground. Roving Wolf imagined the woman arguing to stay. But she would go. The Big Father would not permit this woman to interfere with the fate of two warriors.

"Can a person fit through the opening?" Gannon asked.

The Comanche motioned the gun at the boy to answer.

"I think so," Bosley said.

"She's coming up!" Gannon answered.

"Not you!" Roving Wolf said. "Later."

"Agreed."

The grunts and sharp exhalations of the woman echoed in the throat of the opening. Roving Wolf took a few quiet steps back. It had occurred to him that the quiet conversation might have been the white man giving her instructions to attack. He had made a pact, but white men did not always honor their words. And white women—he did not believe that they often heard what white men said.

The black sky with its partial moon threw very little light on the tableau, but enough to see shapes. The woman was passed up, arms first, and the boy braced himself with foot against rock, leaning back slightly, to receive her.

The woman was a shabby sight. She was wet, her garments ripped and in disarray, her body more snake than human as it writhed through the opening. She did not emerge on her feet but on her knees, and then on all fours. The boy crouched before her, asking if she was able to stand.

Constance turned her dark face toward Roving Wolf.

"I want my horse," she said, panting.

"No. You walk."

"I will lead it, then," she said. "You have taken enough from me. No more."

Roving Wolf considered going back and shooting the animal, but he did not want to do anything else to draw either his people or those of Gannon. Not until he had faced the white man.

"You get—both horses," Roving Wolf said. It occurred to him that sending the pony back as well would be an insult to the white men. The red man had no use for such a small animal.

"Roving Wolf!" Gannon shouted from below the opening. "There's no one waiting for them? No ambush?"

"Nothing. They take horses and go," he promised.

"Constance?" Gannon said. "Will you do that?"

"Yes," she said bitterly. "But Hank—"

"I will be fine," he assured her.

The woman hesitated, but only a moment. Rising on Bosley's proffered arm, she walked to the valley floor. Roving Wolf backed away to give them room. He waited in silence as they passed, the boy slumping and rubbing the bloodied back of his head, the woman striding like a man with her head erect. They were a strange people, these invaders. The chaos in their ranks, with boys and women both posing as men, must be considerable. Even without guns, were their numbers equal, the Comanche would have taken no more than a season or two to push them back into their ocean.

The clopping of the horses as they approached had a tired, even defeated sound. The draft horse came first, the woman before it. Then came the pony and the boy. No Comanche who ever lived wore shame as openly as this boy.

Attack me, Roving Wolf found himself thinking. *Redeem your honor.*

But he slouched onward, behind the woman, until he was lost in the darkness.

Gannon struggled with his efforts to get through the opening of the tunnel. He was either too broad or too hurt. Roving Wolf tucked the gun in his waistband and walked over.

"I'm not getting' out this way," the officer said as he tried to dip a shoulder through. The shape of the opening prevented him.

"Return," Roving Wolf said, pointing to the first opening.

"Against the current—you gonna give me time to rest?"

"Return," the Comanche repeated.

Without another word, Gannon retreated into the tunnel. Roving Wolf stepped from the hole and turned back, toward the place where he had heard the will of the Big Father.

Gannon was an impressive warrior, but he was not a brave. He could not know what was in store, Roving Wolf thought. But he believed the white man would agree to it. If not, the sun would rise on the body of one of them, resting beside the flesh of Wild Buck.

PART THREE
Blood and Resurrection

CHAPTER THIRTEEN

October 21, 1871

Sgt. Calvin was furious when Garcia reported that Evan Bosley was gone.

The Tejano officer had gone for a walk around the perimeter to help stay awake, always with an eye on the valley, always listening for a sound that hadn't been present earlier in the night. He used to do that as a boy, when his father would ride to his post in Veracruz after visiting Garcia's grandmother in their ancestral home of Jalapa. They made the trip several times a year to see to any repairs of her hut and to give her coins for her needs—which, to the frustration of Jesús Garcia, often included generous donations to the Church, which financially supported the conservative rebels.

The two Garcias would leave the jungled foliage by torchlight in order to make their destination by nightfall. That was where the boy acquired his passion for horses; it made him feel large, powerful, almost like his father. They would pass the graves of Hernando's American-born mother and sister, who had drowned in a flash flood, and would then move on. It was an exciting time that stirred the senses of the ten-year-old. To this day, the creaking of wooden wagon wheels gave him a great sense of well-being. It was 1860, and the Mexican civil war had been raging for two years. The lawful government of President Benito Juárez, which was supported by the elder Garcia, was based on the coast in Veracruz. A succession of leaders would assume command of the military junta, and on this particular trip in March, 1860, the forces of the murderous Miguel Miramón were in siege position outside the city. Though favored by the Catholic church, Miramón was a hated figure who not only executed loyalists but anyone who assisted them, including doctors. Warships of many nations, including the United States, were anchored there in support of the Juárez government, creating an inspiring sight but also a false sense of well-being. On the land, Miramón's forces were often searching for deserters whom they could capture and question and even enlist to their rebellious cause.

During these journeys, careful listening meant their survival, from both animal and human predators. When to remain very still, when to hurry, when to use a knife or a gun—all of these were decisions that had to be made, by ear, from dark until late morning, there was nothing to be seen beyond the head of the horse pulling their army cart—and sometimes, not even that if the mists were unusually thick.

They survived, sometimes just barely, and Hernando Garcia saw his first man shot when a deserter from the revolutionary army tried, at saber-point, to steal their horse to make his getaway. The poor, doomed man could not have imagined that the senior "peasant" had a Colt revolver in his lap, part of a shipment smuggled to Veracruz by the United States Navy. The deserter was brought back to the stronghold and thrown from the wall as a warning to the enemy. It took another ten months, but the enemy was routed at San Juan del Río, Querétaro, in December, just before Christmas—a fitting slap at the Church, Jesús Garcia had cheered. The coward Miramón escaped to Europe. He returned several years later and attempted to overthrow Juárez yet again. This time, he was wounded, captured, and executed by firing squad.

By that time, Hernando Garcia was nearly of military age and had been honing the skills he felt he would need. Given his diminutive size, at five-foot-five, he became proficient at infiltration and fighting with his *laguiole* pocketknife. When engaged in the infiltration, Garcia was able to draw upon his greatest skill: being very still, very quiet, and listening for changes in the environment.

Garcia was able to monitor the perimeter wherever he was, and to note if even a single night bird had suddenly fallen attentively silent. If a man was out of place, he knew from the different location of his yawning; to him, the sounds were like a constellation in the night sky. A few moments of failing to hear Evan Bosley's canteen rattle at his belt told him the man was not where he should be. Garcia went to investigate.

Bosley was indeed gone, and it had to be assumed that he heard something to draw him away— something there wasn't time to report to Sgt. Calvin.

Garcia understood that; sound was ephemeral and, losing it, one might not locate it again.

But investigating it was not the boy's decision to make, Garcia knew.

The Mexican officer looked around, listening, before ascertaining that the man had not gone to urinate or had been abducted. There was no sign of a struggle, no hint of blood, no scents on the air that had not been there before. Garcia walked briskly back to Calvin to make his report.

Before the sergeant could decide what action to take, they heard the single shot from the valley.

"One of ours," remarked Rufus Long, who was stationed within easy earshot of the sergeant.

The men waited in rigid silence for any other sounds of combat.

"So we have to assume that Bosley or someone with Bosley's gun fired that shot," Calvin said with unguarded exasperation.

"An Indian was not likely to give away his presence like that," Garcia noted.

"That is a fact, unless he is looking to draw you in," Calvin said. He looked over at the open horizon toward the east. There was not yet a hint of dawn. Setting out now, they would still be in the dark by the time they reached the general area from which the shot had come. It was still a prime area for an ambush.

"I don't hear anything else," Garcia said. "Perhaps he has not been captured."

"True enough," Calvin said. If the Indians had intended to draw them in, they would have begun carving him up immediately.

The sergeant was sick of seconding what one of

his subordinates said. That was consensus, not leadership. But did leadership mean patience or muscle? He looked down. He did not want to feel the expectant stares of the men around him.

Are there policies or are there not policies? he asked himself. *What is the point when the beaver puts one too many logs on the dam and it slides into the river? There are two, now maybe three, of our people out there . . . two men dead here, one gravely wounded. When do we fight back?*

Calvin looked out at the valley. It was mute and impenetrable, like a wrestler he had once drunkenly challenged at a county fair. Because Calvin was big and strong, his men had *expected* him to go into the ring. So he paid his two dollars in the hope of winning twenty—and took a thumping.

This isn't that, he told himself. *It is your* job *to protect.*

Calvin scarcely believed the words as they came from his mouth; it was as if he were simply a member of the unit listening to a command.

"Garcia, tell the men we are going to get our men and the lady."

The Tejano threw off a salute and was about to pick his way from the dark when he stopped, turned to the valley.

There were hooves, faint and slow but out there nonetheless. And getting louder with each passing second. He heard them, then Calvin heard them, then the entire command heard them.

"Hold," the sergeant told him.

The command was redundant. No one was moving.

The blackness continued to daunt them. Calvin

began to feel shame at his own caution. Before too many seconds had passed, he drew his sidearm.

"Garcia, follow me," he said as he started walking toward the valley.

"*Sí,*" the Tejano replied.

Calvin could tell the situation was serious. Garcia always went to Spanish when he was focused.

The ground beneath their boots seemed to crunch louder than before, magnified by their own attentiveness, the absolute stillness of the men, and the quieter, smaller hours of the night. Calvin almost envied the Comanche. They always knew where their people were, what they were doing. They could afford to kill anything that stirred, secure in the knowledge that it would not be one of their own people.

The last man was behind them now. They were in a funnel of larger rocks that had been punched from the mesa to make the valley on this end. They were still small enough to walk upon, not piled high; those were to the left and right, like the waters parted for Moses.

He could tell, now, that the hoofbeats belonged to a pair of horses. The sounds were from a narrow area not far ahead; they were either side by side or one behind the other. The sergeant crouched, raising his revolver and walking behind it. When they were almost at the entrance to the valley, when the walls loomed large and the camp seemed very far away, he half turned and whispered to Garcia to stay where he was. Calvin continued on, a few paces forward and to the west. If there was gunfire, he did not want them both falling at once.

The sergeant was just a few yards from the horses

when the animals stopped, not in an orderly fashion but haphazardly as if one horse had stopped and the other walked into it.

"Is someone there?" a woman asked.

Calvin still believed that this might be some kind of subterfuge. The speaker was not on horseback; perhaps Indians were.

His heart throbbing against his chin, Calvin said, "Sgt. Calvin, Texas Special Police."

Calvin half-expected those words to be his last. But there was no gunshot, no whoop, no charge with a tomahawk. Just the same voice saying, "I am Constance Breen."

"It's Officer Bosley," said a young male voice behind her.

Roving Wolf retrieved the blanket-and-harness construct he had made and lowered it into the opening. Gannon used that and whatever crags he could find to pull himself from the water. It was an arduous and time-consuming ascent, the swim to the south, against the current, having taken whatever remnants of energy remained. His sides ached as if he'd tried to break a wild horse and been thrown repeatedly into the rails of the corral.

"Just let me . . . catch my breath, Roving Wolf," Gannon said as he collapsed onto all fours. Even that caused him pain, and he rolled slowly onto his back.

"Our people fight soon," the Indian said.

"No doubt," Gannon replied.

"We join."

That surprised the officer. He moved slowly onto

an elbow and sought the shape of the Indian in the blackness. "You mean we fight with our men?"

"No. We wait."

"For what?"

"End of battle."

"My men will shoot you on sight," Gannon said. "And yours will kill me."

"They not see," Roving Wolf told him. He swept his hands along the crags.

Gannon was not particularly interested in this conversation, but he needed to catch his breath and figure out how to move without hurting. Talking bought him time.

"I don't understand," Gannon told him. "Why not just do it now?"

"Need rest and strength of pony." He pointed in the direction Constance had gone. "Only one warhorse. Other workhorse. Not equal."

The Comanche made an interlocking gesture with his hands, suggesting that he wanted no advantage for either of them. It was a sign, to Gannon, that he was considered a worthy foe to be met on equal footing—both men on horseback, both men injured.

"You think you can sit out a fight between our people?" Gannon asked.

"If not, we both die. Need healing. Rest."

"They'll call you a coward, Roving Wolf."

"I die in battle, they not say. I bring your head, they not say. Big Father revealed this."

The Indian had a point, wherever it had come from. But Roving Wolf failed to grasp an important element: Gannon felt that he *should* be with the officers when they faced the Comanche, however much they were no longer "fellow" officers. He wasn't as concerned about how Roving Wolf or any other attacking Comanche died, as long as they did so.

"I don't very much like your plan," Gannon said at last. He pushed off the ground to his knees. He winced and stiffened with pain; it took him a moment to say more. "Let's finish this now, right here. Hand to hand."

Roving Wolf stood over him. The Indian still held Bosley's firearm, but Gannon did not think he would use it.

"You are same as all white men," the Comanche said.

"For a man who talks to his ancestors, you have a short memory," Gannon told him. "If what you just said were true, you would have died the day we met."

"Honorably."

"Honorably," Gannon said. "Like what your party did to Constance."

"What *we* did?" Roving Wolf said with what sounded like disbelief. "Your party hear her, leave her! They cowards!"

Gannon flinched as he thought of Constance's suffering, and he had to restrain himself from digging his fingers into the man's raw throat and claw out a fistful of flesh. To be so cavalier to suffering was not only uncivilized, it was the road to extinction for this creature and his people. Unlike the Indian, Gannon allowed his brain to trample down the animal thing his hands and soul had suddenly become. He breathed hard, huffing his outrage into the dirt and stone.

You are not a savage, Gannon reminded himself, though most of his body disagreed. Strangely, he thought of Captain Keel just then and the sandbar the commander had to walk between bitter men who had only known combat or slavery—often both—and the armchair fops in Washington or Austin who issued edicts tied with red tape; orders that Keel was somehow supposed to forge into reality. Gannon's fingers relaxed as he forced himself to consider, *What diplomacy would the captain attempt to wield here?*

Like most Comanche, like most red men Gannon had met, Roving Wolf had a narrow view of the world. Maybe life was easier, better that way; Gannon didn't know. There was no overthinking of tactics and results: you and your tribe either threw yourself at a problem or migrated somewhere else. Things were that simple. Rank was earned using the same yardstick for all, and leadership was hereditary or the result of a robust challenge. Gannon could not dispute that his own existence had been less perplexing and challenging since he'd been out here, away from politics and the demands of economy, away from the judgments and entitlement of colleagues and Constance's family.

This was all too big for Gannon's very tired mind and a body pinched everywhere with injury to contemplate. He replayed the red man's last remark.

"You're wrong, Roving Wolf," Gannon said. "My people are not cowards. They will fight you."

"For pay," the Comanche held out an open palm, snatched it shut. "Go where told, not where heart is." He slapped his closed fist on his chest. "During fight, many hide. Run. Not so our war chief, Buffalo

Eyes." Roving Wolf made a fist, closed it tight, brought it down. "He powerful, will crush you. We are warriors all the time. You, when you put on uniform."

"That may be true," Gannon agreed. "But there are many more of them than there are of you. If we both lost every man tonight, my people would still be ahead. You cannot afford those trades."

"Cannot afford to lose lands," Roving Wolf replied. "Many old and young die crossing mountain, desert. Better die facing enemy than run."

"That is what the Indians of Mexico thought, of South America, of the Caribbean," Gannon said. "They were all crushed. Forgotten."

"Only by white man," Roving Wolf said. "Not by the gods."

That was the problem of trying to reason with Indians; they were not a practical people. Everything was a straight line, without nuance, utterly unchanged from ancient tradition to the present. But the exchange was not without some value. It reinforced Gannon's understanding of the enemy and offered guidance to his own survival. And he knew—as Roving Wolf must—that neither man was going to change his way of life. The talk was simply a pause so that each man could find a weakness in the other, perhaps provoke him, possibly weaken him. It was an oral form of the kind of torture the Indians inflicted on captives.

Except that Gannon was not a captive and he had no intention of letting things go on like this.

Gannon thrust himself forward, one arm wrapping around the Indian's waist, the other reaching for the gun. The Indian braced himself on legs made powerful by riding without a saddle. He stiffened his back, locked his arms, and Gannon had to put his shoulder into the Indian's belly to budge him. With his free hand, Roving Wolf grabbed the back of Gannon's hair and yanked back. The officer rose from his knees and, still gripping the man's waist and arms, pushed into him. The Indian stumbled back and fell over the rocks but did not release his grip on Gannon's hair. The white man landed on top of him, hurting his own arm, which was under the Indian, but jarring loose the grip on his hair. As their free hands fought for purchase somewhere, anywhere on the other man, their other hands struggled for control of the gun. Because Gannon was on top, he was able to let the man raise that arm from the rock, just a little, then apply his full weight and slam it back down. The blow to the Indian's shoulder rippled along his arm to his hand—but the fingers were iron and refused to let go. And while Gannon grunted with effort and pain, the Indian made no sound.

The thought of Constance brought back the feral rage in Gannon's arms and knees and even in his teeth. The Indian's injured throat was exposed beneath the haphazard bandage and Gannon bit at it. Now the Indian made a sound, hissing with pain. Pinning the Comanche with his greater weight, Gannon wrapped both hands on the gun and drove it knuckles-down into stone. Then again. The fingers opened now and, his own fingers spidering through the dark, he wrenched the weapon free. Pushing back from the Indian, he got on his feet, nearly tumbled backward, but landed upright against the wall of the valley. Only blind luck put him on the north side of the opening instead of through it and back into the water.

Without looking back, Gannon turned and ran to the north. It wasn't so much a run as a lope; he was too tired for more. The former officer listened for sounds of movement, heard none, and only now realized that there was warmth on his chin—dripping warmth. The Comanche's blood.

You should have shot him, Gannon told himself.

But if he were to believe his own reflections on barbarity, that would have been the act of an uncivilized man. Even a man—*especially* a man—who had just tried to rip apart the throat of another had to try and recover his humanity.

Wheezing from the exertion of his flight, Gannon slowed, wavered, remained upright . . . and prayed he was alert enough so that if Keel's men were coming in, he heard them before some nervous greenhorn shot him.

The fight had aggravated his injuries, and Gannon's side began to hurt with every step. He knew he would not make it to the end of the valley without some kind of crutch to help support his weight, and there was no way to make one in the dark.

Believing that he had put enough distance between himself and Roving Wolf and suspecting that the brave would not follow him into the police encampment, he hobbled to a natural recess in the wall, snuggled himself into it with his gun hand in his lap, and waited for sunrise.

CHAPTER FOURTEEN

October 22, 1871

The camp of the combined police and guard contingent was alive with whispered excitement at what they first thought was the rescue of the captive lady by one of their men.

The truth spread just as quickly, to mixed reaction.

As much for modesty as for warmth, Calvin threw a blanket around the woman's shoulders. She apparently did not realize how much of her garment had been torn away. Both returnees were taken immediately to the ambulance wagon of Dr. Zachary. A comforting arm around her shoulder, the doctor had done his best to shield her view with his slight body as she climbed inside; nonetheless, Constance gasped slightly when she spied the well-known shape of Captain Keel on a stretcher on the ground.

"Risk comes with the uniform," Zachary said quietly.

That was something he usually said to his patients,

who were mostly men. Nonetheless, Constance seemed to understand. At least, he could feel her shoulders relax.

"Sergeant," the doctor said, "get me more water— about a thumb. Use that bucket," he added, nodding toward a hook on the back of the ambulance.

Calvin grabbed it. They had needed considerably more for Keel. He moved quickly to one of the three casks on the supply wagon.

Bosley waited outside as the medic attended to the woman after rolling down the canvas shades on the side.

The ambulance had been located behind a large rock, and the doctor risked lighting a single lantern. Zachary removed the blanket and set it aside. Lying on her back on the narrow cot, Constance shuddered and suddenly shot upright, trembling; that told Zachary what he needed to know. With gentle hands, he held her arms and said, "When you are ready, Miss Breen, I should see to your injury."

The woman saw him look to her waist then back again. He knew.

"I'm sorry," she said softly.

"There is no need," Zachary smiled in the dim orange glow. "Would a medicinal drink help?"

"Thank you, no," she said. Then she laughed a little, nearly crying. "I—I pass out easily. I am . . . not . . ." she stopped. "My mother says I am . . . too much a lady."

"And so you are," Zachary reminded her.

Constance did not reply to that. She lay back again and when she appeared to have settled, the doctor removed his hands and retrieved a clear bottle. He splashed some on a sponge as he bent over his patient.

"This is bichloride of mercury—just for cleaning," he told her. "It will feel a little damp, nothing more."

"There . . . are there cuts?"

"Don't worry about what there are or aren't, Miss Breen—Constance, if I may. Let me have a little check, all right?"

"Yes. Of course. Thank you."

She started, not from the liquid but from the touch of the sponge, its slow, sweeping movement on her bare leg. She tried to think about Hank, about nothing else, and to pray silently for his safe delivery. What they had been through together, how he had protected her—

"Surely that will matter more," she said aloud.

"Were you talking to me?" Zachary asked.

"No, I was just thinking," she said.

The doctor got a clean sponge and dipped it into the bucket that Calvin had placed in the cart. When he returned and the water dribbled like running blood, Constance Breen screamed.

The men had removed themselves a respectful distance from the ambulance, but the scream carried like the cry of a hawk—raw, high, and angry. No one looked in that direction save for Sgt. Calvin, who was already facing that way. Bosley sat on a flat rock in front of him. He had not been given a blanket.

"By leaving your post you jeopardized the life of every man here," Calvin said after delivering the bucket. "But you say you saved Gannon and the lady."

"I fired a shot that ignited gas in the cavern," Bosley said. "Without that, they'd have likely been slain by the braves."

"And in the pursuit of that you failed to hear the approach of the other Comanche," Calvin went on. "The one who has your gun."

"Yes, Sergeant."

"Fully loaded?"

The officer nodded.

Calvin shifted, dipping a shoulder as he considered the wretched-looking man before him. The first hint of light in the sky showed his contours, nothing more.

"You saw no other Comanche," Calvin asked.

"None. The brave acted very much as if he were alone."

"How does a man act when he is alone, Officer?"

It took a second for Bosley to figure out what he had actually meant by that. "He was only interested in Gannon. He did not look around for approval or ask for anyone's opinion."

"Gannon was still in this subterranean cavern."

"Yes."

"Your impression being—?"

"The Indian wants him," Bosley said. "He told him to stay down there until we were gone."

"Did you see any other weapons?"

"It was very dark, Sergeant."

Calvin considered this. Gannon had no standing with the Texas Special Police. He was a citizen who had put himself at risk. The hostage had been recovered. Bosley had returned. Their mission was to protect, not attack. A defensive position, where the only means of attack was through a bottleneck valley, from a high mesa, or coming around rock walls that afforded very little cover, was a strong tactical advantage.

There is no good, sane reason to enter that valley.

Calvin turned from Bosley. The men were very still. The only sounds coming from the ambulance were sporadic whimpering and the indecipherable but softly consoling words of the doctor.

They tortured an innocent girl, Calvin thought. If the Comanche left now, the army in the west might or might not intercept them. If the Comanche scrubbed off their war paint, there would be no justification to assume they were a war party.

Would *they leave now?* Calvin wondered. *Could they return to their land, regroup—now that they knew the size of the force and tactics that would be fielded against them—and return?*

Anything was possible. That was the weakness of defense: reacting instead of making something happen. Calvin looked to the east. Simply reacting to this, with the sun falling flush upon them, was a bad idea.

Keel would wait for an attack. Calvin ached to launch one.

"Garcia!" he said.

The Tejano ran over from his position nearer the valley. "Yes, Sergeant?"

"Have our men muster on the western side of the outer wall," he said. "I'm going to have Nightingale's men set up a picket just northeast." He looked at the hint of glow to the east. "You got about ten minutes. I want to push those redskin bastards right into the sun—and a line of guardsmen."

Garcia was off with a sharp salute and Calvin walked to where the bulk of Nightingale's men were stationed. Official or not, Gannon had distinguished himself like a Texas Special Police officer should. Whatever that Comanche had in mind wasn't good. No man with a backbone could do less than try to stop it, whatever the cost.

Buffalo Eyes breathed the foul smell of the burnt paint, seared metal, and blackened wood. There was a sense of satisfaction in that stench. Though they had lost their prize, the party had been reminded of what the destruction of white things smelled like. Like the smell of blood, the smoke had whetted their taste for more. They would take fire to the white men and make all of their settlements like this wagon.

The war chief called a council of his eldest braves, who sat in a circle on the ground as the last of the night hours began to fade. Buffalo Eyes explained that they must ride through the valley, along both sides, and use crossfire to pick off any of the enemy who came near while using the stone for protection. By this means, he believed that at least half the force he saw the day before would be killed before a counterattack could be mounted. He also believed that the steep walls would prevent the rising sun from revealing them or blinding them.

Buffalo Eyes also ordered two of the twenty-two braves to ascend the mesa, one on each side. They were to kill any white men who might be up there and set up covering fire if necessary.

There had been thirty-four whites when they met in the plains. There would be fewer now. And by the time the sun rose, there would be fewer still.

When this day was done, there would be nothing to stop the Comanche from riding through Austin and burning both the city and its people.

Neither Albert nor Martha Breen had slept. They left the bedroom shortly before sunup, made coffee, and sat on the front porch looking expectantly toward the south. The air was warm and still, tinged with the hint of dust kicked up by the railroad workers who were already at work by torchlight, moving iron and tools and crates of ties. Albert did not rock in his rocker nor Martha move on the swing bench. The streets were nearly empty, and the familiar clatter of their horse and wagon was defiantly absent. Albert would have done any penance the Lord asked just to hear it coming toward them.

It wasn't just the absence of their daughter that kept them awake, though that was the largest part of it. Their night was filled with Martha Breen verbally moving between anger and disappointment, and Albert Breen silently regretting his action and also inaction toward Hank Gannon. He did not entirely trust the man and his motivations. Constance was a pretty girl, intelligent, but inclined to swoon for a tall man in a vest and gun. He should have taken a more forceful hand early on.

"I should go to the stable and hire a horse," Albert said after a long, dismal silence.

"You don't know where she went," Martha said,

her voice as harsh as the expression he could just make out in the lamplight glowing just inside the window. "And what would you do, drag her back?"

"Talk to her," Albert said quietly. "That's all."

"She hasn't listened to us since she met that man," Martha complained. "What makes you think she would listen now?"

"Because I wouldn't tell her what we've—what you've—told her before," he said.

"To be sensible? To be prudent? To heed her elders who have been where she is?"

"That," Albert began, "is as dead as the Confederacy."

The hard face snapped toward him. "There is something blasphemous about that remark, Albert Breen. Our daughter is not—"

"What?" her husband interrupted. "Rebellious? Seeking to assert her own rights?"

"There is nothing in Constance that aligns with wretched slaveholders, and I won't have you comparing them," Martha said.

"It's just conversation," Albert said, sipping the now-warm coffee.

"Well, it's rude," his wife replied. "We have always fought to better others, whether slave or poor or even ourselves. We built a life here so that our daughter could have a new world, a better world, a cleaner world. Something of refinement."

"As you say, 'we' did that," Albert replied. "Then she found Hank and turned her eyes westward, as we did when we looked to Texas. What might she want for her own children?" He set the chipped china cup on a small wooden table he had built. "I wonder, Martha."

When he did not finish the thought, his wife said, "Wonder what?"

"How much she was running toward Hank and how much she was running away from here?"

The words set Martha back, moved her so hard that her husband heard the bench squeak, the cup rattle.

"She would not do that," the woman decided after a moment.

"I don't see her," he said.

"You're just being impertinent," Martha said.

"No," Albert replied. "Just asking questions. Sometimes, when I'm assembling something I worked out on paper, it mysteriously, spitefully, rigidly will not go together. It usually turns out to be a mistake in more than one piece. Moisture, sevens that I misread as ones, or even—I did this the other day, with that loft in the Masons' barn—I cut pieces from two separate plans."

"Our daughter is not a mute, inflexible piece of wood."

"Which is why you can't 'fix' whatever is wrong by sawing or hammering," Albert said. "And that's just what we've been doing. Do that enough and the plank splits."

Martha shook her head slowly. "I talk to the women who come for pies," she said. "Their daughters accept the guidance and wisdom of their mothers. They want to live better lives, finer lives, be a part of a decent and respected family."

"Are you talking about the daughters . . . or the mothers?"

"You really are trying me, Albert," she said. "You talk as if there is something wrong with raising yourself up. Back in Ireland—what if Hank Gannon had been a Londoner? Or a seaman out of Plymouth? What if his birthright had been the oppression of our countrymen? Would you have been so insinuating then? So ready to forgive a daughter's infatuation?"

"If I cared more for what my neighbors thought than for what my daughter felt, then no," Albert said.

"Another impiety," she said.

Albert shrugged. "Maybe so." He looked down the street, saw the new day just beginning to arrive. "I should really consider a pipe," he said.

"You'd burn the lumber, like that fool who sold hay. Why would you do something so reckless?"

"It would give me something useful to do with my mouth," he replied.

Martha huffed, raised herself awkwardly, in parts, due to a back stiffened by years of bending over pies, and took the coffee cups inside. Albert remained where he was, looking down the street, his eyes damp, quietly telling the Lord that he *would* do whatever the Almighty required to have his daughter return—or at least to know that somewhere out there she was happy.

The Comanche entered the valley in two divided rows, Buffalo Eyes leading the men on the west, Strong Elk in front on the east. The odor of horse was in the air, but not strong; the horses—Buffalo Eyes detected two scents—were no longer present.

With vision as sharp as the knife in his belt, Buffalo Eyes spotted Roving Wolf before any of the others. The brave was upright and leaning against the western wall of the valley, edged in orange-edged sunlight. Buffalo Eyes passed by him and raised his hand for both rows of riders to stop.

"The gunshot?" the war chief asked.

"A white officer," Roving Wolf rasped. "He is of no consequence. Three of our party . . . dead below. The officer, the girl, and the man Gannon have all moved on to the white camp." He indicated the other end of the valley.

"Gannon. He who attacked our camp?"

Roving Wolf nodded slightly, painfully.

Buffalo Eyes had no pony to spare for Roving Wolf, nor would he have been much help in his current state. "You will join us when you are able," the war chief said.

The wounded Comanche nodded again.

Buffalo Eyes indicated for the braves to resume their passage through the valley, and the horses continued at their slow, careful pace.

This white man, Gannon, was formidable. He had rescued the captive and then bested Roving Wolf. Buffalo Eyes was keen to find the man and kill him. His death would not just remove a powerful enemy, it would be great medicine. The war chief desired that privilege for himself. And he would have it soon, he hoped. He had never believed the white men had returned to their city, as the leader had said. He had not expected him to. He had known they would block the other end of the valley—and, so doing, would leave themselves open to being cut down like rabbits in a warren.

The first birds of morning were in motion overhead, along with the larger birds that hunted them. The breeds, the patterns, were known to Buffalo Eyes, who missed his lands and his family to the west. He wondered if he should ever see them again. The ways of war were uncertain, however great the resolve and courage of the braves. With his own eyes he had seen the skins of his namesake piled higher than a small hill—and they, too, once owned this land.

As the Big Father opens his eyes on a new day, and the spirits of the birds and bucks and buffalo move among us, only he knows who shall prevail this day, and who shall end it as ghosts in his great teepee.

So long as he acted without fear, Buffalo Eyes would be content with his fate.

The war chief suddenly raised his hand again and stopped. A few horses snorted and were silenced by their riders. Buffalo Eyes listened. There were sounds of movement in the distance, at the other end of the valley.

He motioned for Strong Elk to dismount and learn what the white men were doing. The big Comanche dropped from his horse, drew tomahawk and knife from his belt, and eased ahead. He stayed hidden from the fresh colors of the rising sun, blending with the crags as he moved among them. He vanished beyond a gentle turn in the valley. But the noise was clear, not echoing. They were not far from the end.

The sounds of men and horses in motion continued—but then there was another sound.

A gunshot.

"What the hell is that now?"

Sgt. Calvin spoke in a loud whisper through locked teeth as he was about to mount his horse. The men had organized into two groups, were preparing to ride out, when the shot popped loudly just to the south.

Almost immediately, and much louder, Calvin gave the order to dismount. Then he asked if anyone had been hit.

No one had been. There was no second shot. It could be Bosley's Colt, which meant it could be the Indian. The Comanche might have been firing at the nearest officer to see if he was in range. If he was willing to waste a shot, it meant he had four more.

"Garcia, spread the men out," Calvin ordered, drawing his own weapon and getting back on his horse.

"Yes, Sergeant? But where—?"

"Watch for an attack from the outside," the sergeant interrupted, "do not advance without my signal, and Garcia?"

"Yes?"

"Don't give me a pain!" With that, Calvin reined his horse around and galloped toward the valley.

The Tejano barked out the order, though most of the men had already begun to move apart. Keel had drilled them regularly not to cluster—or to bump one into the other—under fire. As the dispersal was underway, Garcia pulled his rifle from the saddle holster, squatted behind the nearest boulder, and prepared to cover the sergeant. His Winchester would be able to reach anyone who took a shot from the valley. From here, he could also watch for an assault from around the mesa.

El burro sabe mas que tu, he thought, repeating something his father used to say to him. *The donkey knows more than you.* But Garcia meant it as a show of respect for Calvin's courage, even when he acted impulsively, as now.

It was light enough now to see the plain, and also to be seen upon it. Calvin skillfully maneuvered the horse around the boulders that covered the field—some as large as a man, some as low and flat as a picnic blanket. He had his own .44 Colt in his hand as his eyes searched the still-dark opening. The jagged slash looked like a black lightning bolt, stuck in the earth, as though thrown there by some ancient god. Calvin felt the power of the land run through him. The Indians might have their sky gods and animal spirits, but an armed man on horseback, at full charge, was a thing of cataclysmic consequence.

The dirty sleeves of his white shirt billowed with the speed of his approach, and his brow dipped toward the target to keep dust from his eyes. He was not an easy target, but he was a target nonetheless.

The sun was on the plain and had not lit the lower part of the valley, so Calvin had no idea whether the

Indian was there or not. Perhaps, as was their way, the Indian had fired and moved elsewhere; possibly a tactical retreat to bring him in the way Bosley had been drawn in.

As the sergeant closed in on the opening, the horse salivating, its chest heaving, Calvin peered at a spot in the morning shadow, squinted to see more clearly, then pulled hard on the reins and stopped the horse so fast it reared. Calvin raised his left hand, signaling Garcia to hold his position. The police officer motioned over two other men to form a small skirmish line.

Calvin settled the horse, patting it with his left hand, then took up the reins, steadied his gun, and eased forward slowly.

CHAPTER FIFTEEN

October 22, 1871

With a few choice words flung at fate, Hank Gannon had to admit that for a man who had left the Texas Special Rangers, he had faced an inordinate amount of trouble and pain on their behalf.

Sleep was not possible in the ragged nook, nor was it advisable with enemies on one side and tired, probably scared, restless-trigger police on the other. If he were talking this out with Constance or even with Keel—in a rare moment when he was Amos Keel and not Captain Keel—they would be telling him that this was God's way of showing him that his work was not yet through. That anyone worthy of the designation "man" should be working in the service of family and neighbor, not roaming the lowlands or foothills like a rogue coyote.

They would have a point. From the plantation to last month, Gannon had found merit and purpose in being part of a team. It could achieve so much more than the individual.

But then he would think of Constance and her disapproving mother and tell himself, *The individual deserves something, too, Lord.*

And there had been more value and, more important, peace these last few weeks than Gannon had ever known. Not having to think past the next meal or safe resting place. Having complete freedom of movement. Not having the cold breath of politics in his face, destroying his livelihood in Florida by starting a war, destroying lives and limbs during the war, destroying his own balanced existence in Austin.

Right now, except for the pain in his sides, except for the suffering of his beloved Constance, the firm embrace of the rock around him was a simple damned blessing.

So was finding the gun. It looked like the one Andrew Whitestraw carried. But it could have come from any of the men who did not leave this valley alive or ended up in desperate flight. Gannon tucked it in his belt.

So now, Hank, he asked himself, *how are you different from a field mouse with a gun? Is that what you want?* That image made him chuckle, but then he was beyond exhaustion because there was nothing in his life to laugh about right now. He told himself to shut up and closed his eyes, trying to relearn how to breathe without hurting.

Though Gannon was well-concealed, the wall of his niche, on his left, was slightly recessed; the wall to his right, on the side of the police camp, jutted a bit. He was able to hunker back and still hear everything from the Indian side of the valley. He hadn't gotten very far with his inhaling and exhaling drills when he heard horses to the south. The man did not move his body. He only opened his eyes and drew his gun.

The sounds of the hooves told him there were definitely many horses out there. Comanche, headed for the police encampment; it couldn't be anything else. He not only heard it, he could feel it in the rocks under his seat. The sounds and vibrations stopped, and he wondered if he had been seen or smelled. The two trips through the underground water had left a distinctive musk on his clothes.

Gannon listened, listened hard to his left, to the south. He heard the tumble of tiny stones, the very slight scratch of rock against rock. Someone was approaching. This spot was just beyond a bend, would have been a blind spot for an approaching party; it could be a scout, or perhaps they had encountered Roving Wolf and he had warned them about Gannon. Either way, someone was about to come upon him.

His heart went from repose to action, his limbs tensed, and his breath became painfully rapid as he contemplated his courses of action—of which there was only one, really. If the Comanche saw him, he had to kill the man and make a break for the end of the valley in case the others gave chase. If the Comanche walked by, he could afford to wait and take him from behind—club him, take him to camp, and leave the braves without a report from their scout. The only information they would have is that someone apprehended him.

The dull light of sunup shined on the opposite wall of the valley, a zigzag shape that came through the opening in the mesa. The light brightened very,

very slowly. It briefly took Gannon back to a much better time and place, when he would turn on a lantern before spending the night with his girl in the barn back in Florida. He would adjust the knob slowly, slowly, allowing just enough light to see but not to draw the attention of his mother doing her ledgers at the kitchen table when the house was quiet—

A shape moved in from the south. Black and thick, it reminded Gannon of the observation balloons he saw moving across dark, dawn skies during the War. It was the big chest of a big man, a Comanche, whose proportionately big fists held weapons.

Gannon held his breath, remained as still as possible, and watched as the giant of a man moved past the mouth of the opening. The white man listened for others, heard nothing but the receding footsteps of the Indian. Presumably, Keel would have anticipated this and there would be a point man to handle it.

The world was silent, save for its morning wildlife overhead. Gannon leaned forward slightly so he could hear beyond the slight projection of rock to his right. He waited several minutes, at least, until the scrape of moccasins on rock came back toward him. This was a bastard of a moment, tough enough to handle when he was clearheaded. But he could not let the Indian return with his report.

Gannon pointed the gun at the stone lip that ended about a foot and a half from where he sat. During the War, he had shot men without announcing himself, without giving them a chance to surrender. This didn't feel the same; he wasn't fighting an invader, he was the invader. But it was war just the same. Not quite sure what he would do, Gannon waited until the shape appeared, a little brighter now, before he decided.

"Comanche!" he said in a loud whisper.

The Indian turned toward him, knife raised waist-high, pointing directly at his head. Without hesitation, Gannon fired into the big target in front of him, the man's chest.

The shot kicked the man back on a geyser of blood, and Gannon immediately grabbed the sharp limestone with his left hand to pull himself up. Wheezing with pain, he thrust himself forward, running past the Indian, who was trying to rise, his heels dug in, his hands clawing at things unseen.

Bent to one side but running as best he could, Gannon made for the light, for the encampment that was becoming brighter with every second, toward the man galloping toward him.

Buffalo Eyes heard the report and waited for another that never came. He was surprised to hear just one shot crack from within the valley. The war chief had expected that the enemy would station a man there; but he was surprised that anyone could have seen Strong Elk in those shadows and then killed him with a single bullet. Buffalo Eyes had no doubt that the man was dead; there were no sounds of a struggle, just the continued movement from the other end of the valley.

The war chief thrust his rifle straight up; the

attack would take place as planned, while the white men were in light and they were still in shadow.

The figure lurching toward Calvin was a white man who was also a red man, his face, shoulders, and left side wet with blood. It might have been a trap, bait, if not for the fact that the man held a pistol.

Calvin urged the horse forward at a canter. It did not take many steps for him to realize who the bloody man was. Grizzled, thinner, tired-looking, but he was still recognizably Hank Gannon. Calvin stopped and dismounted at the same time, catching Gannon in his left arm as the man moaned and fell. A quick glance told him the blood was not running, did not belong to the new arrival.

The man was very nearly deadweight; it would have been impossible to get him on the horse. Leaving the animal where it was and turning toward the encampment, Calvin tucked his shoulder under the man's arm. Gannon gasped and the sergeant realized there was some kind of wound there. He held the injured man tighter to minimize the man's movement as they walked back. The sergeant hated turning his back on the Comanche, since they would use it for target practice. But that couldn't be helped.

"Sergeant!" Garcia called.

Calvin heard it at the same time the Tejano had: horses in the valley behind him. They would never make it to the main body of men in time. A shot took the horse down, even as Calvin was looking for cover. The nearest rocks were a disconnected array of chest-high boulders about ten yards away. Calvin ran for them, carrying Gannon's entire weight on his shoulder. The sergeant heaved Gannon to the dirt as a shot whizzed between them, hitting the edge of the boulder and ricocheting; a rock chip struck Calvin in the left cheek as he jumped to the ground beside Gannon.

The police and guardsmen returned fire, a brief drone that Calvin could hear pinging off the valley walls.

"Hold fire!" he shouted.

Garcia repeated the command and there were just sporadic shots from the valley, two more horses falling before the gunfire stopped. Garcia shouted for the animals to be moved back.

There was a break in the shooting, though the scent of gunpowder drifted over the battleground. While the two men were lying there, Calvin moved closer to Gannon.

"How're you injured?" he asked.

"Ribs," Gannon said.

"We'll get that wrapped," Calvin replied. "The blood?"

"Comanche. Thanks for haulin' me in, Sarge."

Calvin lay a hand on his shoulder. "Good to see you, Reb."

"Lay me over the rock," Gannon said. "I can still shoot."

"If we need that, I will," Calvin said. "I'm not sure they're coming out."

Still holding his gun, Calvin had elbow-walked to the other side of the boulder. He looked out across the plain that was marked with sharp shadows cast by the rising sun. The opening of the valley seemed even darker as the dry sands around it brightened.

"Is Constance still in camp?" Gannon asked. He had assumed she made it; he was fearful of the sergeant's response.

"She's here," Calvin told him. "She's with the doctor. I want to hear how you did that, Reb," Calvin added. "Got her out."

"She did most of the shooting," Gannon admitted. He felt unprecedented relief knowing that she was in good hands and at the rear of the battlefield— for now. "What is the captain's plan?"

"The captain is with the doctor, too," Calvin replied. "Indian got in, shot him up pretty bad. Killed the other commander, Nightingale. White-straw is gone, too. So the plans are mine and what I'd intended to do was maneuver around the mesa to the south, pin them inside. I don't think that can be done now. We'd never get across the plain."

"Good news is, they won't be able to pick us off from hiding," Gannon said. "That was probably their plan. Thin us, equal the numbers, charge when we were in disarray."

"Which they could've done if we'd mounted up," Calvin said. "You spoiled their plans. Any idea what they'll try instead?"

"Not sure. You saw yourself, this is a war party," Gannon said. "But when I was in their camp, I noticed something else. They are traveling very light."

"You mean supplies?"

"Yeah," Gannon said. "They packed arms, not water, not food, not tobacco for peace pipes, no spare ponies—they must've planned to take any they needed. Their war chief is Buffalo Eyes. Heard of him?"

"In a dispatch from Blanco Canyon," Calvin said. "Army gave pursuit, lost him, but found several ponies from his war party. Their bellies were burned, bad. Torches, it looked like. That was how he got the animals back up after they'd dropped from exhaustion."

"This war chief did not intend to stop or turn back but to burn and kill as far as he was able," Gannon said. "That's not going to change."

"So what does he do next?" Calvin thought aloud.

"The only thing that lets him get past us, even if it costs him some braves," the sergeant said gravely as he looked back at the encampment. "We better join the others."

Buffalo Eyes had lost the surprise he sought. He did not dwell upon that fact, however. Lamentations were for women. It meant only that they would have to leave the valley sooner than he planned, and against greater numbers, to fight the enemy. In the open, Buffalo Eyes still counted his braves as superior to any warriors, Indian or white. He motioned for the braves to remount. He rode to the center of the valley and faced both rows of the war party. He pointed to four braves and motioned for them to leave the ranks. They understood. Then he regarded the others.

"Puuku!" he cried, then turned the upraised rifle in a circle, indicating for the two rows to form one.

Then he spun his horse around and led his braves from the valley in a single, thundering column.

It sounded to Gannon like thunder rolling in from the sea.

He had not required Calvin's help to retreat. The rocks provided cover, and he was able to bend low without much pain. His appearance drew stares from the men he saw, mostly unfamiliar guardsmen, and until he reached the ambulance wagon and Calvin handed him a towel, Gannon hadn't realized how much the dead Indian's blood had covered him. He wiped it away, intending to see Constance and Captain Keel when the Comanche burst from the valley.

Calvin heard them, too. The horses had to be the Comanche target, and before he could give the order to lie them down, make them smaller targets, the first volley erupted from Garcia's skirmish line.

"Get their horses!" Calvin shouted, repeating the command several times so it could be heard over the constant gunfire.

Some men heard and aimed for the Comanche stallions. A few fell in ugly tumbles, throwing their riders hard. But the Indians surged through them like a spear, and those who survived the initial transit made it impossible for the white men to fire without risking hitting their own people. The veteran police and guardsmen turned their rifles around and used them as clubs, swinging hard at the Comanche who were firing at the horses tethered in the rear of the camp. Almost at once, the

Indians in the rear of the line adjusted their tactics, using an upsweep of their tomahawks to meet the swung rifles, then bringing the stone heads down again on the defenders. More and more of the Indians were able to punch through as the white men backed away, tried to fire, but more often than not missed their targets.

Gannon was at the rear of the camp. He still had the gun, and Bosley was outside the ambulance. Gannon put his back against the nearest boulder to keep his torso steady and fired at the Indians who closed in on the makeshift corral. He was too busy shooting and reloading to see if Roving Wolf was among the attackers. It was carnage in the densely packed rear quadrant as horses were killed or injured, others were pulled to the ground, guardsmen returned fire, bullets pinged off rocks, and Indian braves and their mounts died in twisting, bloody falls. Even in the worst battle of the Civil War, Gannon had never experienced chaos like this. He was glad that the ambulance wagon was slightly to the east and of no tactical importance to the Comanche. Wisely or fearfully—or both— Dr. Zachary had all the flaps drawn tight.

With the amount of dust thrown up by the attack, it was impossible to see how many men and horses had fallen in the main area. What alarmed Gannon was not the potential losses but the potential survivors on the Comanche side. As yet, the braves who made it through circled back to attack the horses. Gannon could not hear Calvin's raw-throated commands, but he noticed more and more police whom he recognized, and guardsmen he did not, falling back to protect the herd. The sergeant had to be concerned, rightly, about what would happen if a substantial number of Comanche broke through and rode on to Austin.

Nearly out of ammunition—he had just loaded the last six bullets—Gannon pushed off the boulder, squinted with the pain that slashed along the middle of his back, and staggered toward the nearest horse. It was already saddled, having been readied to ride out; he pulled himself up, wheeled the horse toward the nearest saddled mount, and grabbed the reins. He drove his steed ahead with his heels, pulling the other behind him; there was an open stretch of plain, without any sheltering boulders, but with the ability to quickly put significant distance between him and the Comanche. The stretch was due east, perpendicular to the valley, and he visually marked the hundred or so yards that would put him out of range of the Indians' rifles.

Shouting at the horse and whipping its sides with the reins, he raced into the clear morning. He did not fear being shot in the back, since the men were not the target; but he was mentally prepared for having the painted shot from under him and either shattering what was left of his rib cage or having to finish the trip on the second horse, if that was possible. He had not yet considered what he would do when he was safe; Comanche would no doubt pursue.

As he rode, he heard shots close behind him but not the whiz of gunfire flying by or the punch of bullets striking the earth. He chanced a look back and saw Hernando Garcia between himself and the massive dust cloud. The Tejano was also on

horseback, not far from the ambulance wagon, but
he had stopped to face the enemy and protect
Gannon's retreat. He quietly thanked God that the
Tejano was such a fine horseman. He could shoot
straighter in the saddle than any man Gannon had
ever met.

Free to concentrate on the next step, Gannon had
to get the horses to safety. Without them, it would
be impossible to pursue the Comanche. He rode
on, using distance as his buffer. Out here, there was
nothing else. He realized that by doing this he
was leaving one less man to protect Constance if
the Comanche spitefully turned on her wagon.
Seeing that the captain was still alive, the Indians
might just do that if any of them made it through the
camp. Gannon felt sick in his stomach but—and he
could thank Keel and Calvin for this—the mission
had to take precedence. And he took consolation
from one thought.

*If Zachary has a weapon in there, Constance knows
how to shoot.*

He looked back. His own dust cloud obscured
Garcia, though he could see flashes of distant rifle
fire in the thick haze. The sounds were muffled,
too. Gannon slowed to preserve the horses.

With his own flight quieted, Gannon heard the
continuing pop of gunfire . . . and the thump of
hooves coming in his direction. *Four . . . eight?* He
turned to face the sound, held his weapon waist-
high so as not to have to raise his arm. Either a pair
of Comanche were coming after him or—

Garcia burst through the mist at a gallop, trailing another pony. The Tejano was looking down,
following Gannon's trail, headed straight for his

position. Gannon looked beyond him, saw only the dusty air—and then a single warrior speared through it on horseback. From the beaded leather satchel around his neck, Gannon knew at once that this was the war chief.

There was another brave behind him. Then another. Gannon suddenly understood Garcia's plan. Several braves were going to break through anyway. He was using himself as bait to give Gannon an opportunity to pick them off, knowing that they'd go for the horses before they went for him.

Gannon dismounted to give himself the steadiest shot possible. He got on one knee, a position he'd mastered behind bushes during the War. He aimed at the war chief's horse. When it was in range, he fired. Gannon was glad he had dismounted; as the war chief fell, so did Garcia's trailing mount, shot by one of the braves. The pursuing Comanche could not stop fast enough and piled into the two fallen horses, falling over them, the horses whinnying and dropping and trying to get up. Only one of the horses succeeded. Almost at once, the war chief had pulled himself on its back, wheeled, and fired into the head of the horse that had risen from the dirt. Then he rode back to the fight.

Still in the saddle, Garcia spun round. The war chief was lost in the dust, and Gannon fired at the other two Indians as they tried to get to Garcia. They went down among the horses.

The Tejano rode over to Gannon—who was looking back at the camp, trying to understand the sudden flight of the war chief. He could have tried for any of the three surviving horses. Or if he had wanted to get away he could have broken for the north, away from the two police officers.

"Christ," Gannon said suddenly.

"What is it, *amigo*?" Garcia asked as he rode up. Despite the battle—or because of it—a smile shone through his dusty face.

Gannon said, "Take the spare horse. I've got to get back."

"What is so urgent?" Garcia asked—though from Gannon's expression, he understood at once what the target must be. If it were not possible for the Comanche to go all the way to Austin, they would leave the kind of carnage that horrified readers in their newspapers.

Mounting, and leaning forward as a lance of pain ran through him, Gannon tore back across the plain, headed for the ambulance wagon.

CHAPTER SIXTEEN

October 21, 1871

Passing through the cloud of dust, Gannon saw a battlefield that was bloodier than the scale and close quarters would have suggested. There were no cannonballs, no snipers, just bullets and blades—but they had wreaked destruction on horse and man both.

The Comanche were retreating to the valley, seven men in all, the war chief at the rear. There appeared to be blood on his right arm. Calvin held up pursuit, which was roughly organizing under one of the guardsmen. The sergeant was still on his horse, his gun raised toward the sky. Like the others, his face was covered with a layer of dirt.

"We should pursue, Sergeant!" one of the mounted guardsman was saying with some urgency. "They're on the run!"

"Not until we count the dead and I talk with Gannon," Calvin said.

"Gannon?" said Long. "Last I saw he was running—"

The police officer stopped talking as Gannon rode up. The men exchanged a heated look.

"He was running to try and save horses in the event of a chase," Gannon said.

Calvin ignored Long, trotted over to Gannon. "I count seven in flight, eleven dead," the sergeant said. "Is that all of them?"

"No," Gannon said. "There were at least twenty braves at the camp and there's one more I know of in the valley."

"So the war chief left people behind," Calvin said. "Either to harass our flank or pick us off if they couldn't break through and had to retreat."

"That would fit their arrogance."

Calvin asked, "How so?"

"We had greater numbers and they still thought they could beat us," Gannon said. "But it was also smart. With all the shots flying, chances were better they would hit white men." His eyes were scanning the ground. "They got seven of ours and double that in horses."

"And they're still out there," Calvin said, peering into the valley.

Gannon pulled the horse around and saw the ambulance wagon. The Indians were technically not his problem, save one, and they could wait. Biting down on his teeth to fight the pain, he rode forward.

As Gannon approached, he saw a rip in the canvas at the rear, a diagonal slash in the solid sheet. He turned sideways so he was athwart the back of the wagon. His heart was beating faster as he spoke.

"Constance?"

The canvas was rolled up noisily, clattering on its ropes. She was behind the cot, which had been turned on its side and wedged on the floor at an angle. The doctor in front of it with a surgical scalpel. There was blood on the scalpel and a fierce, desperate look on the medic's face.

"They've left," Gannon said. He extended his left hand into the wagon, took the knife. "You can relax."

Gannons's eyes returned to Constance, who climbed over the cot, shouldered around Dr. Zachary, and hugged his neck. He crushed his teeth harder so he didn't cry out.

Constance stepped back quickly. "You're hurt," she said, remembering. "I'm sorry."

"Best embrace I ever got," he assured her. He looked down at the scalpel, then up at Zachary. "That was the war chief you cut."

"I was defending my patient," he said defensively, almost apologetically. "Is he here? I—I would like to bind the wound."

"He's gone, they're all gone," Gannon replied. "You'd better see to the field, though. There was a lot of shooting, probably some wounded."

"Of course, yes," Zachary said, turning and looking for where his medical bag had gone in all the upheaval. He found it and hopped over the lip, landing unsteadily but rushing ahead.

Gannon looked up at Constance. "I thank God you are all right," he said.

"And you," she said. Her formality, in public, did not conceal the joy in her eyes. "I was . . . so worried."

Gannon looked down.

"What is it?" Constance asked.

"I have to go back," he said, lightly cocking his head toward the valley.

It took her a moment to understand what he was saying. "For that Indian?"

"If I don't finish what we started, he will come again," Gannon said.

"He was not in a healthy way," she pointed out. "He might not survive."

"I have to know that," Gannon told her.

"Then I have a suggestion," she said. "Come in and at least let me bind your side."

He hesitated. "You won't try to put me to sleep then cart me away?" he said, looking over at the bottles on a shelf.

"You'd only wake up and have farther to travel," she said.

He smiled. He couldn't remember the last time he felt a connection like that. Gannon dismounted and entered the ambulance while Constance relit the lantern and fingered through a stack of linens and selected one that was long and narrow enough to go around Gannon's torso. He bent to try and right the cot, thought better of it as he felt a knife pain in his side.

"Just stand there," Constance said. "It will be easier that way."

"Upper ribs," he said as she stepped over the cot.

The touch and proximity of the woman was a tonic for them both. Gannon closed his eyes and connected with each finger; she savored the gentleness of his presence. The horrors of the previous day and night did not go away, but there was a feeling that everything—the Indians, the valley, the officers—was very far from the two of them. She was firm but careful in the placement and tightness of the binding, and she tied a small knot with the ends in a spot where there was no injury. Gannon took a trial breath which was as much a reaction to the woman's proximity as it was to the bandage.

She did not have to ask to be held. It happened. They were together like that for only a few seconds before a cavalry detachment seemed to arrive next to the wagon.

"Gannon, are you in there?"

The couple separated, their eyes lingering a little longer, as Gannon went to the torn back flap and leaned through. It was Garcia with the three horses.

"Did we win?" the Tejano asked.

"We stopped them, for now," Gannon replied.

Garcia nodded with understanding as he looked across the field at the casualties. Then he looked up. "The buzzards. They always win."

Campfires were made, coffee was served, birds were shot from the sky and cooked. Gannon slept under the shade of a tree for several hours, waking when he felt a poking about his side. He wakened with a start that wasn't as painful as it might have been three hours before. Since he had left the farm in Florida, Gannon had become accustomed to waking in unfamiliar places. He was instantly alert.

Dr. Zachary was bending over him. The man

smelled of blood, and his checkered vest was spotted with it.

"Sorry to wake you," Zachary said, "Now that I'm done with the major injuries, I figured I'd better check your wrapping. Lady did a real fine job. Not too tight—how's it feel?"

"A lot better than before," Gannon replied.

"No lacerations, correct?"

"Just bruises."

"Fine," the doctor said. "I'm going to leave it, then. You can breathe all right? Not too much pain?"

"Long as I don't breathe deep, it's okay."

Zachary nodded. "Bettin' it's muscle, not bone, you injured." The doctor rose and sat on a root that had gnarled up from the wind-eroded topsoil. He looked around, then said, "Can I talk to you a minute?"

Gannon eased onto his elbows. "Of course." He immediately looked around, saw Constance beneath another tree, curled on her side facing him, asleep.

The doctor put himself between Constance and Gannon, spoke very low.

"Constance Breen—I know her from Austin, met her a few times at church and at socials. I've seen you with her."

"I want to marry her."

Zachary nodded and smiled, though his smile didn't last. "It's my understanding that she was probably out here trying to find you."

"She was."

"You are aware, of course, what happened out there." He cocked his head to the valley.

"I was there."

"Yes," Zachary said. "But I'm talkin' about—she bled some, I stopped it, but that isn't the real injury. It's too early for me to know much, certainly not in a field hospital that's mostly good for busted arms and ribs. But . . ." he stopped.

"But she could be with a Comanche child," Gannon said in a voice that showed none of the emotion he felt.

The doctor nodded. "I did what I could—but there are new laws and, anyway, without the proper instruments I could do grave harm."

"I understand," Gannon said. "Did you talk to her?"

"I did not," he admitted. "I believe she is aware, though. After all these years—I don't have to tell a patient what they already know or feel."

Gannon thought back to the cave. "She asked me how I did it, how I forgave old enemies. How do you live with all this?"

Zachary patted Gannon on the shoulder; the connection was more for the doctor than it was for the patient. "Believe it or not, I lean on my patients. They are strong. Oh, scared, yeah. But I have never met a soldier or a mother or even a child who did not teach me about courage."

The doctor smiled down and Gannon smiled back. It was the second time that day the former officer had felt something to be warmed by and proud of. The doctor was about to leave when Gannon called after him.

"How's the captain, doctor?"

Zachary took a few steps back. "Grave," he said

quietly. "He's fighting, but he should be in a bed where there's clean sheets and hot water."

The doctor left, and Gannon turned toward the sleeping woman. For a moment, her repose reminded him of the murdered South, of the simple, almost daily joy of being able to rest under a shade tree. He still could not think, not yet, of what the nation may have gained in integrity, decency, and international respect as he had heard it said. All he could contemplate was everything he and his family and his neighbors and his people had lost.

And then a gunshot shattered his reverie.

"The Comanche are still out there," Garcia said.

Sgt. Calvin did not bother to comment. The shot from the edge of the valley had announced that fact, and also declared, confidently, that the police and guardsmen were going to have to come in to get them. The Indians had not attacked the previous night, preferring daylight assaults. But their plan having failed, there was no telling what maneuver they would try next.

"We don't have to worry about them now," Calvin said. He pointed to the west. "Stack their dead over by those boulders. We'll bury ours on the other side."

"Colonel Nightingale, too?" said Sgt. Philip May of the Texas State Guard.

"Colonel Nightingale, too," Calvin told him. "We can come back and get them, with proper conveyances, when this is done."

"My men will not abide by that," May said. The

wide, swarthy, mustachioed former cannoneer with the 1st Indiana Heavy Artillery Regiment had ceded authority to Calvin because the Texas Special Police knew this terrain. But this was the first time May had challenged his authority. "We will bring him back when this mission is completed—today, I trust."

Calvin walked over to face his counterpart just as Gannon arrived.

"Sergeant," Gannon said, inserting himself between Calvin and May and facing the latter. "Let me tell you, from experience, that you do *not* want to ride into Austin with a dead man without proper ceremony."

May took a moment to study the man's bandage and attire. A flash of recognition spread across his dark face. "Do I have the questionable pleasure of addressing the man who the late Colonel Nightingale referred to as a 'traitor'?"

Calvin moved toward May, but Gannon refused to budge. To their right, Rufus Long overheard the exchange and took a few steps forward. Whatever Gannon's differences with the man, a brawl was the last thing the men needed. He gave Long a look that told him to stay where he was.

"You have that pleasure, Sergeant," Gannon said. "And you can call me whatever name you please, but if you got a thimble of brain you'll take my advice."

May's mouth disappeared tightly under his woolly moustache, and several of his men gathered around him, equally ready to spit.

"I also suggest you turn that hate on killin' Comanche, or we'll be buryin' more of our people today," Gannon added.

The caution was not lost on May, whose glare shifted from Gannon to Calvin to the man who was holding the unit's only two shovels. He strode toward them with his fists tight and a huff in every breath and his men followed.

Calvin came around to look at Gannon. "I remember now why I always liked you," the sergeant said. "You got iron."

Gannon shook his head. "What I got was a nap. Makes me feisty."

Calvin grinned. "What're your plans—Officer?" he asked. "Number 27, wasn't it?"

Gannon smirked. "Yes, Sergeant, but I'm not wearin' the badge again. If I get out of this, I'm goin' west."

"If you get out of this?" Calvin asked. "Why shouldn't you?"

"Because I got open accounts with a redskin. They have to be closed."

Calvin took a small sip from the canteen he carried, offered a swallow to Gannon, who accepted. The warm mouthful brought back the entirety of the Civil War.

The sergeant moved his hat to shield the morning sun. He looked out at the police and guardsmen moving bodies and digging graves. "No one will think the less of you for taking that gal and movin' on. You shouldn't either."

"I'll have to look over my shoulder all the way to California and then some," Gannon said. "Wife, kids—I'll never feel safe. And I'll never feel right." He shook his head. "It ain't iron, 'cause Lord knows I would really rather do what you just said. It is survival and—I have to prove something to men I used to bunk with. I didn't trample a man to get home to my girl. Careless? Tired? Maybe. I think I did right by him. But the only way to prove that to them, and to me, is by doin' right here."

Calvin took another drink and capped the canteen. "I can't argue with any of that. I wish I could, 'cause that gal needs you alive and whole."

"Yeah," Gannon said. He couldn't think of anything to add to that. "This thing is as the Good Lord willed it. I'll stay for a bit until this feels better," he rolled an arm painfully. "Then I'll go find that Comanche."

"Will they let you pass, you think?"

"I have no mortal notion. They just might see me as Roving Wolf's enemy, not as a white man. You know the Comanche, Sergeant. It don't pay to try and think like them. They have a funny set of rules."

"They do," Calvin agreed. "Hell, I still have to figure out what we're going to do. Regulations kind of went downriver."

"Been tellin' Captain Keel since I arrived that they need a telegraph out here," Gannon said. "Texas is just too damn big."

Calvin shook his head and looked back at the valley. "Right now, it seems too damn small."

Gannon couldn't dispute that.

The weapons that had been collected from the fallen Indians were gathered in a stack near their bodies. Gannon had not decided, yet, what exactly to do about confronting Roving Wolf, but he asked the sergeant if he could take a knife and a rifle as well as one of the buckskin tunics. Calvin told him to take whatever he wanted, except a horse.

"They may try again for ours," the sergeant said. Then he asked, "Something symbolic about takin' one of their shirts? Sorta like a scalp?"

"Nope," Gannon told him. "It gets dreadful cold out here at night."

Calvin snickered but looked at him funny. "Prairie life seems t'have made you a bit of a smart-ass."

"Maybe so. You spend a month out here, talkin' mostly to yourself, you get a little funny."

Calvin offered him his big hand. "Well, I hope ya don't stay alone—and if our paths don't cross again, best to you."

Gannon shook the hand. "You'll watch out for her."

"With the lives of every man here," Calvin assured him.

Gannon thanked him and collected what he wanted from the remains of the raid. There was a bison water pouch attached to a dead palomino, and he took that as well. The officers and guardsmen both looked at him as if he were a ghoul, but Gannon didn't care. In the wild, you learned to use every part of an animal—beast or human.

Then, with a slight hobble, he made his way back to where Constance was still asleep. He had seen a pad and pencil in the ambulance wagon and went over to write her a note. The doctor was giving water to the captain, and Gannon had a few minutes of privacy. He left Constance a note, dressed—the tunic was a little small, which actually helped

keep him from straining his sides—and then
ducked under the side flap on the opposite side
of Constance and the doctor. He walked about a
hundred yards, toward the eastern side of the mesa
where he would be out of range of any Indian
sharpshooter. Then he stopped, looked back at the
sleeping woman, and let his eyes drift north in
the general direction of Austin.

He felt, at that moment, what this mesa must
have experienced in the distant past. A river became
a torrent and then nothing was ever the same. If it
had been capable of thought, the vast rock mound
would probably have found itself with a big division
down its center before it even realized it.

That was Gannon's life. An order from Keel to
Calvin to Gannon to go collect a wanted man had
turned into a life in which civilization would no
longer play a part. Whether he remained in the wild,
a trapper, a mountain man, just a rover, or whether
Constance would still want to go with him to the
untamed north of California, that life was dead.

Strangely, Gannon did not feel a sense of loss. He
felt free.

But first there is a dispute to finish, he told himself,
looking south. Finding a stride that would not tax
his side, he resumed his journey around the side
of the valley to where he expected he would find
Roving Wolf.

Constance was not surprised to wake and learn
that Gannon had gone. She was also not surprised
to be handed a note by the doctor.

"I found it pinned to one of the last laundered towels," he said. "Guess he wanted to make sure I found it."

The doctor gave Constance her privacy, and the young woman read the brief message quickly, then again:

> *Dearest: DO NOT FOLLOW.*
> *I will come for you before I head west.*

It occurred to Constance that this was the first written note she had from Gannon, the first time she had seen his handwriting. The schoolteacher in her was impressed with his bold, correct script. The woman in her was moved nearly to tears by his love and devotion. Despite what had been stolen from her, she felt complete in a way she had never known.

Constance folded the note and put it in her blouse, close to her heart. It would live there, she vowed, every day of her life until it hung on the wall of their home, wherever it was.

The area outside the hole in the valley wall was a ring of savage resolve.

After the white men had failed to follow them into the valley, Buffalo Eyes convened a war council. They said words over the body of Strong Elk, which they had recovered, then sat in a circle in the cool shadow. As long as the enemy had horses, they represented a threat. Because both sides had lost fighters, the Comanche had not achieved the advantage Buffalo Eyes had sought.

"They will not come in for us," the war chief told the others. "They do not need to. We must attack again."

There was no dissent among the braves. There was silence as Buffalo Chief considered the best approach.

"I have my own battle to finish, but I would like to make a suggestion," a voice said from outside the group.

"Roving Wolf may speak," Buffalo Eyes told him.

Not having participated in the previous raid, the brave had been excluded from the circle. It was not a reflection on his courage. But it was tradition, which held that only he who fought had a voice.

"My experience with white men over these last few suns has taught me that they are soft," Roving Wolf told them. His dark eyes narrowed with purpose and he put a fist on his chest, over his heart. "They will show a woman's concern if we ask for a truce to bury our dead. This being achieved, our fallen warriors may still serve us."

"How?" Buffalo Eyes asked, though like the other braves in the circle he was already considering the many ways in which injury could be inflicted on the white man.

Roving Wolf said, "With something I learned from the white man."

CHAPTER SEVENTEEN

October 23, 1871

The procession was nothing that Calvin and his men had ever seen, nor expected ever to see. Lee Bates, the reporter from Houston—who had remained in the back of the camp, writing about the heroic Death River Valley stand of his fictional hero Archer Barrington—came over to witness the sight. Calvin wondered if it was the closest the reporter had ever been to an uncivilized red man.

A line of Indians, minus the war chief, had emerged from the valley under a white flag. There was a small population of the remaining Comanche force, five of them, walking single file, their hands free of weapons, toward the sergeant.

Calvin undid his gun belt and left it with Garcia. "Send someone to keep the lady in the ambulance wagon," he said and walked forward.

"I'll go," Rufus Long said, overhearing. He ran off.

"Stay with her!" Calvin shouted after him.

Bates stepped closer to the Tejano. "Do you think they're surrendering?" he asked.

"No."

Garcia's certainty caused Bates to recoil several steps. His literary Indians were mindless savages, like the Cossacks of Russia he also wrote about in *The Adventures of Prince Sergei Novgorod*. He did not know at all what to make of Indians who did not simply scalp and burn.

"What do you think they want?" the reporter pressed.

"Nothing less than they wanted when they got here," Garcia replied with equal confidence.

Calvin continued to approach the men with long strides. He noticed a few minor wounds that had not been attended to. One of the braves seemed to have added to his war paint with his own blood, judging from the way the markings on his face glistened. He did not think they were here to assess the strength of the white men; they could just as easily have determined that from the valley. When the sergeant met the leader, the first brave lowered the flag to his side.

"We take our dead," the Comanche said. "Then go." He pointed back to the valley, not to the west.

So this was only a truce, Calvin decided. He had suspected as much when the war chief remained behind, unwilling to parlay with the enemy. Just the same, Calvin asked, "Are you sure you don't want to end this thing altogether? Go home to the Comancheria?"

"Bury dead," the man repeated.

Calvin stepped to one side and walked down the

row of braves. None of them carried any weapons. They appeared prepared to do exactly as they said.

"You will bury them where they are?" Calvin asked when he returned to the front of the line.

The man nodded once.

"We don't have any extra tools," he said.

The man held up his strong left hand.

"Why don't more of your people come out and help?" Calvin asked.

The Comanche pointed his hand away from his chest, swiped it from side to side. That, plus his expression, told Calvin that they didn't trust the white men.

"I don't trust you either," Calvin told him, though he did not repeat the gesture. Something had to be up; he just could not figure out what it was. His biggest concern was that they might still make a run at the horses, either scattering them or jumping on the backs of five of them. The Indians did not need a saddle to ride.

The Comanche don't play by our rules, and they don't deal in goodwill, Calvin thought. *They're as likely to keep my officers tied up watching them and launch another attack from the valley.*

Calvin stared at the Indian, who was the tallest of the braves. "You attacked our camp, defiled our woman, and ask for courtesy," he said. "But I do not wish to become like you. Gather your dead. But if you do anything except that, you will be shot."

"White men would shoot unarmed braves," the Comanche said. "Then call us savage."

Calvin didn't feel like debating this further. He gave the order to Garcia to assemble a group of guards, one for each man, as they gathered the bodies. He did not trust this man and his people, but even if their plan was as simple as infiltrating the camp and distracting the police and guardsmen, the Indians were already here.

I should have had them shot on sight, he thought, feeling a strong sense of foreboding. Calvin did not have much schooling, but he had heard, somewhere, at some point, the story of the Trojan Horse.

The braves went about their business slowly, reverently. The dead Comanche had been laid side by side, and the Indians dropped to their knees at the feet of each fallen brave, bowing and remaining low over the body as he sang words in the Comanche tongue. Five police officers stood a barely respectful distance behind the warriors, their rifles or sidearms pointed down, barely, and ready.

Calvin's sense of omen increased. He had collected his gun belt from Garcia, who had his own revolver in hand. The sergeant held the belt in one hand, the firearm in the other. He checked the barrel, filled it up, snapped it shut.

"Why are they doing a ceremony *now*?" The Tejano leaned toward the sergeant.

"I don't know," Calvin said as he glanced back toward the valley. "And I don't like it. I don't like the way they got us all watchin' two spots simultaneous—"

Suddenly, in a blur of movement, Calvin's five men gagged, dropped their weapons, and fell to the ground like sacks of grain. They were indistinguishable from the braves who were tangled among them. The only clear difference was that the leather bands which had been clandestinely removed from the ankles of the dead were pulled tightly around the throats of the white men.

The men and their attackers were too close and tangled to shoot at, so other men ran forward—just as Buffalo Eyes and his braves charged toward the eastern end of the camp and the horses. This time they were not in a row but, with clothes and blankets and a few branches tied to their tails, brushing the ground, in a surging mass hidden in dust.

The peace outside the valley was disturbing. The high, sloping, wall of the mesa was to his right, the flatlands leading to the lowlands leading to the dead, dark mounds of Pilot Knob were on the left. To think that so little could be happening here—a light wind stirring occasional dust devils, lizards scurrying on rocks, dead brush blowing by now and then—while cultures were at a deadly standoff on the other side filled Gannon with deep sadness.

Leaving Constance also gave him an enormous sense of discomfort. He believed that this time, this leave-taking, she would stay where she was. But he questioned his own insistence on that. Was he thinking of himself or her?

Roving Wolf would have tracked me, he told himself. *If we had left together, headed west from here, and if I had been killed—? No,* he told himself. *It was the right decision. The Comanche had to die.*

And if the Comanche were victorious, at least Constance was with people who could get her home.

Unless they were slaughtered, Gannon told himself. Then Constance would once again be in the hands of the braves. His only consolation, and it was a miserable one, was that if the Indians were somehow victorious, they would not burden themselves with hostages. They would slaughter every survivor, quickly, and move on to Austin.

"Lord," he said aloud, his eyes turning heavenward, "I have not had a Comanche-type vision for all the time I been out here. If you'd care to send one, Sir, I would be most indebted."

But the only uncommon sight was the rippling waves of heat rising from the warming earth as the sun rose higher in the sky, dropping the illusion of water or sky on the ground. Perhaps that was a foreshadowing after all, Gannon thought: the bright, blue sea of the Pacific.

Gannon's side actually began to feel better the more he worked it, which made him think—with relief—that the doctor was probably right, that no ribs had been damaged. He was lucky he hadn't been killed. Gas like they were flirting with down there had been known to bring down entire mine systems and the mountains that contained them.

The sun had moved a little across the sky when two things happened at once. First, Gannon thought he heard the distant drum of hooves. It sounded as if it were rising from the northwest—the direction of the police encampment. Whatever it was, there was nothing he could do about it. The sound was too far from where he was.

The other event—that was different. It was very near and very perplexing.

* * *

It was a devilish and brilliant tactic.

Either the Indians killed five men and had five braves at their flank; or five, six, seven men would have to go to their rescue. That left the horses vulnerable to a party of mounted braves . . . Comanche who would ride on toward Austin, unopposed. And there was no way to signal the citizenry. The Indians might not want to fight in darkness, when the spirits could not watch over them. But they could wait until dark, sneak into the city, and start fires or kill families in their sleep—there was no limit to what a guerrilla party could do.

Calvin should have shot the white-flag Comanche on sight.

"Shoot the Indians and their horses!" he shouted, then shouted it again as he ran toward the northeastern end of the camp. The job was protecting the city, not themselves.

This kind of chaotic, close-quarter fighting was the birthright of the Comanche. It was not the kind of fighting for which any of these men had drilled; not in the Civil War and not in their respective services. But most of these men had served in the War and had experienced brutal, hand-to-hand and muzzle-to-gut fighting. Almost at once, the veterans exploded in remembered fury, more aggressive than in the last attack, where ranks had broken into pockets of war.

Indian horses fell, crippled or wounded, when the riders were too far to hit with precision. But the way the charge had been bunched together, horses had to be killed to get through to the animals behind them. When Indians were within easy range they were targeted by gut-shot, rifle butt, and by men leaping from where they stood at passing Comanche, grabbing at a leg or blanket in the hope of unseating them. The gunfire was frequently so close that it was muffled in the clothing or occasionally the flesh of the Comanche.

The Indians did not fire at the soldiers, saving their bullets for the riderless horses. It was a wave with two clear purposes: to leave the white men stranded and to break through to the plain beyond with as many braves as possible

Calvin stopped firing and grabbed Garcia by the collar.

"We have to get ahead in case they get past us!" the sergeant yelled.

Garcia nodded and, ducking low, the two men ran around the back of the camp to where the horses were spread over a wide area—three of them already having fallen. Calvin paused only to take a clear shot at one of the party who had come to claim the dead, punching a red hole in the small of his back and saving the guardsman who was beneath him. Hacking and gasping, the young man threw the body off and clawed to his nearest comrade— who was no longer moving. The Indian who had killed him was beneath him and threw him off, only to get a rock in the face, crushing his skull.

Crouching low and using the boulders as cover, Calvin and Garcia reached a spot where two horses were, for the moment, protected by rock and landscape. There was no time to saddle them. Garcia had grown up riding bareback; Calvin was less experienced, but he had the strong legs for it. Side by side, their fists full of mane, the men steadied the uneasy mounts and waited as if for a starting gun, watching ahead.

The police and guardsmen had managed to form an arc on the southern side of the thinly grassed grazing area. The fighting there was a fierce confusion, with cries of rage and pain and hints of motion within the dusty fog.

Garcia was openly disturbed by his inability to join the other police. He saw men fall along with Indians and grimaced with his forced inactivity.

"Steady, friend," Calvin cautioned.

"I don't like them thinking we deserted."

"No man is thinking of anything but his fight," Calvin assured him.

The Tejano nodded sharply, and the sergeant saw his fists tighten around the mane. Soon the battlefield was too dusty for them to see anything.

"Walk 'em north," Calvin said. "Slow."

The men moved carefully, trying to keep enough of the dust between them and the Indians so that they would not be noticed.

And then it happened.

Three Comanche emerged from the northeast side of the perimeter and raced into the plain. Calvin had placed two men there to make sure the Comanche did not avoid the valley altogether and go wide around the mesa, but those men had moved in to save the horses.

"Go!" Calvin yelled.

Like a coiled spring, Garcia launched ahead in pursuit of the enemy, Calvin several paces behind.

* * *

Rufus Long was standing outside the ambulance wagon, in back, watching the battle taking place roughly 150 yards to the southwest. He had a pair of Colts in his hands, both from dead police.

Constance Breen had heeded his advice and remained in the ambulance with the doctor, who had Long's own sidearm and ammunition.

The black officer was perspiring and his lips were tightly pursed to keep the sweat from his mouth. Apart from the rivulets, his eyes were the only things that moved on him beneath a rigid, attentive brow. In his head he was thinking, *Come on, come on,* aching to be part of this fight but not wanting to waste any shots.

And then a Comanche on horseback surged through the haze in his direction. The Indian was bent low behind the pinto's neck and there was no target but the horse that was coming straight-on. Long aimed and shot at the area below its windpipe, between both shoulders. The animal went down silently, somersaulting and snapping its neck, and throwing the Comanche free.

Buffalo Eyes landed flat on his chest, arms splayed, and was either uninjured in the fall or sufficiently enraged to ignore any pain and scrabble to his feet. He had lost the spear he was carrying and did not bother to search for it. Instead, he drew his tomahawk from his belt as Long fired a second shot from the other gun, piercing the war chief's side. That did not stop him, and in one motion he twisted away from the third shot while simultaneously bringing the stone head down on Long's neck. There was a crack of bone and a ripping of skin, and the officer screamed as he went down. His mouth twisted with fury, Buffalo Eyes barely paused as he picked up the two guns and thrust himself through the flap. His eyes were not adjusted to the dark and he would not have known where the doctor was if Zachary had not fired. The bullet struck the war chief's shoulder but did not stop the two stolen handguns from coughing. The medic's arms flew back and he fell with a pair of uneven red cavities straight through to his spine.

Buffalo Eyes looked ferociously at Constance, who was crouched behind the still-upended cot, the doctor's gun out of reach. The war chief was angry at having been unhorsed and kept from immediately joining the rest of his party and intended to take it out on the woman.

Before the Comanche could advance, his back arched so hard he would have fallen from the ambulance if a lance hadn't been propping him up. It was his own weapon, thrust through his ribs, scraping his spine, and emerging from the front of his chest through his heart. It was held there by Captain Amos Keel, who had dragged himself to the ambulance when he saw Rufus Long go down. The captain's expression was wild, his eyes big circles, as blood ran down the shaft onto his hands. Only when the Indian went limp, became deadweight, was the officer forced to drop the spear and stagger back himself, falling to the ground almost simultaneous with the Comanche.

Though the gunfire around them continued, Constance stepped over the cot and left the ambulance, jumping down to the commander's side. He was gasping for breath, bleeding again through the bandages, and staring wide-eyed at the sky.

Constance gently untied the wrappings around his wounds, removed the swabs that had been placed on them, saw the blood running. She went back to get fresh gauze to pack against the bullet holes, oblivious to the tumult and dust around her. The fighting all seemed so far away. She looked away from the broken, marionette-like figure of Dr. Zachary, who was sprawled with his legs over the cot, his back on the floorboards, his arms akimbo, head twisted to the right. She opened the cabinet with the surgical supplies and retrieved a roll and scissors.

Captain Keel was barely breathing when she reached his side. His eyes were moist and red and still staring. She set the supplies aside and took his left hand between both of hers. That seemed more important, more relevant somehow. Her own eyes began to tear.

"You saved my life, Captain," she said.

His jaw moved slightly and his brow wrinkled, as though he were frustrated by his inability to reply.

"It's all right," she said, forcing a smile. "Please . . . just rest."

His mouth struggled to form a word.

"For . . . forg . . ."

The rest of the word never came, only a long exhale and his eyes drifting shut.

"Forgive?" she asked the dead man. It took her a moment to wonder whether he meant Gannon. There was no one else *to* forgive.

On her knees beside him, Constance bent low and prayed.

The gunfire faded, the voices of officers and

guardsmen were heard—relatively calm tones, organizational voices, voices that were victorious but not unaware of what victory had cost.

Laying Keel's hand on his chest, Constance went to the still form of Rufus Long and prayed over him as well. And when she was done she remained on her knees to pray for the doctor . . . and for the safe return of her beloved.

The charge across the plains was as much about staying on the backs of the horses as it was about pursuing the three Comanche. The Indians had become aware of them, and the five animals were charging at a gallop. At this pace, none of them would get anywhere near Austin.

The Indians must have realized this and one of the riders peeled off to face the two officers. Mounted but not moving, he shouldered his rifle and took aim.

The rifle was pointed at Calvin, who pulled the mane hard to the right and, despite the strength in his thighs, slid off. The Indian's shot hit nothing as the riderless horse swung away from the fallen rider, shook its head, and just stood there catching his breath.

Calvin drew his gun, got to his feet, and ran as fast as he was able at the Indian as Garcia continued to charge. The Tejano fired twice at the Indian, missed, and the Comanche returned fire. His shot hit Garcia's painted and the animal's four legs went dead. Garcia flew over its head, bracing himself with his hands, and snapping his left wrist.

The Indian had to reload and Calvin ran until he knew he had a good shot. He stopped, aimed, and put a bullet through the red man's throat. Then the sergeant continued running.

"Get my horse, Garcia!" he shouted over his shoulder as he jumped over the dead Indian and vaulted onto the back of his horse. He took the reins, cracked the animal's ribs with his heels, and raced ahead.

The other two Indians were in sight. Once again, a Comanche stopped, wheeled his horse around, and prepared to fire at Calvin. This time the sergeant didn't stop. He had five shots and let them all fly in the direction of the target while silently praying he hit something.

He did. A single bullet grazed the Comanche, whose rifle discharged down and wide. Unarmed, Calvin drove his horse into the other, causing both animals to bolt and buck before going down. Both men were disoriented after the fall, the Indian partly beneath his horse, which was struggling to get up, Calvin with his leg bent beneath him and apparently broken. His own horse, the one he had stolen from the Indian, got up and ran away.

The battle was still not over, the bitter enemies down but still moving.

"Shit!" Calvin said, repeating it several times as he looked for something to use against the trapped Comanche. There was nothing around him but sand, nothing on his person but clothes. The sergeant didn't know what the Indian might bring to bear if he got free. A moment later it didn't matter, as there was a loud crack. The Comanche's head jerked and then went utterly still with a single bullet wound in the forehead.

Calvin turned and saw Garcia, on foot, bent over and panting. The sergeant thanked him with a nod and looked ahead at the retreating cloud that was the last Comanche.

"I—I couldn't ride and shoot," Garcia apologized, pointing broadly toward the horse with a muscle-weary arm.

"I understand," Calvin said in a dry, hoarse voice.

As Calvin looked back at the animal, which was still standing where he'd left it, he saw a cloud approaching. After a moment he could make out two horsemen coming rapidly in their direction. A few moments more and he could see Sgt. May and one of the guardsman who had obviously set out in pursuit of the escaped Comanche. He saw the two dead Indians and when he passed Calvin and Garcia he threw them a salute without stopping. The police officers didn't bother returning the courtesy; May and his man were already past them, headed east.

"I guess we won back there," Garcia remarked.

Calvin nodded, thinking about how many more men lay dead just outside the valley, and whether trading life for life constituted "winning." Especially when the army still had to fight Comanche in western Texas and beyond and would continue to do so for God knew how many years.

"I could sure use a drink," Garcia said, flopping on his seat. "Even water."

Calvin nodded again, his mouth too dry to form words. He just sat and tried not to move his leg while Garcia cradled his left hand in his right. The Comanche's horse finally managed to gain its feet. The Indian's lower half was disfigured; his pelvis had been crushed. Calvin felt detached from the brave's dead and broken body. His war was over.

The men made no effort to get on either horse. It wouldn't have been possible to ride, let alone mount. As they sat in the dirt, they heard a pair of shots in the distance ahead of them, like twigs snapping.

The two men exchanged looks, but even Garcia was too parched to speak. They just waited until the two guardsmen appeared in the wavering heat above the plain. They were like fallen branches on a river that was rolling toward them, finally taking shape when they were just a few dozen yards away.

Sgt. May stopped beside Calvin, dismounted, and handed him his canteen.

"There will be no Comanche in Austin," the guardsman reported.

Calvin took a long swallow, washed it around his mouth, and passed the canteen to Garcia. He looked up at the sergeant, who was blotting out the sun.

"How bad is it at the campsite?" Calvin asked.

May's voice was somber as he replied, "Captain Keel . . . the doctor . . . too many, friend. Just too many."

"The captain?"

"Died saving the girl," May said.

Calvin did not bother responding. There was nothing to say. He feared the worst for Rufus Long.

"Keep the water," May said. "It's bound to get pretty hot out here before I can get some men out here to help you. Sorry I don't have anything for a makeshift tent." The mounted sergeant looked around in the dirt, saw no weapons. He handed Calvin his revolver. "For buzzards," he said.

"Thanks," Calvin said.

The two guardsmen gathered up the other horses, roping them together, and rode off. Without the animals here, there was no shade and no sense of life beyond the two spots where they sat helplessly. Garcia returned the canteen and capped it for the one-handed man. Then Calvin shifted off his sleeping good leg and cried out as he moved the broken one slightly. The injury reminded him about Dr. Zachary, who would not be setting or splinting the breaks . . . and about Captain Keel. For all the sergeant had found to complain about in the officer's kowtowing to politicians, Keel was first, foremost, and at the last a great soldier.

Garcia's voice snapped him from his reflection.

"My father used to say that pain is God's fire and death is His ice," the Tejano said, frowning. "But my wrist is numb—I do not know what to think of that."

"Be glad you're a police officer and not a guitar serenader," Calvin told him.

It took Garcia a moment to realize that Sgt. Calvin had made a joke, and he chuckled at it, though there was probably more relief behind his laughter than there was wit in the remark.

Exhaustion quickly caught up with both men. They stopped speaking, let their chins fall to their chests, and caught brief snatches of sleep as they sat facing one another on the hard, hot ground.

CHAPTER EIGHTEEN

October 23, 1871

Hank Gannon had expected to come around the mesa, enter the abandoned Comanche camp, and find Roving Wolf where he had left him. It had been his intention, then, to negotiate their showdown.

But the Comanche would not be in the valley. He appeared to be ahead, crossing the lowlands on foot. Gannon could not imagine where he was going or why, but there was nothing to do except follow him.

The distant reports of gunfire alarmed Gannon, but he was helpless to do anything about it. Sgt. Calvin was a good and very capable man, and he would handle whatever came up. That didn't make it any easier for Gannon not to be with Constance, but as he had been reminded time after time since the start of the war, fate did not work at his convenience.

Gannon's side didn't hurt as much as his hips did. His life had been one of riding, not walking, and this last day had been little else. His feet were swollen inside boots he had intended for weeks to replace with moccasins, though he had never gotten around to doing so. It wasn't just the strain on body and soul, he was also plagued with the awareness that he could not afford to let any of that stop him. Not now. Not until this was done.

Un-Christian as it was, he could only hope that Roving Wolf was suffering no less. Given what the Indian had been through, he could not believe the man was willingly on the move.

The terrain became less even, hillier, with more tangling scrub underfoot as he followed the Comanche. There was no relief from the heat and Gannon rationed his water, since he knew from having traveled in this region the past month that there was no water for miles around.

And then, Gannon realized where they were . . . and where they were going.

To the southeast, roughly a quarter-mile distant, was the spot where Gannon had first encountered the grave, right after Roving Wolf murdered Joseph Williams. That was not where they were headed. They were going northwest.

To the spot where his companion was shot, Gannon thought.

So much of Indian thinking was circular. It was how they measured their lives. The movement of the sun and moon, the cycles of the seasons, even the lazy circles of birds of prey, which were used to pinpoint rabbit warrens and other sources of food. It would make sense that he would want to live or die in the place where this all began for him.

Gannon followed with an increased spirit in his step, a call to this final reckoning.

* * *

The campsite was carnage and blood, though the only gunfire was occasional shots at birds and varmints that came to pick at the dead.

Constance had been to a carnival, as a girl, and this felt like that: grotesque bodies, distorted faces, fire, and noise. People moving this way and that with individual purpose, no sense of community or order. Nothing sane to hold onto, except the hand of her father.

In her mind, she held on to Hank. And she was suddenly, then, very afraid for him and for herself. He had to come back to her. They were now whole and inseparable. Until this day, she had only understood what courtship was. She did not understand what a bond was between two souls.

Upon his return to camp, Sergeant May had ordered the ambulance hitched and sent out for Sgt. Calvin and Officer Garcia. Captain Keel and Officer Long had already been carried to where Nightingale and the others had been laid. Now it was necessary to remove the doctor. Constance watched as he was lifted from the wagon. In a strange way, the guardsmen who removed him seemed almost as lifeless as he, their movements dull and rote.

The other cost of war, she told herself.

The dead. The wounded. And the survivors who would forever be shrouded by both—some more, some less. Maybe their curse was that the only people who would ever understand were those who had been through it, too, or something similar.

Which company will only keep it vividly alive, she thought sadly.

Whether she wanted it or not, that would forever be part of her bond with Hank. The silent nights, perhaps on a patio, perhaps by the fire, perhaps in their old age—when this day returned like a demon spirit.

With sadness, she realized that as much as her mother had never understood her desires before, Martha Breen would be openly hostile to this. Home, too, was a casualty of war.

Men had been wounded in the last attack. After conferring with the three men who were going out with the ambulance wagon—only one of whom had any experience with field dressings—Constance removed some of the bottles, tools, and bandages to see to their care. In the face of each man she sought to help, she saw a boy like those in her classroom . . . frightened, hurt, alone. She tried to patch bullet wounds, and used parts cut from saddles and the boots of the dead to fashion splints. Where the injuries were grave, she offered laudanum. But as she moved among the men, Constance found that it was her voice, her touch, her expression that was the best balm. Men who felt no pain because their wounds were too severe spoke words they wanted passed on to family. Constance was sorry she had not thought to take the pad from the ambulance so the men could write a note themselves. She vowed to remember every word.

By the time the medical wagon had returned, the battlefield had been organized into something resembling a functioning campsite. There were campfires, food and water had been distributed, horses had been corralled. The living—nine men plus Constance, a wide-eyed journalist, and then the five men on the wagon—organized for the return to Austin.

Constance helped make room in the ambulance for the transport of the injured: four men on the floor, Garcia beside the driver, Calvin on the cot, which had been set up over one of the wounded men. His leg and Garcia's arm had been splinted with shelving from the wagon. Constance had tied the slats together herself, trying not to cry when Calvin asked if he would ever dance again. There was a knob of bone straining at his flesh, just above the knee. She wondered if he would even be able to keep the leg. The war veteran did not appear to wonder; he seemed to know.

"We'll get him back," the sergeant told her before she left him. "The captain was sorry for what he'd done—as soon as we get home, I'll send men to find him."

Constance was barely able to thank the man. So little had come from the heart these past few days that his remarks caused her to choke up.

By early afternoon, when it was time to leave, Constance rode one of the ponies, which, ironically, were greater in number than the men available to ride them. Behind her was Evan Bosley. If living man could be said to have a dead face, a missing soul, it was he. He was muttering apologies to no one in particular, and she did not believe they were merited. He had saved her life. But she did not feel he would ever find forgiveness for being taken by the Comanche.

Led by Sgt. May, it was a limping, bloodied train that set out for Austin. It seemed to Constance like that old carnival she had watched departing for another town. Behind them, the white men were beneath rocks for now, to be recovered later; the red men were in shallow graves where they would remain, and the horses lay where they had fallen. Even as they left, animals were beginning to gather, some of them feasting on the remains of their own kind that had been shot earlier.

Constance felt no revulsion at that. She was numb save for the emotion she felt for Hank, and her only thoughts were for his safety, for Sgt. Calvin to send men to find him—alive, she prayed again. Before turning her eyes toward home, she took a last, longing look at the mesa where she had last seen him . . .

Whatever his wounds had taken from him, Roving Wolf strode to the ledge like a man who had never known infirmity or sorrow or any human emotion. He was, like his namesake, prowling toward his destiny.

He did not know what the Big Father had willed for the war party. From the distant sounds, it appeared as if the second assault had met with little success. Otherwise, weapons would have been discharged at the air in celebration, as a signal to all who could hear that the braves had triumphed. That had not happened. What Roving Wolf could be certain of was that the Comanche had fought bravely and to the last breath. More than that could be asked of no warrior.

That included himself.

The light of day could not erase the darkness of what had occurred here. But the Comanche did not allow himself to linger in that shadow. He stayed in the light, for the light would lead him to what he sought. He walked among the rocks and scant vegetation, looking down, examining large cracks in the rock, short falls into clumps of stone and shrub beyond the ledge—

It was there in a bush that had split the rock to find sunlight: Great Bear's weapon, the hilt facing up as if clawing the sky. The Indian fell to his knees, his palms crossed on his chest and then unfolding to face the domain of the Big Father. Roving Wolf reached down carefully so as not to dislodge the bandage around his throat, which was stiff with caked blood. The cloth had dried, attached to the wound like skin. So much of the brave made him more than man: the wrapping was made from fiber of the earth; his headband was adorned with an eagle feather above, the tail of the wolf below.

He retrieved the knife that had been meant for the son of his sister. Rising, he held it aloft like the Great Spirit ready to challenge the Demon of Many Faces, showing the Big Father that he was unafraid.

The power of bear, eagle, wolf, and earth filled his arm and his chest, and he knew even before the white man arrived that he had come. The Indian turned to where Gannon was standing, at the foot of the ledge—and Roving Wolf's face twisted with anger. The white man was like the Demon of Many Faces, dressed with the trappings of both his kind and Comanche.

The battle was for more than just the Comancheria. It was a fight for the spirit of a people.

* * *

Gannon had never imagined that a final encounter with Roving Wolf, whenever it came, would
be a matter of man versus man. He had been in
Texas long enough to know that the Indians had a
way of drawing strength from the unseen world.
Whether such forces were real or not, the Indians
did not doubt its existence. Like the heroes and pa-
triarchs, martyrs and saints whose tales were told in
church every Sunday, belief was a power in itself.
Gannon wished he had some of that faith in his
heart here and now.

But he was not spiritually unarmed. Gannon
had an iron-solid resolve to return to Constance.
It was time to discover whether the spirit of this
Comanche was equal to the soul of this white man.
Nothing greater would be decided than that; they
were a sideshow to a sideshow, the kind that even
Captain Keel would have had no difficulty explain-
ing to his superiors.

Gannon drew the Indian knife and spread his
arms. Since walking up the steep slope could hurt
his side, he had decided to make the Indian come
to him. Maybe Roving Wolf would take the eagle
feather seriously, jump the ten feet or so to the
ground, and break his neck. Gannon had nothing
to prove. He was here to protect his future.

Full of the spirit, Roving Wolf strode down the
rocky incline, as surefooted as any creature of
the wild. Gannon got a good look at the weapon he
had been looking for the night they met, a bone
knife with the claw of what looked like a bear.
Gannon had carried a knife in Florida, had killed

crocodiles, skinned foxes and rabbits, and once fought a drunk over a woman. He had trained with the police—a little. If he stood a chance of winning here the combat would not have to be about fighting skill but tactics.

Gannon's belly boiled with anticipation. It wasn't fear; he had experienced that earlier, walking after Roving Wolf. And it wasn't fear of death, but only of what he had to lose by dying—his future with Constance. Now that the action was begun, the end in view, he was almost relieved.

He removed the waterskin but left the tunic on. It would not afford much protection against the claw, but it would be better than bare skin and bandage.

The sun had arced somewhat to the west, so Gannon moved in that direction. Roving Wolf seemed so intent on the man himself that he did not seem aware of the direct light of the sun or anything else. Roving Wolf stopped just a few yards from Gannon, facing him.

"I bear you no malice, Roving Wolf," Gannon said. "We don't—"

The Comanche cut him off with a lateral swipe of the blade, then crouched in a fighting stance, the blade behind his wrist, the claw out. Held that way, the bony paw could rake or the knife could slash with an underhanded swipe of the wrist. Gannon stood with his legs apart, arms wide, the knife pointing forward in his right hand.

With a howl meant to paralyze any foe, Roving Wolf ran forward, simultaneously sweeping the bony blade outward, like a scythe. Gannon stepped back; the initial attack missed but the sharp, fast return swipe connected with his tunic, cutting through it to the bandage below. Gannon lunged forward with his own knife, but the Comanche hopped to the side. The strike missed him, the men quickly faced one another, and they were back where they started—though the sun was no longer entirely to Gannon's back.

That was why Roving Wolf didn't care where we started, Gannon realized.

Gannon was about to run in and thrust up, under the Comanche's arm, when the Indian slashed again. This time Gannon moved with the blade, circling wide around the enemy. The Indian's sweeping arm was briefly frozen between Gannon and its owner; Gannon jabbed out with his own blade, striking the back of the Indian's exposed forearm, drawing blood. With a growl, the Comanche swung his arm back, lower and more viciously than before. Gannon leapt away, bending deeply at the waist to avoid the blade. The edge missed his belly, but Gannon pulled his injured side, leaned in that direction, and the Comanche seized the moment to run at him.

Gannon felt as though he'd been hit by a charging bull. He was simultaneously doubled over and knocked backward. He threw his left arm behind him to take the brunt of the fall and held tight to the knife in his right hand. The Indian fell on him and tried to rake him with the bear claw, but Gannon met it with his knife plunged through two of the fingers. The blade clanged and the men wrestled for a moment, back and forth, locked together, Gannon pushing up and the Indian pressing down. Roving Wolf raised his left hand, tried to claw

Gannon's face, but was met with the white man's strong grip.

The Indian's weight sent fire through the other man's chest, an endless wave of it. The men were both animals now, grappling, pushing, Gannon releasing a primal scream that was part pain, part fury. He managed to bring a knee against the Indian's belly and thrust up, shoving him off. Both men immediately scrambled for advantage, bear claw and blade seeking flesh, finding an arm, a thigh, a waist, staining the earth with spatters of blood.

Gannon was still below the Indian, protected only by the upraised knee, which the Comanche finally, angrily pushed away with his hip before sitting fully on the waist of his intended victim. Gannon was stuck on his back, his legs unable to do more than wriggle. But in the moment after Roving Wolf succeeded in straddling him, Gannon saw an opening. The Comanche had moved to pin the white man's left arm to the ground as he raised the claw to strike down in his eyes. In what was only a moment but seemed much longer, the man's body seemed frozen, like a historic tableau in a saloon show; though brief, it was enough time for Gannon to move his free right arm and thrust the knife upward into the Comanche's chest, beating the downward drive of the bear claw by a heartbeat.

The bone weapon scraped Gannon's cheek before clattering to the ground. The Indian sat motionless atop his foe, the knife in his breast. Gannon's fist was still on the hilt and rage was still in his eyes as he yelled and pushed the knife in harder. He was aware of the warm blood coursing over his hand, down the inside of his sleeve. Roving

Wolf was still looking down at Gannon, but the feral turn of his mouth softened into something human, the eyes ceased to burn, the nostrils no longer flared. With a sigh, the Comanche rolled slowly off the white man, onto his side, onto the ground, where his left arm flopped outward.

Gannon rolled what was left of the Indian on his waist to the ground. Roving Wolf was on his back, the knife jutting from his chest throwing a long cruciform shadow on the dirt. He was breathing deeply but otherwise did not move.

Bleeding where the knife had initially cut his side and arm and clutching his right arm to his ribs to keep from using those muscles, Gannon struggled to his knees and looked down at the dying man.

There was nothing to say, nothing the Indian would have cared to hear. They were from different worlds and their only common ground was war.

So the battle has been fought, Gannon thought without satisfaction. *Now we have nothing.* He looked down as the Indian shut his eyes and breathed his last. *You have even less than that.*

And yet there was the hint of a smile on the face of the dead man. It didn't appear to be a trick of light and shadow; perhaps he had found the boy who had been taken from him up here. The white man hoped so. If there were one heaven, there might be others.

Gannon got to his feet with effort. He sheathed his knife and held his side. It was going to be painful, but he would pull over as many rocks as he could to cover the body. He decided he would keep the bear-bone knife. Not as a memento—he had one of those, dug into his cheek. But it seemed to have a history that should not be buried; maybe it would speak to him one day.

First, though, he recovered the waterskin and took a drink. It felt good to be alive—even the ache of his muscles, the sting of the cuts. Gannon looked down again at the bloody remains of the Indian. He remembered the last time he had looked down at a dead man in these lowlands—Sketch Lively. Another man who hated so hard it got him killed. Gannon couldn't say whether any of it was right or wrong. Only that somewhere, right now, both the Big Father and the Lord God Almighty could only be feeling a helpless kind of sad.

CHAPTER NINETEEN

October 23, 1871

Gannon had taken his time leaving the scene of their struggle. He hurt too much and, until he had nearly run out of water and needed to eat, there was no reason to move.

He headed back to the valley, where he knew he would find water not only to drink but to thoroughly clean his wounds. He had also seen lizards among the rocks and suspected there would be small mammals nosing around the horse and the stone grave of the Indian they had left there. During the war it was what spies and sharpshooters and trackers who were out in the field called "survival rations." As a boy, he had learned that Florida salamanders, cooked on a stick, weren't bad, if not terribly filling.

Though he knew that Constance would be worried, Gannon couldn't bring himself to stir much. There was much on his mind, yet so much of it scattered. He walked a little one day and a little more the next, trying to sort out how he felt about the Comanche and what they had done—and what he would have done in their place. After four years of war, he did not think that fighting was the best solution to any dispute. Unfortunately, talking never seemed to get anyone anywhere and he couldn't think of a third option. With no disrespect intended to the Lord, turning the other cheek reminded him of saloon doors. People just pushed through on their way to one side or the other.

Gannon also walked because, as a matter of pride, he wanted to be able to stand upright when he saw her parents again—if he saw them again—to ask for their daughter in marriage. Sgt. Calvin or someone with the police might be persuaded to lend him clean clothes for that. Hopefully, Captain Keel would not object.

It had been nearly two full days before Gannon heard horses approaching from the northern end of the valley. Though he was feeling stronger, Gannon was not up for scaling the limestone crags or going back into the subterranean passage. He hoped that, coming from the north, and making no effort to conceal their approach, it was not a party of Comanche.

It was not. It was a small contingent of guardsmen and police led by one of their own. The four horsemen were greeted by Gannon, in trousers and bandage, holding his Indian knife and his bearclaw weapon. He lowered the weapons when he saw the men more clearly. He recognized one, a young German-born officer named Gustav Schündler who had joined the force a month before. The men were trailing a horse and wagon.

"Officer Gannon," said May as he approached.

"Mister Gannon," he corrected.

"Officer," May repeated. "As personally ordered by Captain Amos Keel to Sgt. Richard Calvin shortly before the commander's death."

The words caused Gannon to start. "Captain Keel?" he said.

"You didn't know?" the mustachioed sergeant said.

"No."

"I'm sorry," May said. "He was protecting Miss Breen—who is fine and waiting for you back in Austin. We were dispatched to look for you. She said we should start here."

"I . . . I was gonna get there, eventually," Gannon said, absently speaking his plans. For a moment, the revelation of Keel's death and his thoughts for Gannon's well-being made it difficult to breathe. He had been out in the valley for two days, off and on contemplating the futility of the hate men had for one another. To learn of the captain's sacrifice moved him deeply.

"How is . . . Sgt. Calvin?" Gannon asked cautiously, braced for the worst.

"Alive, if not quite kicking," May said. "He has a badly broken leg, but the army doc is hopeful he may keep it."

Gannon thanked the dark-skinned sergeant for the information but didn't ask about anyone else. He had learned during the war that too many names, too soon, did not permit him to reflect on any one man. There would be time enough for more.

Gannon had not even noticed the blond, square-jawed Schündler dismount and come to his side.

"Will you come to the wagon, Officer Gannon?"

he asked with a thick accent. "We have it padded with blankets. It should not be too bad a ride."

"Yes . . . thank you," Gannon said absently. He sheathed the knife and stuck the bear-bone in his belt.

"I've never seen anything quite like that," May said, nodding toward the ivory-colored weapon. "Did it belong to one of the hostiles?"

"The man I killed," Gannon said, touching his face. "It—it was special to him."

"I would like to hear about it sometime," May said. "Indians have some strange notions, eh?"

Gannon made no reply. He just walked to the wagon with Schündler, let the man help him up, then collapsed on the blankets as if they were clouds and he was an angel who had earned his space among them. It seemed impossible that he was going home after—was it more than a month? He had lost track of time. He wondered if the same people who had turned out to see his last entry into Austin would turn out again. What would they be thinking or saying, how would they look at him?

He had no answers, nor did he think of any before the side-to-side rocking of the wagon lulled him to sleep.

Gannon slept through his entry into Austin.

He woke in a hospital bed in the military garrison, a fact he discerned from the flag on the wall and the uniformed private at the door. The bed was smaller and lumpier than the one he'd enjoyed in the back of the wagon.

There were a few men to his right and the cot

directly to his left was occupied by Sgt. Calvin; in a chair beside the sergeant was Hernando Garcia. The men were playing cards. There was sunlight coming through the high windows and a smell of something tart and medicinal in the air.

Gannon saw Garcia poke Calvin with his elbow; the arm itself was bound in a thick splint. The sergeant looked over.

"Good afternoon, Officer," Calvin said.

Gannon was busy feeling under the thin sheet and the flimsy nightgown he wore. The touch-touch-touch was something he had seen with some regularity during the war: men who woke wanted to make sure they were still intact. He determined that his torso had been rebandaged, the wounds on his arms had been treated, and there was gauze on his cheek.

Only then did he look over and say, "Good afternoon, Sergeant." His eyes went up a little. "And Officer Garcia."

"Hello," Garcia said. He touched his own chin. "They shaved you. You're thinner than I remember."

"You cannot get fat on lizards," Gannon replied.

There was a clean wooden table between the cots with bottles of various color, glasses, and spoons.

"My things?" Gannon asked.

"Footlocker, end of the bed," Garcia said.

"And Miss Breen?" he asked, still waking from what was beginning to feel had been an artificial sleep. No doubt a doctor had given him a draught of some kind.

"She is at home," Calvin told him. And that was all he said, despite an expression that was eager to hear more.

"She has been to see you," Garcia added. "Twice, that I saw. She will come again, I'm sure."

Gannon lay back, his thinking a little muddled.

"You heard about the captain?" Calvin asked.

Gannon nodded.

"He asked that you be reinstated."

"For a hearing," Gannon said.

"A formality. My report talks at length about your courage in the field."

"Thank you. Back wages?"

"You will get them."

Gannon was glad. That would make things easier . . . and quicker. He glanced at the construct of wood and leather poking from under the sheets of Calvin's bed. "Your leg?"

"Crushed by a horse chasin' down escaped Comanche," Calvin told him. "We got two, Sergeant. May got the third."

"Well done."

"Except for the very end," Garcia remarked, pointing to the leg.

Gannon tried to get up. He was bound a little tighter than before, did not have the same pain—or freedom of movement.

"You probably shouldn't try getting up till the doctor's seen you," Garcia noted. "Do you wish me to get him?"

Gannon nodded and, setting his cards on the bed, far from where Calvin could reach, he left the room. The sergeant had never been a man to make conversation, and he didn't try now.

"I was wondering about clothes," Gannon said as he began to collect his thoughts.

"I've had some sent over. Clean, pressed, ready for courtin'." Calvin pointed. "Also in the footlocker."

The door squeaked open and a tall, balding man strode in. He was dressed in shirtsleeves, rolled tight, with blue military trousers, spectacles, and what was probably a perpetual scowl. He greeted the few other men by name as he passed.

"I'm Dr. Breeding," the man said when he reached Gannon's bedside.

"A surgeon," Garcia said as a warning.

"How do you feel, Gannon?"

"Good, thank you. And thanks for what you've done."

"If you can walk, you can go," Dr. Breeding said. "Just sign out with the steward at front and make sure you drink a lot of water, and you might have a few of Mrs. Breen's pies. You've been living in an arid wasteland and you look it. Oh"—he paused as he turned to go—"if you do leave, come back to have the dressings checked by a nurse. Though the marks on your face are going to scar regardless."

"I suspected they might."

"You will be fearsome," Garcia said.

Gannon thanked the doctor again as he walked away.

"It will be a few weeks before we have a replacement for Dr. Zachary," Calvin said. "Breeding is not happy having to work for the army *and* the police."

"Especially former Rebs," Garcia said.

"I see," Gannon said. Another war that resolved nothing, he thought sadly.

"You'd think he'd at least be happy not having to saw off any more arms or legs," Garcia said.

"'Butcher' Breeding, I heard 'em say he was called during the war."

"Maybe he liked the work," Calvin offered. "I told him not to come near me with a saw or I'd kick him to death with my good foot."

Throwing off the sheet and pivoting on his backside, Gannon was able to put his feet on the floor and work himself erect, holding on to the bed and table. His feet were blistered and untreated, but other than that he felt better than he had in days.

Garcia said helpfully, "I can get a nurse to help you dress, if you like. She isn't very pretty, but at least you won't be embarrassed."

"I think I can manage," he said, hobbling over.

By using one hand to prop himself on the iron bedpost, another to work the footlocker, Gannon was able to remove the garments and dress with a minimum of grunts and relative ease. The bandages held him together. The clothes were a good fit, though the new boots were not broken in and were more of a problem. Gannon had to sit and have Garcia help him, pushing one-handed on the heel, to get them on. When he was finished, Gannon rose with a sense of resurrection and collected the two weapons and the waterskin.

"You planning to sell those as souvenirs?" Garcia asked.

"No," Gannon said as he walked stiffly toward the door. "To use them."

Walking down the sunlit streets of Austin, it seemed to Gannon as if he had never been away; and then, as he would see a new sign, a new window, a curb that had been repaired, fresh paint, it felt as though he'd been away for years.

It was later in the afternoon than Gannon had imagined. The slanting sun gave everything a bit of an orange cast while shadowing and brightening angles along both sides of Pecan Street. In the open spaces crafted by nature, not man, one did not see gradations like these, only big spaces that were light or dark.

Most people did not recognize the tall man walking very erect, due to the bindings, and at a leisurely pace, in unbroken boots, nor pay the unfamiliar face, half-hidden in a fawn-colored Stetson, much attention. He carried a small canvas bag in his right fist, U.S. ARMY stamped on its side, containing his two weapons and the waterskin. A few citizens smiled and nodded courteously as they would at any stranger. If Gannon had made an impression during his unconscious arrival, it was as a wild man in the back of a wagon and not this clean man, neat and reborn. There were children in the street, which meant that school was out, so he made his way directly to the Breen house. Gannon did not doubt but that Constance would have gone back to class as quickly as possible. She was dogged that way. Not even her own affliction would keep her from her pupils.

Only you could do that, he thought, remembering with even greater emotion now how she left everything to be with him.

He arrived at the house and stood for a moment outside the gate. The flowers and shrubs just inside the white fence were looking a little weary so late in the season. The aroma of freshly baked pie was absent so late in the day and—

The wagon would not be here, he realized suddenly. *You destroyed it.*

A woman moved behind the pulled-back curtains of the living room. Gannon could not tell, in the shadow of the eave, whether it was Constance or her mother. It did not matter: the alarm would be sounded. He intended to raise the latch and cross the slates to the door, but he froze. His gut burned. He was afraid in a way he had not been in any of his confrontations with Roving Wolf.

It was Constance he had seen, because in just seconds she was out the door and running toward him. He drew his hat from his head and held it in his left hand, beside his private little medicine bag.

"Hank! I was just coming to see you!" Constance said—quietly, conspiratorially. "What are you doing *out* like this?"

"The doctor said I could leave," he said.

The girl reached the gate, about to hug him, but hesitated when she saw how stiffly he was standing. Instead, she dropped her arms on the other side of the plumb-straight gate and boldly took his free hands in both of hers, twining her fingers in his, clutching them, drawing on their strength. She looked well, other than for the tears that suddenly lined the bottom of her eyes.

Before they could speak again, Martha Breen emerged from the house after her daughter.

"Constance, come back inside!" she said. "You are creating a scene."

Gannon had not taken his eyes from the young woman. Peripherally, he noticed two men and one woman stop, look at them, and move on. He didn't care. He didn't have time for nosy passersby or a woman who had been dismissive of him since the day they met, who almost certainly blamed him for everything that had befallen her daughter these last few days.

"They don't know you've been to see me, do they? Your parents?"

Constance shrugged. It didn't matter. Her beaming smile did not diminish. Gannon let his thoughts about anyone but Constance go. In nine years of war and assimilation, he had become accustomed to being disapproved of.

"I had intended to ask for your hand," Gannon said, "but I wouldn't want to create another scene. Constance, will you marry me and come to California?"

Constance smiled up at him but was distracted as she saw her father running down the street. Apparently, during his walk from the hospital, someone *had* recognized Hank Gannon.

Albert Breen arrived breathless and wearing an apron that held a hammer and a chisel in loops on the side. His expression was one of anger, barely contained.

"Constance," he panted, "please go back inside. I wish to talk to Mr. Gannon."

"Officer Gannon, sir," he corrected, looking down at the head-shorter man.

Breen's eyes narrowed. "I see. I did hear, when they carried you back, that you performed heroically *after* you left my daughter to the savages."

"Father!" Constance said.

The older man brushed her away. "I will have my say in *private*!"

Constance released his hand, turned, and brushed silently past her mother on her way inside. The two men stood in the street, Breen waiting for a horse and rider to pass before speaking.

"Dr. Breeding, at the hospital, told us what happened to our daughter," Breen said through his red-cheeked rage and tears. "Do you know, I actually defended you and her girlish infatuation. I did not see the harm." He laughed mirthlessly. "The harm? It may well have destroyed her life. I—I tried to understand when she rode out, then I tried to forgive her and you when she returned with the police. But I keep returning to this, Officer Gannon. You—you were a soldier. You have known women. You know how they get swept away. If you loved her, you should have watched out for her!"

"That is why I'm here," Gannon said. "I came to ask your permission to marry."

Breen snorted. "And take her to San Francisco, as she told us, where there are nothing but hooligans and roughnecks?"

"They need police there, too."

"And half-breed children?" he hissed. "Do they need those, too?"

Gannon did not know how to answer that. He hadn't thought the topic through himself, not entirely. He had not gotten further than wanting to be with Constance.

"I can't answer for the city, only for myself," Gannon said. "I want to be with Constance—as wife, as mother, for better or for worse."

Breen moved closer, his fingers tight around the head of the hammer. "It will be better if we cut the thing from her, before it has a chance to take root!" he said. "She still has a chance for happiness here, for a proper life and marriage."

Gannon looked to his left, to the small, sweet home. There were no faces in the window.

"Do the decent thing and leave," Breen said, so close that Gannon could feel his hot breath. "Go to the dance halls and docks of the Barbary Coast where you belong. *You*, not my daughter. Go to your plantation in Florida—"

"It was a farm."

"With slaves?" Breen said. "Like the man you killed?"

Until now, Gannon had not understood that this was not just about him but about any man, Southern-born, who would have courted his daughter. Even an aristocrat from the former Confederacy would have been spurned—though very few Southern gentlemen, other than blatant collaborators, had anything left that would give them status.

All of which made the plan he had roughly formulated even more important.

Gannon put his hat back on his head, tipped the brim toward the man he had hoped would agree to be his father-in-law. He saw now how ridiculous that was.

"I wish you a good evening and a good life, sir," Gannon said. He held the man's eyes a moment longer. "I am not sure you are destined for either."

"I will tie her to the bedpost!" Albert Breen yelled,

then immediately shrunk into himself as he saw that his customers, the Spicers, had heard.

Gannon reached into the canvas bag and showed the man the knife. "With what, sir? Chains? The Gannons would never have done that."

So saying, he turned and walked briskly toward the office of the Texas Special Police, where he had business.

EPILOGUE

December 24, 1871

The old and stately Mission San Luis Rey de Francia loomed large against the darkening sky, its tower and Spanish-Moorish-inflected façade dimly white under the nearly full moon. Riding the two horses Gannon had purchased with his wages, the former police officer and his wife had crossed the Southwest into California, camping in the open as he had learned to do, enjoying the company of each other without concern for anything else.

It had not been necessary for Gannon to further disrupt the Breen household. Constance had taken care of that. She could not see the front of the house from her bedroom, but she could see the southern side of the street. When she saw him leave, and make a turn onto Congress Avenue, she knew where Officer Gannon was going.

Her father had stormed into the house, slammed the door, and was yelling with her mother, in chorus. It would be a few moments before they got to her. She had already removed her green day suit and slipped into a walking dress more suitable for movement. She also took her wool coat from the wardrobe. Constance left by the window, wanting to hear no more harsh words about the man who loved her, the man who had saved her life. They met at police headquarters and went directly to the stable, where Evan Bosley was working with his brother Gary. The woman could not help but wonder if the damage inflicted on the officer was as great as the hurt she had suffered. The elder Bosley sold them two horses, not presently needed by the depleted force.

"I do not believe I will lose my job helping you," the stable hand had said.

The couple was away from Austin before her parents had discovered her missing and realized where she had gone.

The couple journeyed through the Southwest, traveling wide of Indian encampments and reservations. It was a revelation to Constance how unpopulated so much of the land was and how much of it was desert or plain. There was, nonetheless, ample food and water, courtesy of the skills Gannon had acquired in the wild. Nights were spent under the sky or, when it was cold, in a cave or in burrows Gannon dug with a shovel he purchased in Fort Mason. Constance missed her pupils and she missed teaching, but she had never experienced a time in which she felt so free and so loved. Not protected or instructed but truly cherished.

Upon reaching the California border at Fort Yuma—having followed, in part, the mail route—the couple rested before deciding to ride on to the Pacific Ocean and follow the coast north from

San Diego. It was by chance that they reached the mission when they did. It was a chill night, with cool air from the sea, and Gannon thought it best to be inside.

Unable to go on in the dark, they turned at the well and followed an irrigation ditch and a row of pepper trees to the mission. Under torches, they saw Mexican and Indian converts moving content-edly among the few padres who had remained at the secularized Franciscan outpost. Preparations for Christmas were underway, and the couple was welcome.

"As Mary and Joseph were wanderers, we are honored by your presence," said one of the old men in brown, Father Cornelius, with a warm smile.

While Gannon stabled the horses, Constance fol-lowed the padre along the tiled patio that rounded an inner courtyard.

"Do you require the assistance of a nurse?" he asked, looking back at the woman. He wasn't en-tirely sure, judging from her buttoned coat, but said, "There is a lovely one, a Cajun all the way from Louisiana, who is also a midwife if you stay so long."

"I am very well, thank you," Constance said, smiling graciously. "And we will be leaving in the morning. We have a long way to go and would like to be settled before our child arrives."

"I understand, and may the blessings of God be upon the three of you," the padre said as he showed her to a small, candlelit room. "You will join us pres-ently for our evening meal?"

"Very gratefully," Constance replied, adding, "Father."

As the sun went down and the brilliant moon

rose higher, Constance and Hank Gannon went to the window of their room before going to the dining hall. They stood in close embrace, eager and ready to face their life together in a free and welcoming land.

Turn the page for an exciting preview!

ONE BAD APPLE . . .

John Apple, a gardener and preacher,
has a good life in Ohio in 1834—until a failed
romance sends him fleeing to the south in search
of a new life. An encounter with a very drunk
Jim Bowie sets him on a path to the Texian
Revolution. There, as indignity upon indignity
is piled on the settlers by Mexican President
Santa Anna and his soldiers, Apple learns
he has a third skill: Killing.

. . . CAN SPOIL THE WHOLE BUNCH

Working with Bowie, Sam Houston,
Stephen Austin, and their ragtag army,
Apple becomes a secret courier and bloody
advocate for the cause. His calling card is
distinctive and fills agents of the tyrannical
generalissimo with terror: Apple plants apple seeds
deep in the chest cavity of every soldier he slays,
his way of bringing new life from old.

For Apple, the road leads to the Alamo, where he
is sent on a dangerous mission in an effort to
stave off disaster. Yet the fall of the bold defenders
does not deter him. For him, the war—and a
particular case of revenge—is just beginning!

BAD APPLE
by Lancaster Hill

Coming soon, wherever Pinnacle Books are sold.

Prologue

Save for the steady *plick, plock, plick* of the longcase clock across the room, it was another cemetery-quiet night at the Hickory Bar. That was the saloon I established two years ago, shortly after graduating from school back east, coming west, losing my wife Lidyann and child in childbirth, and finding just enough silver in a sandstone deposit to buy out the barbershop and the cooper's place. I knocked down the wall between them and used the barrels the cask-maker left behind to start distilling my own brands. One day, I hoped to sell them. First, I had to keep from going broke.

The Hick, as she's called by those who love her, is just a big jump past Fort Gibson, whence came most of my legal clientele. The illegals—Creeks mostly—had a special knock they used at the back door in the small hours of the night to make their own private, illegal purchases. As of this evening, the Indians were my only regular customers, sometimes paying in gold dust; I hadn't much use right now for the animals they also brought in exchange for alcohol, since there was no one around to enjoy my celebrated Three-Hare and a Frog Stew.

The Hick was a very private place. The entrance was not at the front but on the side, on a broad alley. That kept the dust and the sound to a minimum. It also allowed me to focus on my job tending bar, not listen for every potential new customer. But there's private . . . and there's dead.

Right now, we were dead.

I take the liberty of sharing this little bit about myself and my place of business because, frankly, this is all the time I get in the footlights. Hereafter, the stage belongs to another. Another who is unlike any man who ever passed through my swinging doors. A man who would become a legend different from the legends he would talk to me about.

This night—the sixth in a row, by my mournful reckoning—the Hick lay as hollow and silent as the Liberty Bell. The chalkboard hanging behind me had the same scant menu it had a week ago. There was a section of the wall across from the door where I hung pictures drawn by customers of the strange things they had seen on their journeys, from man-bears to contraptions that flew. One of my regulars from the fort, a Frenchman, was an expert with the rapier and had given me such a relic to hang there. I looked at it often, thinking about the weapon that helped to conquer an old world compared to the new and better firearms that were spreading us west and south.

I had not added anything new to the wall for weeks. Things had been that way since the troops and harder-drinking officers of Fort Gibson had been sent south to babysit the war. Old Hickory, the President of the United States—for whom this institution was respectfully named—the great Andy Jackson had drug every man in uniform, and some who weren't, from the garrison and sent them to the Texas border in case any Mexicans tried to enter the territory in pursuit of rebels. I didn't know how that struggle for Texian independence was going, save that everyone was upset about the massacre at the Alamo. But I kept a flintlock musket under the bar in case any of Santa Anna's weasels tried to enter the Hick. The only ones who liked those kill-minded loons were the Indians, only because the Mexicans were hated more.

I did have one customer at the moment, though. I'm pretty good at reading my customers, but this was a puzzle of a man.

The oil lamps nailed to the wall behind me, athwart the big mirror, cast just our two shadows across the half-dozen empty tables, the unlit lamps upon them, and wooden floors, planks that were scuffed from boots on the bar side, scarred with barrels being rolled and tugged across the other.

The man at my bar was about sixty. He might've been younger; it was tough to say with a face so cracked and lined it looked like sunbaked clay. He wore a beard though that might be from inattention rather than choice. It was careless and naturally uneven. My customer hadn't bothered to take off his hat, so I couldn't see anything above the middle of his nose. But the tilt of his head said he was looking down. Remembering, from the stillness of him; tired men don't sit still, they pass out. I couldn't tell the man's trade either. He didn't stink like a trapper or a ranch hand, which was most of my trade that weren't soldiers or Indians. There was a faint smell of gunpowder about him, possibly from the two Colt revolvers I saw him wearing when he walked in. The firearm was new but these did not gleam in the light. They looked as toughened as their owner. There was also a long, sheathed knife tied to his right leg.

The man's clothes looked as weathered as the man who wore them. He had on a sheepskin vest, dirtier I'm sure than the sheep who once wore it. His slouch hat was probably gray under its uneven, dusty coat. His beard and moustache were as ungroomed and wooly as his vest, though they were definitely gray. He had likely washed his face in the horse trough after riding in from wherever he'd come. The mouth tucked amongst the whiskers was pencil straight and only moved for the intake of liquor.

This gentleman's tall, lean frame was bent over slightly, like there was a slow-leaking sack of grain on his shoulders; they had risen just a little since he sat down. He was leaning mostly on his left hand, which was flat-open on the bar. The other hand did not release the glass. I'll get to those hands in a moment.

He was drinking the house whiskey—Wildnut by name, on account of the bit of walnut I brewed in with the alcohol, sugar, and chewing tobacco. He had sat there for maybe ten, fifteen minutes before gulping the glass down. Then he sat there some more, not moving, not saying anything. I gave him a shot on the house, not even sure he could pay for the first one, but what the hell. Another one might open him up, help me pass the night. The man acknowledged by raising a finger. He didn't look up, he didn't say "thanks," he just lifted that finger—which, like the rest of him, looked like it had seen better days. Now I've seen stranger fingers since I draped that big Open for Business sign outdoors that got blown away the first day. I saw one that got flattened by a cow and looked like a spoon; one that got shot off by an arrow at the knuckle, leaving little notches in the adjoining fingers; one with a tattoo of a naked squaw who danced when it moved. There's a lot of uncommonness comes through my swinging doors.

But these fingers were not simply grotesque, they were—I once heard a traveling salesman describe a brass nutcracker as "utile," and I would use that word to describe eight of these fingers. They were straight and they were filed or stropped sharp, except for the trigger fingers. Those nails were sawed-off at the tip. The skin was also utile—rough-looking, almost like tree bark. Taken as a whole, each hand had four sturdy little knives like some beastie from the English penny awfuls I read when I attended the Philadelphia College of Apothecaries. The creatures and unnatural beasts of those stories gave me the shivers, and so did these devilish little fingers. And they hadn't even done anything, except one of them coming briefly to attention.

That was the thing about this man. Based on absolutely nothing that he had done, he seemed like a coiled snake, just waiting for the wrong thing to make him strike. I didn't want any question of mine to be that wrong thing, so after pouring the second drink I walked away to blow dust from the bottles that lined the wall under the mirror.

But I glanced at him again, though, at his reflection. And I saw something I did not expect to see.

A single lamplit tear on his left cheek.

There being no minted money in these parts, not yet, I was always curious to see what my customers would offer for payment. This man had a pouch under a kerchief and used a long nail to hook out a lump of gold. He dropped it like a shovel emptying dirt. I swept it up, put it in the till behind me, and turned back to him. "Do you have a place to stay?"

After dusting and polishing and stepping outside to look at the full moon, I risked asking that question because it was not personal, it showed polite concern, my voice quiet like I was talking to a spooked mustang, and it was the kind of thing any barkeep would hospitably be expected to inquire about.

It was the first time I heard or saw the man breathe. He drew air through his nose, the mouth still not moving—though, while I was distracted by my busywork, he had managed to empty the second glass.

"The question I have been pondering, sir," he replied in a deep, quiet voice, "is do I have a place to go?"

He obviously did not mean for the night. His searching question—though directed more at the surface of the bar than at me—prompted me to ask, "May I inquire where you have come from?"

I thought he had gone dumb on me again when

he finally answered in a voice barely more than a whisper, *"El degüello."*

That was Mexican death music. It signified the slitting of the throat, murder without quarter. I had heard it discussed by the soldiers, in particular a bugler who played the damn thing and brought the kind of silence to the Hick that is reserved for churches and piano recitals.

The man's dull, mournful reply suggested one answer to all the questions I had.

"You were there," I said.

I didn't have to say where "there" was. His silence was my answer.

He had come from the Alamo.

I moved away slowly, respectfully giving him room to reflect without distraction. But he did not seem to need—or want—privacy. He looked up for the first time, that single streak now dry on his cheek. The face was like something on a Creek totem, stiff and grim. But the eyes were bright and green, almost like emeralds with a touch of mint.

"I was there but I was not," he said. "God Almighty, I was unable to help my brethren."

As he spoke, and probably without realizing it, he used the sharp middle finger of his left hand to cut what looked like a small cross in the drink-stained surface of my oak bar.

"What's your name, if you don't mind my asking?" I asked anyway.

"John," he replied wearily, as if he were falling asleep and already had one foot in a dream.

"I'm Nedrick," I told him, a little more sprightly. "Nedrick Bundy."

If he heard, he made no indication. "The *degüello*," he said again.

"What about it?" I asked.

A pained squint slowly closed in around John's eyes. "They needed guns. Men. You know what I had?"

"Tell me," I said.

He was still looking through me with those narrowed eyes. A second tear followed the first. It was not a dream but a nightmare he was in.

John uttered a single word with such sadness, such longing, that it uncorked a bottle of hurt that just flowed . . .

CHAPTER ONE

Mansfield, Ohio, December 1834

For half the year, the hills and the farms are easy. The two fingers of the Mohican River were touched by God with fertility, as surely and whole hog as the rambunctious Adam and Eve. The town that grew there was just as fecund, producing farms and businesses and population with rapidity that at first intrigued the local red men, then perplexed and alarmed them.

I got there in 1832. I was in my fifties, then, and a little less patient than I had been in my youth. No, maybe that's not the word. I was patient to watch things grow. I was unforgiving—that's a better word—unforgiving for things that grew bad. I could nurse blight or bugs from my plants but that was a natural, God-created competition. What people do is rarely that.

Where I lived before, in Warren, Pennsylvania, was showing signs of smoky, noisy blight. Too many forges, too many mills, too much hammering, too many people hollering to be heard, too many horses complaining, too many cartwheels turning, too many youngsters shouting and crying and getting yelled at.

Too much civilization.

I worked on a sheep and goat farm nigh the Allegheny River and wasn't attached to a thing but the earth. I would always stay out until sunset and took that moment to look west and admire what remained of the uncorrupted work of God. I would go to my shack, then, and read the Good Book by the failing light before joining my employers, the elderly Brandons, for supper in the main house. It was over apple pie one night that I announced my intention to leave. I hadn't planned to say that, hadn't even planned to go; it just, suddenly, felt right. I waited till a replacement could be found, and set out on a spring morning, at dawn, with just a rifle, my Bible, and a grain sack generously filled with produce I had grown.

It took me about six months to arrive at where I didn't even know I was headed. I was meandering west, and Mansfield got in the way. I planted myself there for two reasons. First: the soil was so rich I wept when I touched it. I swear, if there were seeds, those tears would have grown them. It was like God had sent me a vision instructing me to work this land. Second: that good earth was the only sign of God in the region. Oh, people had dutifully built two churches, but few parishioners passed through their doors and the parsons lacked enthusiasm. One of them told me he had agreed to this sinecure just to be close to Pittsburgh for when some aged clergyman there hung up his frock.

"I want to be in a real city," he told me, "with real sin."

I was not sure how the padre meant that, but I decided to trust the calling and not the man.

With more faith than planning, I elected to use what money I'd saved to buy a small plot, plant my own fruits and vegetables, and use the unsteady old barn for Bible meetings.

I did not grow up prayerful. I was born and raised on a small farm in Massachusetts before, during, and after the War for Independence. We were the people who constantly broke the King's peace, and we suffered the first and enduring wrath of the Red-coats. Floggings, hangings, deprivation of goods and services. I learned to shoot at a young age—at game, since my pa was off fighting. I learned to work the land. When the war ended and pa didn't come back, me and my younger brother Nathaniel stayed on till my ma went, too. From sadness, I believe. She was the one who had turned to the Holy Book and found solace in its lessons. I often sat by her as she read, more for her comfort than mine. She taught me reading, and soon I was reading to her—right up till the end.

Nathaniel apprenticed with a granite-carver—he had the stocky build and arms for it—but I did not want to stay. The spirit of freedom smelled too much like blood. It still does, only then—well, then I was younger and thought a new place would clean it from my nostrils. I picked and hunted my way through New York and into Pennsylvania. I read verse by the light of many a campfire. I felt the presence of God Himself under the million eyes of night—the stars above and the lesser ones lurking in the shadows, "all kinds of living creatures" that were created amidst the innocent coming of the world. I stopped in Warren, partly to share my faith but also to put my hands in soil again, to make things grow. When the choke of man became too great, I departed.

You know of my reaching Mansfield, about me growing food outside the barn and over the next two years, one by one, then two by two, and eventually in groups of ten or twelve growing souls inside the barn. They grew me, too, a community of loving souls as surely my God had intended. Eventually, I fell hard in love with a member of the flock: Mrs. Astoria Laveau, a New Orleans–born widow who used her inheritance to found and run a library.

I knew how to read, but it was there, from her, that I learned how to *read*. How to understand what was in the mind of the writer, why words were chosen just-so, why some writers described everything in detail and while others did not. Why some stories were told by narrators and others were not. A world opened for me, and with it—my heart opened, too.

Everyone, if they're lucky, has love. She was deeply mine. She was spiritual. She had all those many books—not a day went by that I did not learn from her. She was worldly and desirable yet we did not cross into sin. Not that I did not desire it. I went to kiss her, one time after a springtime walk, but she bowed her forehead to me. It was love-made-chaste . . . at least, for me. Alas, when I finally summoned the gumption to propose an official courtship I was spurned. Astoria said she loved me as a preacher, as a friend, as that accursed word "brother," but not as a man. I learned that at the same time I was considering betrothal she had feelings for another man, a blacksmith. It was just gossip, whispers, until they came to a dance together and I saw how affectionate she could be within the bounds of public decency. My heart stopped beating for anything but getting away.

I left carrying what I had left Massachusetts with. It was nearly winter, last winter, and at my age and lack of girth, it meant the only direction I could plausibly head was south.

CHAPTER TWO

Fort Gibson, Oklahoma, May 1836

"So you got away to Texas," I said. "Love broke your heart. Did Texas heal it?"

"In . . . in a manner of speaking," he replied.

John was still looking ahead. He had told the story without stopping, without hesitation, and without emotion. Just like he was reading from the Bible, but to himself.

When John didn't answer, didn't nod, didn't even blink, I approached the bar with a cloth and pretended to wipe it. I had already done that before he'd arrived, and it was spotless.

"You got to Texas a year ago," I coaxed. "That was before things boiled over."

His eyes shifted to the mirror. If he saw his own reflection, he did not react.

"So few people . . . so much anger," John said. Then said no more.

"I heard people talking here how Santa Anna upset his own people when he threw out the Constitution," I said. "Do you remember that?"

"Central government, more power to him, less to the states," John replied, nodding. "I remember that. And the revolts. We heard about the revolts in Oaxaca, Zacatecas, others."

"We?"

"Colonel Fannin. Colonel Bowie."

"Jim Bowie? It must have been exciting to know him," I said. I took a second look at the knife visible on his hip. It was as sure a carte de visite as any.

"It was—a time," he said vaguely with the first hint of a smile. "I learned that Bible, fist, and gun were connected. Knit. Security, life, and salvation did not exist separately."

He was becoming talkative, and I went to pour him another drink. The hand uncurled from the glass and settled on top.

"Thank you, no," he said. "Any more would be vulgar."

I had no idea what that meant, except that he didn't want any. I set the bottle down. "I have bread . . . some rabbit in the back."

He did not respond. I shouldn't have led him down another road. His story interested me, and I wanted to hear it.

"Where did you meet Colonel Bowie?" I asked.

He replied, "Just outside a war, in Mexico."

Connect with Us

Visit us online at
KensingtonBooks.com
to read more from your favorite authors, see books
by series, view reading group guides, and more.

Join us on social media

for sneak peeks, chances to win books and prize packs,
and to share your thoughts with other readers.

facebook.com/kensingtonpublishing
twitter.com/kensingtonbooks

Tell us what you think!

To share your thoughts, submit a review,
or sign up for our eNewsletters, please visit:
KensingtonBooks.com/TellUs.